SWORD OF THE SUN

SINÉAD O'HART

Illustrated by Manuel Šumberac

Piccadilly

This edition published in 2024 by
PICCADILLY PRESS
4th Floor, Victoria House, Bloomsbury Square
London WC1B 4DA
Owned by Bonnier Books
Sveavägen 56, Stockholm, Sweden
bonnierbooks.co.uk/PiccadillyPress

A CIP catalogue record for this book is available from the British Library.

ISBN: 978-1-80078-510-6
Also available as an ebook

1

Typeset by Envy Design Ltd
Printed and bound in Great Britain by Clays Ltd, Elcograf S.p.A.

Piccadilly Press is an imprint of Bonnier Books UK
bonnierbooks.co.uk

This one's for you.

The Burren

The Forge of
the Cailleach

Shannon

Boyne

Prologue

1979

Unseen and unheard, two figures moved near the summit of Mweelrea, staring out at the Atlantic Ocean from the top of that great mountain. Both were tall – one so much so that it was clear he had not been shaped or formed by any part of nature. He looked like magic striding on two legs, his long silver hair blowing in the frosty breeze and his skin almost blue, though not with cold. In one great hand he held a sword. Beside him walked a woman, her steps unimpeded by the snow. Her hair flickered like a black candle flame, wreathing her head in darkness. The trail of her footsteps was littered with feathers, like those from an old crow. Her eyes were rimmed with shadow that seemed to move of its own accord, and within the murk her irises shone with an eerie violet light. Her lips were as red as crushed beetles, her cheeks feverish pink and her robe skittered about her like it was afraid to touch her skin.

The footprints she left as she climbed Mweelrea were sometimes made by one set of feet and sometimes three. Indeed, the woman herself – had any human eye been there to see her – looked, at times, as though she had two companions, one on either side; sometimes she turned to speak to them. And in the next blink they were gone, and she was one person again.

'The Cailleach rises,' said the man. His voice was like the shifting of rocks beneath the earth's surface.

'Let her come,' the woman replied. She spoke in a voice that was not one but three, a sweet, melodious tone with a sharp, harsh croaking tucked underneath, and above both of these could be heard the sound of warbling, cracked words, like they were being uttered by a person of immense age. 'I do not fear the Hag of the Hills. Nor should you, Nimhfola, son of Nuada.'

The tall figure turned to regard his companion. 'You would do well, She-Who-Is-Three, Battle Crow, Shadesinger, not to underestimate your enemy. Particularly when she comes wrapped in the power of the Old Magic –'

There was a strange skittering sound in the room, and the man looked up from the book he'd been reading. His papers sat in the pool of light thrown down by his lamp, like an island in a sea of murk. How had it grown so late? Surely the children would already be in bed . . . He glanced at the small clock he kept on his desk. Nearly midnight. He sighed. Maura was probably asleep herself by now, and he imagined her seething anger, settled around her as tightly as any blanket. *You're never here to help me with the girls! They don't even* know *you, Brendan! They might as well have a hat stand for a father!*

Brendan sighed, moving in his chair. His back ached, his head thudded. The November night was cold and still outside his window. Snow glinted on the straggling hedgerow, and the ground was slick with ice. He looked out into the dark, seeing the reflection of his 'office' in the glass – a desk, a chair, a stack of books, some of which he'd written himself, an empty ashtray, a pinboard on the wall with all manner of notes stuck to it, his daughters' drawings and notes buried somewhere at the bottom, like treasure waiting to be excavated. He sat in the middle of all this industry, floating and golden, suspended in the night.

He could see the muffled shapes of the mountain on the horizon, and at the end of the garden, the cave . . .

Quickly, he darted out of the chair to pull the curtains closed – *too* quickly, according to the muscles popping in his back and shoulders. He hissed in pain, rubbing at the sore spots, before turning back towards his desk.

There was someone standing at the far side of it.

Brendan stopped, his heart thocking wildly in shock. He opened his mouth, but the words were somehow stoppered in his throat. The person – the *woman* – looked up and smiled, and Brendan swallowed his question.

It was as if she had stepped out of the pages he'd been reading. He knew who she was, for she was unmistakable.

'Greetings,' she said. There were only the barest traces of her other voices in her words, but Brendan could hear them. They were there, like discordant, echoing whispers, somehow lingering, even though their owners were mere memory.

'Get out,' Brendan said, finally unsticking his tongue from the roof of his mouth. He coughed. 'Get out of my house, or I'll call the Guards.'

The woman laughed loudly, harsh and sudden. 'The telephone is in the hallway, Brendan. I know I'm not,' she waved a hand, 'of this *era*, so to speak, but I do know how certain things work.' She took a step, and Brendan fought to hold his ground. 'And how long do you think they'll take to get here, anyway? This house, in the middle of nowhere . . . Bad conditions on the roads . . .' She tutted, pretending to be concerned. 'I really don't think we need to worry about the Guards.' Her violet eyes flashed. 'Guardians of the *Peace*,' she said, almost spitting the words. 'Such a thing was never known, in my time.'

'Your time is long past, Anand,' Brendan said. The woman flinched at the sound of her name, and something in Brendan's chest flared hopefully. She preferred to be known by her title, which she used when all three of her Aspects were together, the name that described them all. *Morrígan*. Great Queen. The Battle Crow. But her other Aspects – her sister-selves – were long gone now, banished by the Cailleach, and by Manannán Mac Lir, one hundred and forty years before.

But the woman before him was much, much older than that. Old enough to have walked with gods.

Old enough to have fought in battles that had passed into legend. Old enough to have watched humanity rise and fall and rise and fall again, in war and peace and bloodshed, each revolution nourishing her like a prayer.

She narrowed her eyes as she regarded him, and Brendan felt his hope sputter out.

'And yet, I live,' she said, her voice low. 'Perhaps there is still some space in this modern world for She-Who-Is-Three.'

Brendan swallowed hard. 'She-Who-Is-One. Your sisters are gone.'

Anand glanced down at the book Brendan had been reading. 'January, 1839,' she intoned, reading from the text. '*Oíche na Gaoithe Móire* – the Night of the Big Wind.' She looked back at Brendan. 'The night that the Cailleach of Mullaghmore and her lackey, Mac Lir, stole from me the people I hold dearest, banishing my sisters to places even I cannot reach.' She smiled, a cruel twist of her lips that was barely there before it was gone. 'And that was not all they stole from me that night. I am heartened to see, at least, that our battle is remembered, even if history has recorded it as a mere storm.'

Brendan held her gaze. 'Hundreds of people died. It was more than a mere *storm*.'

Anand seemed to hold herself straighter, as though mentioning death gave her relief. 'Yes,' she whispered. 'I remember.'

Brendan tried to push away his fear, but his thoughts were panicked. *The children. Maura. I have to get them out . . .* 'What do you want?' he asked, willing himself to stay steady. He was an O'Donnell, and this was his duty.

'What do I *want*? You know what I want, Brendan O'Donnell, son of Hugh, son of Liam, son of Seán.' She stared him down. All Brendan could see were her eyes, shining like polished blades.

'I will not give you a single thing,' Brendan said, unable to stop his voice from trembling. 'My people have stood as guardians here since the Cailleach brought you down, and we will stand here forever. My father, his father before him, and his –'

'Enough!' she hissed. 'For you *have* no sons, Brendan Finian O'Donnell. Only two daughters, mewling brats who have no love for you.' She took another step, around the desk. 'Nobody to keep your name. No O'Donnell to continue your line.' She licked

7

her lips. 'You are a weak link in the chain.'

Brendan blinked against sudden tears. 'My daughters are fine girls, who will understand why I had to work so hard. They'll know, when they're older, and they'll carry on their duty with as much heart and courage as any O'Donnell before them. You wait and see.'

Anand leaned against the desk. She picked up a photograph in a frame and scoffed at it, before turning it to Brendan. He didn't need to look at it, but he did anyway. The image showed two small girls, one newborn – Aisling, who was heading for two years old now – and her then three-year-old sister Niamh, cradling her. Brendan's chest filled with panic. His babies . . . And his wife, asleep, with no idea of the evil that was in their house . . . *And it's all my fault.*

'The only way they'll carry on anything,' Anand said, replacing the photograph, 'is if they are trained, and schooled, as you were. No warrior can face the field without first being formed. Wouldn't you agree?' She toyed carelessly with a lock of her black, black hair as she spoke. 'And without a master, a warrior might as well be a lump of rock.'

Brendan's heart picked up pace. 'I won't let you –'

'You have precisely *no* power to stop me doing anything,' Anand growled, becoming a swirling dark cloud for a blink before solidifying once more, so close to Brendan that he could feel the fierce heat from her skin. Brendan stumbled back, almost colliding with the window behind him.

'Don't harm my children,' Brendan said, in a strangled gasp. 'Or – or my wife. They're innocent.'

Anand's cruel eyes glinted. 'There are no innocents. But be assured, I'll let them live. I'll watch them fail, confused, not even knowing what their duty is, undoing through their own ignorance all the work you've done, and all the work your forefathers did, and I'll watch your family crumble.' She smirked. 'Yes, believe me. I won't deny myself that joy.'

'No,' Brendan gasped. His heart was galloping now, like a panicked horse. It hurt, the pain crushing, like a band of iron slowly tightening around his ribs.

Anand levelled her cold gaze on him and, as he watched, her eyes turned blood-red. He felt like all the air had been sucked out of the room, and his brain filled with screaming taunts and accusations. *You didn't even fight! You weakling! You're unworthy*

of the name O'Donnell! Everything that follows this will be your fault!

Brendan clutched his chest and dropped to one knee. At the same moment, Anand burst into a cloud of crows, which shed feathers like snowflakes. The crows swirled around him, the feathers pressing against his face, smothering him in darkness. All the while, the voices kept shrieking inside his head. *Your daughters will hate you! They'll never understand! You're a failure, a pathetic excuse for a guardian . . . Everything will fall, and when the world burns, when I have the Sword once again and my sisters are free, your family will be the first to die . . .*

Brendan struggled to his feet, fumbling for his chair. He collapsed into it and picked up a pen, desperately trying to write something – anything – to explain, to warn Maura, to tell his daughters . . . to tell them how much he loved them, and how he wanted to protect them, and how he'd got it all wrong . . . But his hand was weak, and he couldn't keep his grip. His vision grew dark around the edges as he stared at the photograph of his children.

He slumped forward, his head landing on the still-open book in front of him. Slowly, the crows stopped their spinning, the feathers blanketing the floor. They each found perches, and they watched, impassive and calm, as the life drained out of Brendan O'Donnell.

Once his last breath had hissed out into the dark room, the crows leaped as one. They swirled together, becoming the woman once more. She stared down at Brendan's body, her lip curled in disgust, before turning and walking out of the room.

Anand left the house as silently as she had entered it, watched by no one.

The present

'Aw, *what*?' muttered Ben, as his avatar shrivelled up, turned a funny colour and trickled to the bottom of the screen. He stared at the game in disgusted disbelief.

'Everything okay, pal?' said his dad, from the passenger seat of the car. He turned to look back at Ben. His mam, who was driving, glanced at him in the rearview mirror, but said nothing. Ben thought she looked weird in her driving glasses – like some sort of bug-eyed alien.

'Just the game,' Ben replied, already tapping the Restart button. 'I made a mess of it.'

'No harm done, then,' Dad said, leaning on his elbow and turning back around, staring out of the passenger window once again.

'Yeah, s'pose.' Ben swallowed his irritation as the game began reloading. His brother Fin, sitting beside him in the back of the car, made a sudden and disgusting noise in the back of his throat, and Ben glared at him. Now that he wasn't concentrating on his game, he realised he could hear sounds trickling out of Fin's earbuds – the crashing, grinding, multilayered noise that passed for music, in his brother's world. He glanced at the screen of Fin's phone, which was balanced on his knee. He saw a weird-looking figure, like a skeleton with skin. It had glowing eyes and gritted teeth, and its long, grey, wispy hair was blowing in the breeze. Around what passed for its torso was a thick metal corset, red-hot, with rivets and rust all over it. The metal was pulled tight, squishing the figure almost to nothing. One arm, with long bony fingers, was busy trying to pull the corset off, but judging by the expression on its face, the creature wasn't having much luck.

Girdle of Agony, read the display. Ben guessed that was the band name, and the scary skeleton-person was the image on the album cover. The song title was too small to read, but they all sounded the same to Ben anyway.

Fin cleared his throat and turned to stare at his younger brother. 'What?' he snapped.

Ben shrugged, looking back at the phone in his hand – his dad's, borrowed for the journey – as Fin refocused on the view out of the window. Fin's hair was long at the front and shaved tight at the back, falling over his face and hiding his expression, but Ben had a feeling it would be the same as always: a twist of faint horror at having a brother, or a family, or having to be in a car with other humans, travelling to live in a place none of them – besides the boys' mam – had ever been to before.

Ben's stomach rolled slightly, making him feel carsick. He killed the game and locked the phone, then leaned forward to hand it back to his dad. Sometimes looking at the tiny screen, or trying to read, made his travel sickness worse.

'You want some air?' his mam called, looking at him in the mirror again. Ben nodded, and his mam pressed the button to make his window roll down a little, just enough to let a snake of cool, fresh breeze push its way into the car. It was welcome, but there was a tang of something disgusting in it too.

'They must be spreading on the fields,' Dad said,

turning to Mam with his nose wrinkled in distaste. She nodded.

'Spreading *what*?' Ben called.

'Slurry,' Dad told him, turning in his seat. 'Cow dung, basically. To make the grass grow green, and all that.'

'Oh my God,' Ben said, his stomach lurching again.

'Country living, boys,' Dad laughed, turning back around. 'We'll have to get used to it now.'

Ben breathed deeply. The smell was almost gone, and his stomach was starting to settle. He tried to focus on the road ahead, as the greenery whipping past the car windows could sometimes make him feel ill too.

Fin sucked phlegm into his throat again, and his mam turned briefly from focusing on the road to stare at her oldest son. 'Finian Ferdia O'Donnell-Mulhern,' she snapped. 'If you do that one more time, I swear to God!'

Fin swallowed, making Ben's stomach heave. 'Or what?' he called, too loudly. His earbuds meant he couldn't hear his own voice properly.

'You mind the way you speak to your mother! And turn that rubbish *down*,' Dad grouched. 'It must be wrecking your ears!'

Fin rolled his eyes, flicking his hair out of his face, but Ben noticed his finger clicking the down button on his phone's volume. The tinny noise faded, just enough to be bearable.

'How much further, love?' Dad said.

Mam glanced at him as she replied. 'Another twenty miles or so. The roads are fairly bad, so we'll have to take our time.'

Dad nodded, and Ben hoped his stomach would hold out. The last thing he needed was to decorate the back of Mam's seat – again. He glanced out at the passing countryside. It was all so different to where they'd come from, and he thought about home – the house they'd lived in since he'd started in Junior Infants. The house they'd had to leave, once he'd finished his last day in fifth class, because their landlord was selling up and wanted them out.

So now they were coming here, to the middle of nowhere, to live with his Aunt Niamh and her wife, in the wilds of County Clare.

Ben had never even *been* to Clare before. It was just a mystical notion, the idea of a place, the county where his mam and her sister had been brought up. Mam had left her childhood home the second she'd turned eighteen and had never once been back there, not even to visit her own mam when she was dying. She'd gone to see her in the hospital, of course, and she'd stayed down for a week when Nanny Maura had actually passed away a few years back, but she'd slept over in a hotel in Ennis, the nearest big town, despite Aunt Niamh's protests. Niamh had inherited the house, as the oldest of the sisters, and had made her own life in it since Nanny's death – she had a whole family now, one that they didn't really know. Ben swallowed nervously at the thought of meeting Aunt Niamh again, and of meeting her wife and her wife's daughter, for the first time. *Eun-Kyung*, he repeated, inside his head. *Ji-Ah*. Those were their names. His aunt, Dr Kang Eun-Kyung, and his sort-of cousin, Park Ji-Ah.

Fin, unexpectedly, pulled out an earbud. 'I can't believe we're actually going to have to live here,' he snapped. 'This *sucks*, more than anything has ever sucked.'

'It's better than sleeping under a bridge, son,' Dad said, rubbing his forehead with one hand. 'You know we've no choice.'

'Is there *nowhere* closer to Dublin we could've

stayed? Like, nobody we could've crashed with?'

'You try getting someone to let two grown adults and two teenage – or, *near* teenage – fellas just *crash*,' Mam freed one hand from the wheel to make air quotes around the word, 'and see how well you get on. Nobody has the room, Fin. And we looked.' Her voice dropped. 'This is the last place on earth I want to be, lads. Trust me.'

'We're going to be grand. All right?' Dad turned again, looking first at Fin and then at Ben. 'Mam and me will get ourselves set up with new jobs, and we'll have a safe place to lay our heads, more or less rent-free, for a few months while we get things up and running. It's not ideal, guys, I know. But it's a heck of a lot better than any of the alternatives.' He gave them a tight, pained smile. 'Dublin's just so expensive. It was out of reach, once we lost the house. And I know you're missing your pals, and your old routine.' Ben pulled his lips tight as he listened. Dad had no idea how much he was missing their old house, and the green just outside their door, and the neighbours that had been like family, and the library within ten minutes' walk, and his coding club every Saturday morning . . . 'But this is a chance to set up *new* routines and get to know new people. It's a great opportunity, all right? We've just got to make the most of it.' He nodded, his gaze flicking between his sons again, before turning back around.

Ben and Fin shared a sidelong glance, united for once. Fin gave his younger brother a look that could almost be sympathetic, before tossing his fringe again and pushing his earbud back in. Ben focused on the road. It had started to rain, enough to speckle the windscreen but not so heavily that Mam had to set the wipers going. All he could see were flat fields and a rolling hill in the far distance. The sky grew darker as they drove and the rain eventually began to come down hard. Mam finally switched on the wipers as the car's headlights came on, automatically reacting to the sudden loss of light.

Moments later they reached a black metal gate. It was standing open, and Mam indicated to turn. The engine roared as she urged the car up the driveway, rocking and bumping up the potholed road towards the isolated house Ben could just see. A room near the top had its light on, and in the porch, with a brightly coloured cardigan wrapped tightly around her, stood a woman who was like Mam in every feature, except her hair was red where Mam's was golden-brown. As the car came to a halt beside a massive four-wheel drive with an eye-catching logo on it – a bear, its head lifted to roar – another woman came to join Aunt Niamh in the porch. She had thick black hair, thrown over her shoulder in a loose braid, and a welcoming smile on her face.

Ben gulped. So, here they were. This was the house. And these were his aunts, Niamh and Eun-Kyung. And here, in this rain-soaked gloom-fest, was the rest of his life.

2

'Come on in and get something to eat – we don't have long before the movers get here,' Niamh said, flapping her hands to usher Ben's family in out of the rain. 'We'll have hugs in the kitchen!'

Ben shivered as he stepped inside. The house was old, and cold. It might be July outside, but it felt like October in here. He wondered which box his jumpers were packed in, and whether anyone would mind if he dived right into it as soon as their stuff arrived, but until then he busied himself having a look around. Right inside the front door was a large open space. The floor was tiled. Straight ahead was a huge staircase, its treads wide and its polished oak handrails dark and gleaming. To the left were some open double doors which seemed to lead to a sunroom or conservatory.

'Kitchen's this way,' called Eun-Kyung, turning to the right and heading down a narrow hallway. Ben followed her, glancing around warily. The ceiling was high, the walls smoothly painted in an odd greenish tint. The lampshade was made of coloured glass, which threw out an interesting pattern. Everything smelled slightly antiseptic. They passed a heavy door on the left that gave way into a living room with an empty fireplace, and on the right, facing the living room, was a closed door. A nameplate had once been screwed into the wood and the small rectangle it had covered was still paler than the rest. As they walked on Ben wondered, briefly, what was in there, and then Eun-Kyung pushed open a door at the end of the hallway into a warm and welcoming kitchen with a cast-iron range. It radiated heat and Ben made a beeline for it, all other thoughts falling out of his head as the warmth started to bring his fingers back to life. The table was laden with sandwiches and a cake, still in its box from the shop where it had been bought, and steam was rising from the spout of the kettle – it had just boiled. Cups and teabags and a sugar bowl lay on the worktop around it, waiting to be put to use.

'Grab yourself somewhere to sit,' ordered Niamh, bustling in behind the others and making straight for the kettle. 'Everyone for tea?' She didn't wait for answers before popping a bag into each cup and flicking the kettle on to reboil. 'What about Ji-Ah?' she said, glancing at her wife.

Eun-Kyung rolled her eyes. 'She'll come down when she's ready.'

Ben remembered the upstairs room with the brightly lit window. *Must be where she's hiding out*, he thought. He glanced at his family, crowding awkwardly into the small kitchen, and felt a jolt of sympathy for Ji-Ah. If all this were happening to him, he'd probably be holed up in his bedroom hoping it would all just go away too.

Niamh had started carrying cups across to the table. 'It's stretch or starve around here,' she said, grabbing a sandwich as she made her way back to collect the rest of the tea. 'If it's not nailed down, grab it before someone else does!'

Ben pushed himself away from the range, reluctantly, and pulled a sandwich out of the pile. It looked like plain cheese – his favourite. Fin was hiding behind his hair, though Ben could see a sandwich disappearing into his unseen mouth. Mam and Dad just cradled their warm cups, Dad lost in thought and Mam eyeing the room warily, like she expected the shadows in the corners to leap out at her.

Finally, Aunt Niamh ran out of things to do, and flopped into a seat. 'Well,' she began, putting her free hand over Eun-Kyung's. 'How are you all?'

Mam and Dad exchanged a glance. 'We're grand,' Dad finally said. 'I mean – considering.' He cleared his throat gently. 'We're very grateful to yourself and Eun-Kyung, Niamh – I mean, there aren't words for it, honestly. Only for you, we'd be lost.'

'Shocking, what happened,' Niamh said. Eun-Kyung nodded sympathetically. 'It shouldn't be allowed, to just turf a family out of their home.'

'That's the reality, when you're renting,' Mam said. She hadn't drunk any of her tea yet, and Ben didn't think she'd taken any sandwiches either. It was like she thought she was a character in a fairy tale where if you ate or drank anything in another realm, you'd be stuck there forever.

'It's still wrong,' Eun-Kyung said. Her voice pulled Ben out of his fairy-tale daydreams, and he forced himself to push all that aside. They had enough to worry about, right here. 'There ought to be better protection in place. We're really sorry for everything you've had to deal with, Aisling, John. And of course, you boys too.' She glanced at them kindly.

'Thanks,' Ben said, giving Eun-Kyung a quick smile. She returned it, her eyes warm.

'And hopefully we'll have Miss Ji-Ah down here to say hello to you soon too,' Niamh said, in a loud voice, aiming her head towards the room's open door. Eun-Kyung chuckled lightly, gazing fondly at her wife.

'She won't hear you,' she said. 'And even if she does, she'll ignore it.'

'Oh, I know,' said Niamh, picking up her mug of tea. 'I'm just venting. Don't mind me.'

Eun-Kyung gave Niamh's hand a gentle squeeze. 'So, boys,' she said. 'You'll be starting at the school where Niamh teaches in September, Brendan, won't you?'

Ben nodded. 'You can call me Ben, Aunt Eun-Kyung,' he said. 'I'm only Brendan when I'm in trouble.'

'Oh – sorry!' Eun-Kyung laughed. 'And please, drop the "Aunt", all right? Just Eun-Kyung is fine.'

She glanced at Fin. 'And Finian, you'll be off into Ennis for school, right?'

'It's Fin,' he replied, flicking his hair out of the way long enough to look her in the eye. 'And don't remind me.'

Noise from outside made their ears prick up, and a girl's voice shouted down from upstairs. 'There's a truck,' it called. *Ji-Ah*, Ben thought, with a jolt of some unnamed feeling.

'Right.' Niamh sighed, as they got to their feet. 'Here we go.'

The moving contractors were fast and efficient, carrying boxes and furniture into the house. Most of it was stacked neatly in the front hallway, but the adults helped to lug some stuff to different parts of the house. Ben and Fin perched on the stairs, one behind the other, keeping mostly out of the way. Ben felt the urge to let his fingers flick, so he slid his hand down out of the way, where nobody would see. Sometimes his parents gave him grief when they saw him doing it, in case other people thought it looked weird. Ben found it comforting, and felt that other people thought he was weird anyway, so it didn't really matter.

'Can you actually believe any of this?' Fin said, his

voice listless. 'Where even *are* we? It feels like we're living off the edge of the map, or something.'

'I know,' Ben replied.

'And what's with that *bird*?' Ben looked in the direction of Fin's gaze. There was a huge crow, grey and black, its beak as sharp as an insult, sitting on the sill of the porch window. It watched the comings and goings with a beady eye, wind ruffling its feathers. 'It's been there for ages,' Fin continued.

'Nothing better to do, I guess,' Ben said.

As he spoke, the crow seemed to look through the window and into the house, right at the two boys. Ben blinked, staring at the bird, until Niamh – passing by the window with a box under one arm – noticed it. Her face creased with distaste as she banged on the pane with her palm, making the bird leap into flight. The noise shook Ben out of his thoughts, and he shuddered suddenly, the chill finally getting right into his bones. 'I'm going to find a jumper,' he said, getting to his feet. 'This place is Baltic.'

'Hey – watch that,' Fin called, ignoring his brother. One of the contractors had come into the hallway with a sleek black guitar case in one hand and an amp in the other. 'Take care, okay?' He leaped up and pushed past Ben, almost knocking him flat as he rushed to intercept the person carrying his bass.

'Oh, brilliant,' came a voice from behind Ben. He whirled on the spot. A girl stood there, a few steps higher up the stairs. She wore check-patterned trousers, a sloppy black jumper and clear-framed glasses. Her hair was long with a shiny fringe cut just above her eyes. 'Not just boys, but *noise* too.'

'You're Ji-Ah?' Ben said, frowning slightly at her.

The girl flicked her gaze towards him. 'No,' Ji-Ah deadpanned. 'I'm your *other* mystery cousin.'

Ben laughed, a bit nervously. 'Hi. I'm Brendan. Ben. Pleased to meet you.' He stuck out his hand, feeling awkward, but Ji-Ah's arms remained folded. She blinked slowly, heaving in a deep sigh as she did.

'Tell my mothers I'll be in my room,' she said, turning away and stomping back up the stairs.

Ben let his hand fall to his side again and turned back to survey the chaos. Fin was arguing with Dad over the best place to put the bass, while Mam was deep in discussion with a moving contractor about where to put a bookcase. Niamh and Eun-Kyung were trying to stack boxes more neatly, in an attempt to stop them completely taking over – and that weird crow was back, staring in through the window as though it was enjoying the scenes within. Ben swallowed hard against the feeling in his chest. It felt like he was pushing a ball of cold, hard metal right down into his stomach, and he shuddered again.

It was going to be a *long* summer.

3

'Did someone eat the last slice of pepperoni?' Ji-Ah surveyed the table with disgust. 'You guys *know* I can't deal with any other topping.'

'Sorry,' came a muffled voice, as Fin tried to speak through a doughy mouthful.

'Fantastic,' Ji-Ah sighed, sitting back and folding her arms. Niamh tossed a crumpled paper napkin at her. It bopped off her nose, making her blink.

'Don't be such a misery guts,' she said. 'Get another piece of garlic bread into you and let that be the end of it.'

Ji-Ah shook her head, muttering under her breath as she leaned forward again. She lifted a slice of garlic bread and stared at it for a moment. 'I hate this country sometimes,' she muttered, before stuffing it into her mouth.

'What's wrong with the country?' Eun-Kyung laughed, turning to look at her daughter.

'We live miles from nowhere, so our pizza delivery is always cold!' Ji-Ah retorted, once she'd swallowed. 'I *know* we reheat it in the oven, but it never tastes right. And whenever I'm at Dad's, there are, like, *a hundred* times as many options for pizza. Here, it's like you've got pepperoni, cheese, ham, and a handful of sweetcorn if you're lucky. And if you don't like it, then it's tough luck.' She gestured with the remains of her garlic bread. 'You guys haven't lived until you've tried bulgogi pizza. It's literally *magic*.'

Ben gave her a puzzled look. 'What is it?'

Ji-Ah glanced at him. 'It's, like, a top-secret ancient recipe. And this place near Dad's apartment in Seoul uses it as a pizza topping. It's to die for.'

Eun-Kyung gave an amused grunt. 'It's basically barbecued meat, marinaded for flavour,' she said, glancing at the others. Her gaze lingered longest on Ben, and she winked at him. 'Top secret and ancient, not so much. But tasty? Sure.'

'So, your dad lives in Seoul, does he?' John asked.

Ji-Ah slumped a bit in her chair. 'There, and LA,'

31

she replied. 'He sort of goes between them.'

Eun-Kyung swallowed a mouthful of cola. 'His new wife is American,' she explained. 'They've just had twins, so they're staying in LA this summer so they can be close to her parents.'

'Which means our Ji-Ah has to stay here with her mammies, as Dad and Stepmom are just too busy,' Niamh said, leaning forward to tickle Ji-Ah.

'Stop it,' Ji-Ah said, but she couldn't stop herself from grinning.

'So you're normally in, like, Seoul or LA right now?' Fin said, looking up properly for the first time, his wide-eyed gaze landing on Ji-Ah. 'I thought *we* had it bad, but jeez. It doesn't compare to that.'

'Solidarity,' Ji-Ah said, raising her cola cup. Fin raised his in response.

'But you're here most of the time, aren't you?' Aisling said, grabbing a napkin from the pile as she spoke. 'To go to school and that.'

Ji-Ah nodded. 'Yep. Just finished first year in Ennis, same place Fin will be going to. Only he'll be the year above.'

Eun-Kyung beamed. 'Oh, just look at us,' she said. 'Already a happy family.'

Niamh gave her wife an incredulous look. 'Bleurgh,' she said, pretending to vomit.

Everyone at the table, including Fin, began to laugh, and Ben felt something inside his chest – was it relief? He couldn't be sure.

They got to work tidying the table and, as Ji-Ah and Fin did the dishes, Ben was tasked with unlocking the back door and finding his way to the bins, all while balancing a stack of pizza boxes. The wind threatened to rip them out of his grip, but eventually he got them stuffed into the right bin and its lid closed over them.

He walked to the garden gate and opened it, making sure to wedge it with the block of angled wood that he figured was there for that purpose, and then crunched his way through the gravel around the front of the house. This place was *vast*.

He stood and looked around, breathing deeply, trying to take it all in. The rain had lifted and evening was drawing in, painting foreboding shadows across the earth and sky. All that met his eye was eerie emptiness – no roads or power lines or buildings, or anything Ben would have found familiar. He focused on the furthest thing he could see, pushing back against the overwhelm, and when he was ready, he looked around again.

It was flat in every direction, though there were hills in the distance and even the house itself was on a slight incline, with fields on three sides. But beyond the end of the garden was the very edge of the Burren National Park, a huge karst landscape, where the ground was covered in massive limestone formations. He let some facts roll through his mind, each one calming him as it went: the Burren was home to hundreds of rare species of flower, some of which didn't grow anywhere else in Ireland, and humans had lived there for thousands of years, so it had loads of old settlements and burial places too, as well as caves beneath the earth. He'd learned all that from Eun-Kyung as they'd eaten, as it was her job to talk about karst and teach people about it. She worked in the Visitors' Centre a few miles away, and the large four-wheel drive vehicle he'd spotted as they arrived was hers, for getting to and from her job.

'Amazing, isn't it?' Eun-Kyung's voice came from behind him, and Ben jumped in surprise. 'Sorry!' she said, smiling, as he turned round.

'You're all right,' he said, relaxing. She came to stand beside him.

'I like to stand here too,' she said, gazing out at the view. 'It makes my soul happy.'

'It is pretty amazing,' Ben agreed. 'What's that, over there?' He pointed at a large-ish hill, almost a mountain, on the horizon.

'That's Mullaghmore,' Eun-Kyung told him. 'The highest place around here, though not the highest point on the Burren. It means "the great summit" in Irish. Or so I believe.' She gave Ben a sidelong glance, full of fun.

'Do you speak Irish?' Ben asked in amazement.

'About as well as Niamh speaks Korean,' she laughed.

'Is it hard? Being away from home?'

Eun-Kyung smiled softly. 'This is home now,' she said. 'Wherever Niamh is, and Ji-Ah, and my work.'

Ben nodded, and said nothing. He looked back at the landscape. *Maybe home is like that*, he thought. *Not a place, but the people who make it.* Then something caught his eye, near the summit of Mullaghmore, like a sudden flash of light. A silvery glow that seemed to encircle the mountaintop, just for a moment, like a veil that appeared briefly before being pulled away.

'Did you see that?' he asked, breathlessly.

'See what?' Eun-Kyung asked.

'The light, on Mullaghmore,' Ben said.

Eun-Kyung gave him a curious look. 'Sometimes, people report seeing a light there,' she told him. 'There's a story that's been told for almost two hundred years, about the lightning that burst from the mountain on the Night of the Big Wind.'

'The Night of the Big what?' Ben stared at his aunt.

'It was in 1839,' Eun-Kyung began. 'The biggest storm that has ever raged in Ireland. It tore across the country and wrecked houses, trees, boats trying to shelter in harbours. It killed over three hundred people.' Her voice grew low and mournful as she spoke. 'It destroyed lots of the crops being stored over the winter, meaning there was nothing to feed the livestock, so a lot of people and animals suffered in the months after it.'

'But what about the lightning?' Ben reminded her.

Eun-Kyung turned to him. 'Nobody's really sure what it was – maybe something meteorological? Who knows,' she said, her voice back to normal. 'But the contemporary reports all say that anyone who witnessed the light on Mullaghmore that night said there was something otherworldly about it. "Like sparks from heaven," one account said, and others talked about a noise, louder than thunder, like hammers clashing on metal.' She tried to sound light. 'But it was probably just the storm, mixed with people's fertile imaginations.'

Ben looked back at the mountain. 'I did see something though,' he said, quietly.

'I'm sure you did,' Eun-Kyung said. 'Stories say that people still see light on that mountain. Special people. Those with a sense of magic in their bones – what some of the legends like to call the Seandraíocht. The Old Magic.' She gave him a gentle nudge with her elbow. 'Maybe you're one of those.'

Ben drew in a breath and let it out slowly, through his nostrils. *Magic in your bones.* His teachers at his old school had never tired of telling him he was a daydreamer. Sometimes, he had to force himself out of his thoughts and back to real life. *Mam and Dad need me to get with it*, he told himself, severely. *This is such a huge change for us, and I have to start getting real. So no more messing. No more magic.* 'Yeah,' he replied, his voice flat, 'or maybe it was just the sunlight flashing off glass, or something.'

'I should hope not,' Eun-Kyung said. 'Those who visit the park need to bring their trash home with them, especially glass.'

Ben gave her an apologetic look. 'Sorry,' he said. 'I hope I'm wrong.'

Eun-Kyung sighed, gazing out again at her beloved landscape. 'It's a forever sort of battle,' she said. 'Sometimes I think people forget how we're all in the same boat, all on the same planet, all breathing the same air. Some think they can take more than their share, or that there will always be another right behind them, just hurrying along, waiting to pick up their trash or clean up their mess. But of course, that's not always true. Sometimes, it's just up to us to do the work!' She turned to him, her eyes contrite. 'Anyway. I didn't come out here to give you a lecture,' she said. 'Niamh wanted to know if you'd like some ice cream.'

'The answer to that is "always",' Ben said, walking back towards the garden gate with Eun-Kyung. She ushered him through and, as she kicked the wedge out from beneath the gate, Ben looked back at the mountain once more. It seemed quiet now, and there was no light to be seen.

But I did see it, said a tiny voice inside. Ben pushed the voice away, doing all he could to pretend it wasn't there, as his aunt closed the gate and the mountain vanished from his sight.

38

4

'*Oh my God, get out of the bathroom*!' Ji-Ah's voice was loud enough to pierce the fog of sleep that was wrapped around Ben's brain. 'Fin! You've been in there for *twenty minutes*!'

Ben pushed himself up on one elbow. Fin's side of the room was already a mess, and the chaos was encroaching on Ben's space in a worrying way. Fin's bass was leaning against the wall, his amp was serving as a clothing storage area and the walls were covered with posters, including one for Fin's own band, Eddie Ate Dynamite, as well as a brooding Aragorn from the family's favourite film trilogy, *The Lord of the Rings*. Fin's bedcovers were also tossed so completely off the bed that they mostly lay on the floor. Ben groaned, flopping back down on his pillow.

He'd *known* sharing a room with his chaotic older brother would be a disaster.

In the corridor outside he heard Eun-Kyung's voice, low and quick, as she spoke Korean to Ji-Ah.

'Eomma!' Ji-Ah said in reply, her voice tight with irritation. 'Come on, English, please! And get that *boy* out of there!'

'You can come and use the ensuite in our room, Ji-Ah,' Ben heard Eun-Kyung whisper. 'Stop making a fuss!'

'*They're* making a fuss!' Ji-Ah said. 'I hate this!'

Ben rubbed at his eyes, hard enough to see stars. *You're not the only one*, he thought. He remembered what had happened the previous evening, once they'd all stuffed themselves silly with ice cream. Ji-Ah had tried to call her dad, but she hadn't been able to get through, which put her in a foul mood. Then, they'd tried to find something for everyone to watch, which was complicated by the fact that Ji-Ah had seen nearly everything already and none of the adults could agree on a movie. And *then* Fin had got entangled in a conversation about music with Ji-Ah in which he'd grossly insulted her favourite band of all time, Atomic Eyeroll.

'They're *rubbish*!' Ben remembered him saying, his face reddening. 'All twangly voices and terrible production.'

'You are not seriously telling me that their last album wasn't *perfection*?' Ji-Ah shouted back.

'Oh my God, can we talk about literally anything else?' Niamh had yelled, pushing them apart.

In the end, everyone had gone to bed in a temper, having watched nothing on TV. Ben had been awake most of the night listening to Fin snoring, and now here he was, dealing with his first full day in his new 'home', and it felt like being thrown into a sack of rats. He hoped his parents had slept well at least, and that they might be persuaded to bring him on a drive somewhere – anywhere – away from here.

'This place,' Fin grouched, as he burst into the room. 'I'm sick of it.'

'Is the bathroom free?' Ben asked, pushing himself up and putting his feet on the floor. He did his toe-scrunches quickly, one-two-three.

'For now,' Fin replied, darkly. 'Unless *she's* in there.'

Ben made his way out of the room. There was no sign of Ji-Ah, Eun-Kyung or any of the grown-ups, so he made a dash for the bathroom – only to be foiled at the last minute by his dad, who appeared out of nowhere.

'Ah-ah,' John said, wagging a finger. 'Age before beauty.'

'Oh, Dad, come on!'

'I won't be long. I promise. Ish!' John locked the door behind him as Ben leaned moodily against the wall. He was going to at least make sure he was next in the queue.

At the end of the corridor was a large window, giving a view of the landscape for several miles. The sun was shining through fast-moving clouds, which dappled the ground below with strange shadow-patterns. Ben watched it, letting the hypnotic movement distract him from the discomfort in his bladder, and thought about how it was going to be from now on – living and working and going to school here, in Clare, instead of Dublin, the city he'd spent literally every other second of his life in. He could find a new library. Maybe they'd even have a coding club? And maybe there'd be other kids there who liked to game. And maybe –

His thoughts were cut off by the sight of a huge

black-and-grey crow, which fluttered to land on the windowsill. It was quickly joined by another, and then a third, and Ben felt something cold crawl over him as he looked at them. The black-and-grey bird, the largest of the three, looked just like the crow he'd seen yesterday, the one he'd thought had been looking at him.

Don't be stupid, he told himself, shaking away the idea. *How can a bird be looking at you? And why would it care?* He tried to ignore the crows, but they were large enough to take up a lot of the window and somehow he found he couldn't look away from them. The breeze ruffled their feathers and occasionally one would turn its head, as if keeping an eye on the countryside, but for the most part they focused their black-eyed gazes in, as if peering at everything – or everyone – inside the house, and him in particular. Ben saw their beaks opening and closing. The thick glass prevented the sound of their cawing from reaching him, but he could hear it anyway. In his imagination, the astringent sound was like a human voice trying to shout for help, while being strangled . . .

'All right, bud,' came his dad's voice, right in his ear. Ben yelped in surprise, jerking away from the wall like he'd been stung. Out of the corner of his eye, Ben noticed the birds leaping away from the sill and flapping off, right at the same moment his father spoke. 'For God's sake, son! I was only telling you the toilet was free,' John said, staring at Ben with concern. 'You don't need to act like I've stuck you with a needle.'

'Sorry,' Ben said. 'I was – I was just thinking. Didn't expect you to come out so suddenly.'

'You and your daydreaming,' John said, his eyes kind. 'You're a great kid. Your mam and me love you, no matter what way you are, and we always will – but try to keep yourself from wandering off, all right? We need you, down here on earth.' John ruffled his son's hair as he spoke, giving him a quick smile.

Ben returned his dad's smile, but he didn't really mean it. 'Got it,' he whispered.

'Now. Go on. Maybe we'll take a drive into Ennis today, see what's what,' his dad said, as Ben stepped into the bathroom. 'Would you like that?'

'Sounds great,' he said, before closing the door, locking it and leaning against it, his heart hammering in his chest like a trapped animal.

*

Ben pulled up the neck of his hoodie and tried to settle in his chair. A foamy-topped fruit juice sat in the plastic cup in front of him, violently green, its paper straw gradually getting soggy. Across from him sat his dad, his cup almost empty and his eyes on the sports pages of the newspaper he'd pulled from the display near the till at the coffee shop. *Property of Full O Beanz* was stamped across the masthead, just in case anyone forgot to return it.

The coffee shop was small and loud, in that weird way coffee shops always are – the sudden *kussssssshhhh* of the milk frother interspersed with crashing crockery and the occasional *clang* as a spoon or a knife hit the floor, and always dotted through with voices: talking, shouting, exploding into unexpected laughter. Ben usually found them a bit much to take, but his dad found them restful places to think, so Full O Beanz was where they'd ended up.

John flicked the paper shut and looked at his son. 'Hold on a minute there, Ben, you're talking so fast I can't quite catch what you're saying.' His smile was rueful, but kind.

Ben returned the grin, shifting position in the chair again. 'Sorry,' he mumbled.

'Enough of that "sorry" business,' John replied. 'You've nothing to be sorry for. How are you doing?'

Ben thought. He'd asked Fin – and Ji-Ah – if they wanted to come into Ennis with him, but Fin had pretended not to hear through his headphones and Ji-Ah had given him a disgusted sneer before slamming her bedroom door in his face. Mam was busy with Niamh, and Eun-Kyung had work, so it had been a silent car journey in, and so far a silent trip around the town. 'Lonely,' Ben finally managed. A bubble of misery surged up through him as he said the word, and he did his best to push it back down. He was afraid what might happen if it popped.

John tried to chuckle. 'How could you be lonely, in a house full of people?' He caught Ben's eye and his face softened. 'I know what you mean, son,' he said. 'I know this is hard. Mammy and me are doing our best, and maybe when we get our own place . . .' His words trailed away.

'I know,' Ben said.

'And when you start school!' John continued, brightly. 'I mean, you're bound to make a ton of pals there. And you'll have Aunty Niamh.'

Ben gave his dad a withering look. 'She's a *teacher*, Dad.'

John winced. 'Fair enough,' he said, holding up his hands in defeat. 'But it's only one year, and then you'll be off to secondary with Fin and Ji-Ah.'

'Brilliant,' Ben muttered.

'Give them a chance,' John said. 'It's hard for them too.'

Ben closed his eyes, suddenly aware that the noise inside the coffee shop was pounding like a piston inside his head. It was all too much – like the laughter and the shouting and the clashing and the gushing and the radio playing were going to make his brain burst. 'Can we – can we go? I need air.'

Ben was up and heading for the door before John had a chance to swallow his last mouthful of cold coffee and grab his jacket from the back of the chair. 'Hang on!'

Ben pushed his way out through the coffee shop door, gasping for breath. On top of the bin directly outside the shop sat a huge black crow, sleek and shining, its beak frighteningly massive and its eyes gleaming with intelligence. It let out a raucous caw which was answered by another bird, perched on a lamp-post a little way down the path. This one was black and grey, and it eyeballed Ben and the milling crowd all around before fluttering to join its friend on top of the bin. Ben's heart started to kick a weird beat inside him. These couldn't be the same birds he'd seen at home – could they? If so, they'd flown a long way just to stare at him in the street.

'Where's your other pal?' Ben whispered. The black-and-grey crow opened its beak, but nothing came out – at least, nothing Ben could hear. But its eye never left him. Ben focused on it, feeling himself being drawn into the smooth dark sphere, looking at his tiny upside-down reflection in the gleam, having an unbearable sensation of being sucked forward, and then –

'What are you like?' His dad's voice made him jerk awake again, and Ben caught himself. It felt like he'd been about to faint, or sprawl face down on the pavement. Again, as soon as his dad appeared, the birds scattered. 'Standing out here staring at a bin.'

Ben turned. His dad had just finished putting his jacket back on and was looking at Ben quizzically. 'Sorr—' Ben began, then stopped himself before he could let the word *sorry* out of his mouth again. Instead, he clamped his lips shut.

'Come on,' said John, reaching over to wrap an arm around his son's shoulders. 'Let's go and see if there's a bookshop or something. That might snap you out of it.'

As they walked, a single black feather floated down to land at Ben's feet. He kicked it away, trying to ignore the gurgling hollow fear in his stomach. *Stop being stupid!* he told himself, sharply. *Take your head out of the clouds. They're just crows!*

But somewhere deep down, Ben didn't believe it.

5

The crow's beak dripped with something terrible, the drops leaving a trail on the ground as the bird hopped forward. A bright red glow burned in its eye, a glow that looked like the face of a huge animal, roaring. A bear? A bear made of light and anger, its teeth bared. And then the crow took wing, carried by gusts of heat from down below – a foul heat, stinking of rot and corruption and death, and from its beak poured a stream of blood, dark and red as terror –

'Ben!' John's voice was irritated. Ben felt himself being shaken awake and he came to with a snort, trying to put things together in his head. He was in the passenger seat of the car. They'd arrived back at the house and his dad was staring at him.

'Sorry,' he said, which caused another muttering tirade from his father.

'It was like trying to wake the dead,' said John. 'Did you not sleep last night, or what?'

Ben shrugged. 'Not much.' He tried to put together the fragmentary dream. Crows, again? And – and *blood*, this time, and fire . . .

John tutted. 'Will you come on?' he said, opening the driver's door. 'We have shopping to put away.'

Ben undid his seatbelt and tried not to get tangled up in it as he pulled himself out of the car. His dad unlocked the front door, telling Ben to start unloading the boot. Ben did his best to follow instructions, all while feeling like his hands weren't his own, like his *head* didn't belong to him, like there was something wrong, *really* wrong, and he couldn't understand or explain it . . .

'Have you fallen asleep again?' John's voice broke into Ben's thoughts, and he turned to see his dad come striding around the back of the car. He reached into the boot and drew out two bags in each fist, hauling them out of the car while throwing Ben an exasperated look. 'Standing staring at the bags won't lift them into the kitchen, son.'

Ben shook his head and tried to focus. He grabbed a bag in each hand and followed his dad, trying to let the bustle of the busy house settle his mind. He did what he was told, stood where he was put, peeled carrots and potatoes and got them in the pot, all without really thinking about what he was doing. Around him conversations were had, music was blared, arguments were settled, dinner was cooked and dishes done, all while Ben felt like he was on another planet. He was *there*, but his mind was somewhere else.

'Earth to Brendan,' said Fin, waving a hand in front of Ben's face. 'What is with you today?'

His mother frowned. She put down her cup of tea and reached for him, placing a hand on his forehead. 'Are you feeling all right, love?'

'I'm fine,' he said, wriggling away from his mam's touch. 'I really am. Just a bit tired.'

'Hardly surprising,' grouched Ji-Ah. 'The noises that were coming from your room last night – it sounded like a *bear* was in there.'

'Hey!' Fin retorted, but the rest of his words disappeared beneath the fuzz in Ben's brain. *A bear?* 'Aren't you going to stand up for me? Your brother? Against these *vile* accusations?' Ben snapped back into focus again. Fin was laughing, but his cheeks were flushed a little pink. He was embarrassed but trying not to show it.

'I mean, you *do* snore like a bear.' Ben shrugged, while Ji-Ah punched the air in delight.

'What about the Bro Code?' Fin wailed.

'Justice is the only code I serve!' Ben called, making Ji-Ah laugh.

They shared a grin, and Niamh chuckled as she watched them. 'You're a bunch of eejits,' she said, fondly, which made them laugh again.

'Did you get anything nice in town?' Aisling asked, picking up her mug of tea once more.

Ben shrugged. 'Couple of books. A new pencil case for school. Nothing much.'

'Anything strange or startling happen while you were in?'

Ben knew this was just his mam's way of asking if anything interesting had happened in Ennis, but something about her words made him feel weird. *Strange. Startling. Well, Mam, as it happens, there was something strange and startling in town . . .*

His thoughts were interrupted by Niamh's mobile ringing. She looked at the screen and her eyebrows rose. 'Ji-Ah, it's your dad,' she said, handing the phone straight over.

Ji-Ah got to her feet as she took the phone, hurrying out of the room as she started to speak. 'Dad? Hi! How are you?' The rest of the conversation was lost as Ji-Ah slammed the kitchen door closed behind her, and all anyone could hear was the gallop of her footsteps on the stairs as she raced up to her room.

'Brace yourselves,' Niamh said.

Ben blinked at her. 'What do you mean?'

Niamh looked at him with tired, resigned eyes. 'After phone calls with Min-ho, I'm afraid our dear Ji-Ah is either on top of the world, or fit to rip anyone who crosses her path into shreds,' she explained. 'We won't know until she's finished, but it's better to prepare for the worst. Her dad has a particular knack of *really* getting under her skin.'

'Min-ho? That's her dad?' Fin asked.

'Park Min-ho, the very same,' Niamh sighed. 'Gorgeous and wealthy and a *total* messer when it comes to the ladies in his life.' She rolled her eyes. 'He loves the drama.'

Aisling cleared her throat. 'Didn't he and Melissa just have twin girls?'

Niamh gave her sister a meaningful look. 'Blessed is he amongst women.' The sisters shared a grin.

'Anyway,' John said, dragging the conversation back on track. 'I found the library, when we were in town. It should have everything we need, Ash – you know, what we were chatting about the other day.'

Aisling nodded. 'Great stuff. We can get started soon, in that case.'

Ben looked between his parents. 'Get started with what?'

His dad glanced at him. 'Looking for a place of our own. Trying to get work for Mam and me. That sort of thing.'

Ben's gaze dropped to the tablecloth. He found his fingers were tracing the pattern, without him even realising it, and he forced them to fall still. 'So, we're never going back to Dublin?' His voice was small, but his words hung in the air like a spell.

'Not in the immediate future, sweetheart,' Aisling said. 'You know that Dad and me had to give up work, and we've nothing in the bank to get us set up, and Dublin's gone so expensive . . .' She wrapped her fingers around her cup, staring into it as though she hoped it would hold the answers. 'It looks like this is a permanent move. At least until you lads finish school.'

Something shifted inside Ben's chest. He wondered if it was the last spark of hope finally going out. He *knew* his parents were doing the only thing they could, and he knew too, deep down, that he'd always understood this change of scenery was going to be long-term. But there'd been that tiny, stubborn light, the idea that maybe he'd wake up one morning and they'd be back in Raheny, and everything would be exactly as it had been. Now, all he felt inside was cold.

'Fantastic,' muttered Fin. 'I'm sure I'll get a record deal down here, in the armpit of nowhere.'

John chuckled, though his eyes were sad. 'Now there's the perfect title for the first album – *The Armpit of Nowhere*, from Eddie Ate Dynamite.' He lifted his hands in the air, his index and little fingers raised in the rock salute, and pretended to mosh, but Fin snorted in disgust and looked away. 'And isn't it all about streaming these days, anyhow?' John continued, laying his hands flat on the table. 'You can do that from anywhere.'

'Anywhere with decent broadband,' Fin retorted. 'Which does *not* include this place.'

John raised one eyebrow at his eldest son. '*Hence*, your mam and me were checking out the one place where there *is* excellent broadband, which is the *library*,' he said, in a 'gotcha' tone.

Fin muttered something in response, but before anyone could ask him to repeat it, Ji-Ah stormed into the kitchen and tossed Niamh's phone on the table. Without looking at anyone, she spun on her heel and left the room, once more disappearing upstairs. Niamh winced in preparation for the distant *bang* of her bedroom door. 'Yep,' she said, pocketing the phone. 'I thought as much.'

'When is Eun-Kyung due home?' Aisling asked.

'About seven or so,' Niamh replied. 'Though I doubt it'll matter.' Faint music could be heard pumping from Ji-Ah's room. It sounded like strangled wailing over clashing guitars to Ben, but Fin's face crumpled in what looked like agony.

'I've got to get out of here,' Fin muttered. 'Literally talking to sheep would be better than this.'

'You're in luck, so!' his dad quipped as Fin loped out through the back door into the bright evening.

Aisling looked at Ben. 'I don't suppose you have plans?'

Ben felt like his brain was a washing machine, spinning fast. Nothing was staying still long enough for him to understand it properly, and his whole body felt like it was fizzing with some weird energy. 'I'll – I might go and read, or something,' he said, weakly.

'You could go for a walk,' Niamh said. 'Go after your brother, and make sure he doesn't get eaten by any feral wildlife. Just remember what we said about the caverns. Right?'

Ben stretched his memory until the relevant details popped into it. 'Oh, yeah,' he said, remembering Eun-Kyung and Niamh's serious faces as they'd given him and Ben 'the Talk' about what was off-limits and what wasn't. 'I'm not to go into any caves, particularly the big one just past the end of the garden,' he recited in a drone.

Niamh and Aisling shared a look. '*That* one,' Aisling muttered.

Ben frowned at his mam. 'What do you mean?'

'Our dad,' Niamh said, stretching in her chair and fidgeting with a loose bit of the tablecloth. 'Out of what little he left us, he made sure we knew: that cave is off-limits. It's been closed off for years, certainly since I was a kid. Maybe Dad even put the gate up himself. Whatever you do – you stay away from it.'

'Is it dangerous?' John asked.

Aisling looked sad as she answered. 'It must be. Dad never said. I mean, I don't remember him talking about it, but Niamh does.'

Niamh snorted derisively. 'All I remember is the back of his head, bent over some book or other, or him waving at me to get out of his study, roaring that he was busy. And then he was gone, and so much good all his work did him.' She pushed herself up out of her chair. 'Anyway. Enough about that. Just stay out of the caves if you're going exploring, Ben. God knows where you'd end up.'

'And I know how kids think,' Aisling said, staring at her son. 'Adults tell you something's off-limits, and it makes you twice as determined to do whatever they tell you not to. But seriously. I don't want your bones discovered by some explorer in five hundred years' time, right? So, stay out.'

'Whatever,' sighed Ben, getting to his feet. 'See you later.'

'Say hello to the sheep for us!' called his dad, as Ben followed his brother out of the kitchen.

6

Fin was sitting on the back fence of the garden, his feet hooked around the middle plank. He had his earbuds in, but he popped one out as Ben approached.

'Are you here to drag me home, kicking and screaming?'

Ben gave him a quick grin. 'Nope. They told me I was to protect you against man-eating sheep, or something.'

Fin half-chuckled, without much humour in it. He turned his music off and stuck his phone and earbuds in his jeans pocket. 'So all this sucks, right,' he said. All Ben could see, when he looked up, was Fin's hair hiding his face.

'Yup.' Ben heard the sigh in his own voice. He leaned on the fence's top plank, using his arms as a cushion for his chin. In front of the boys, the landscape of the Burren stretched out like a huge, patterned tablecloth – bumps and hollows made by the limestone, with green patches in between. The only road anywhere near them was the one that led to the house, and traffic on it was practically non-existent. The only other houses were four or five fields away. It felt like they were on the edge of the world.

'It's sort of no wonder it got into Grandad's head,' Fin said, unexpectedly. He tossed his hair out of his eyes and looked down at his brother.

Ben straightened, meeting Fin's gaze. 'What did?'

Fin gestured at the landscape. 'All this. The *space*, and the emptiness, and the weirdness of it.'

'Did Mam tell you much about him?'

Fin looked back out towards the karst. He was drumming on his knees with his long fingers, to music only he could hear. 'Nah, not really,' Fin began. 'Only that he lost his marbles or something, and that he wasn't that nice of a guy.' Fin shrugged. 'That's all I know.'

Ben let his chin settle on his folded arms again. 'Mam warned me about the cave,' he said. 'The one

Grandad blocked off. She says we're not to go near it, even if that makes it sound more appealing, because she doesn't want some archaeologist in, like, a million years to discover our bones and wonder who on earth *these* fools were.'

'My awesomeness would be there, even in my bones,' Fin said, and Ben could hear his grin. 'They'd turn my skeleton into a drum kit and I'd live on – *forever*!' He shrieked the last word, rock-star style, and from somewhere close by three crows flew into the air, startled by the sudden sound. Ben watched them, swallowing back a mouthful of sour discomfort. Had they come from the cave? It was down in that direction . . . Fin laughed, tucking his hair behind his ears and looking down at Ben. He frowned. 'Are you okay? You look weirder than usual.'

'Those crows,' Ben whispered. 'They're, like, following me around.'

Fin snorted. 'No, Brendan, they are not, because they're animals and they have better things to do than follow a walking snot like you around the most boring place on earth. Trust me.'

'We both saw them, the first day,' Ben insisted, staring up at his brother. 'And then I saw them again, the next morning, like they were staring in at me. And *then*, when Dad and I went into Ennis, they were there! On a bin, eyeballing me.'

Fin took in a deep breath and let it out slowly, giving Ben a pitying look. 'My friend,' he began, 'sometimes, a crow is just a crow. You're worse than Aunt Niamh – she's forever pulling faces at any crow she sees, giving them the evil eye. And they all look the same anyway. My bet is they were just ordinary birds, and it's your *brain*,' he knocked his knuckles gently on Ben's head as he spoke, 'which is making things seem freaky. So, chill out. Take a breath. Touch some grass.'

'There's nothing wrong with my brain,' Ben grouched.

'You have an amazing brain! When it's not zooming past Jupiter, or whatever,' Fin teased. He unhooked his feet from the gate and swung himself back into the garden. 'But most of the time?' He reached out and pulled his brother in. 'You're all right.'

Ben relaxed against Fin's chest. He was almost up to his lanky brother's shoulder. 'I want to go home,' he said.

'Yeah, buddy, I do too,' Fin said, with a sigh.

'But, I mean, I guess all we can do is try to help the old pair, and do our best not to be monsters. And,' he added, with feeling, 'do whatever it takes to help get us out of here and away from *her*.' Ben didn't have to wonder who he was talking about.

'Ji-Ah's not so bad,' he said.

'In comparison to what?' Fin asked, genuinely incredulous.

Ben shrugged. 'That cave troll? From *Fellowship*.'

'Ooh, nice. Yeah, I need to get my Legolas on, right?'

'You have my axe!' Ben said, in his best Gimli voice.

Fin laughed, and Ben was glad it sounded sincere. 'We'll always be a fellowship, right? I mean, we mightn't always be *friends*, but – you're my bro. I'll always have your back.'

Ben looked up at him. 'Me too.'

'But until then, I reserve the right to knuckle your head,' Fin said, making his free hand into a fist and waving it menacingly at Ben's skull.

'No!' Ben yelled, half-laughing. 'No *way*! Get off!'

They hit the ground in a tangle of limbs, laughing and breathless. 'It's either going to be a mouthful of grass, or a head-knuckle,' Fin said, straining with the effort of keeping his brother pinned down. 'Make your choice!' His voice boomed like a character from a video game.

'Oh my God! All right!' Ben braced himself. 'A head-knuckle. Do it!'

'Nah,' Fin said, ripping up a handful of grass. 'It's no fun when you've got permission.' He tried to force the grass into Ben's laughing mouth.

'Wow, you guys are idiots,' came a voice from behind them. They turned, covered in blades of grass and red-cheeked from laughter, to see Ji-Ah standing a few feet away, her arms folded.

'Finished listening to your screeching cat music?' Fin asked, pushing himself up. Ben groaned as his brother's elbow dug into his midriff.

'It's better than your brainless noise,' Ji-Ah retorted.

Ben sat up, shaking grass out of his hair. 'Why are you out here?'

Ji-Ah sighed. 'I was sent to make sure you pair weren't doing anything you aren't supposed to. Like, breaking things. Or disappearing into caves.'

'They are *so* in a knot about the caves,' Fin said,

slightly out of breath. He leaped to his feet, before leaning down and offering his hand to pull Ben up. 'Don't they trust us?'

Ji-Ah raised one dark eyebrow. 'Of course they don't,' she said. 'Look what you've done to the garden.'

The boys glanced down. Their scuffling had torn up some of the grass, and their careless feet had pulled out chunks of the lawn. 'Ah,' said Fin, staring at Ben in a slightly panicked way. 'Right. Good point.'

'I *knew* this would happen,' Ji-Ah said. 'I told Mam and Eomma that having *boys* here would completely wreck the place. There haven't been men here since Mam and Aunty Aisling were kids! And there's no point having them here now either. The last one caused enough trouble.'

Fin narrowed his eyes as he looked at her, like he was trying to figure something out. 'You mean Grandad? Is that who you're talking about?'

Ji-Ah rolled her eyes. 'Well, *yes*. Who else?'

'What do you mean, he caused enough trouble?' Ben asked.

'He hurt Mam and Aunty Aisling,' Ji-Ah said, staring at them. 'Do you really not know?'

'Our mam never talks about it,' Fin said.

'She probably doesn't remember. She was only a toddler,' Ji-Ah said, her voice loaded with regret. 'And I suppose I shouldn't talk about it, if your mam doesn't want you to know.' She gave the boys a look full of pretend apology as she started to turn away, but Fin was faster. He darted around in front of her, dragging Ben with him.

'Cut the nonsense,' Fin said. 'And spill it.'

Ji-Ah pressed her lips tight as she stared at the boys, making a smile that wasn't really a smile. 'Well, you know, he had an obsession,' she began. 'With something that had to do with this house, or the land it was built on, or both. And he spent all his time – like, every single second – researching it, or writing about it, or thinking about it. He never spent time with his family, they never had a holiday, Mam never remembers him even playing with her. They basically had no relationship. She didn't know him. And Aunty Aisling was younger, so as bad as it was for my mam, it was worse for yours. At least Mam remembers what her dad *looked* like.' She shrugged suddenly. 'And then he died, unexpectedly, and sort of *young* for a grown-up, like in his mid-forties?

67

So Granny basically pretended for the rest of her life that none of it had ever existed – that his work, like, just wasn't a real thing, and that her husband had spent the previous twenty years researching daffodils, or whatever.'

'It was all for nothing,' Ben said. The words dripped something cold down his spine, like a trickle of freezing water.

'The only thing his quote-unquote "work" achieved was to create two daughters who hate his guts,' Ji-Ah said, using air quotes around the word "work".

'But what was it? The stuff he was obsessed with?' Fin asked.

Ji-Ah tucked her hair behind her ears, looking thoughtful. 'Nobody's really sure,' she said. 'As far as Mam remembers, whenever she asked about it, Granny's face would go all hard and she'd say something about *magic*, or *curses*. And he was so insistent that nobody went into that cave that he put a completely illegal gate up, to block it off. Granny was going to take it down, but she never did.'

'So, did she sort of believe in Grandad's stuff?' Ben asked. 'Or why did she leave the gate up?'

Ji-Ah shrugged. 'Who knows?' she said. 'Anyway.

We don't go into Grandad's cave, and that's sort of that. Okay?'

'And where's all his stuff now?' Ben asked. 'You know, his papers or his research, or whatever.'

'*No* idea,' Ji-Ah said. 'In the house, maybe? His office is still there, only Mam uses it as a junk room now. It's opposite the sitting room and usually locked, but she keeps the key in the kitchen somewhere.' Ben's memory flashed to the door with the vanished nameplate that he'd noticed the day before. *So that's what's in there.*

'Maybe his stuff is in the cave,' Fin said, shooting Ben a look of dark amusement.

'Anyway, look. It's nearly dinner. Come on and get washed. You guys look like you were rolling in cowpats.' Ji-Ah's nose wrinkled as she turned away.

'Last one there eats a handful of grass,' Fin said, darting after her.

7

Ben woke the next morning feeling like he'd been put through a tumble dryer. He was hot and sweaty, and his mouth felt parched and full of fluff. He sat up, grabbing the glass of water he kept on his bedside table, and downed it in one gulp. His head was fuzzy too, like sleep didn't want to let him go. He rubbed his eyes, hoping to clear them, and to sort out his head.

He sat on the edge of the bed for a few minutes, scrunching his toes in the carpet. *This is real*, he found himself thinking. *The carpet. The bed. This house.* He looked out of the bedroom window, squinting in the daylight. Fin had already pulled the curtains open. On the horizon he saw the slope of Mullaghmore, the mountain his Aunt Eun-Kyung had talked about.

The one with the light, he reminded himself. *The light that not everyone can see.* He swallowed hard. *The light I saw.*

He stumbled to the bathroom, and as he was brushing his teeth, he remembered some of the dream he'd been having. *There was a bear*, he thought, holding his toothbrush beneath the gushing tap for too long. *Wasn't there?* He was sure there had been – a huge thing, with blue-flame eyes and claws like knives . . .

'Hurry up in the bathroom!' His mam's voice sounded sharp, and her knock on the door even sharper. 'Ben, is that you?'

'Coming, Mam,' he called, turning off the tap and sticking his toothbrush back in the cup. 'Keep your wig on.'

'Cheeky monkey,' his mother teased as Ben unlocked the door. She gave him a quick kiss on the cheek. 'Go on down and get some breakfast. The others are up.'

He sloped back to his room and got dressed before making his way downstairs. His head still felt like it wasn't quite there, or like he'd left some vital part of himself in dreamland. He thought about bears, and how they hibernated in caves, and wondered if this was how they felt when spring came and they had to wake up. *No wonder they're grouchy*, he thought.

'Morning!' trilled Niamh, resplendent in a bright orange dressing gown. Ben winced but gave her a half-hearted wave.

'Yeah,' he grumbled, as he found his way to a chair.

'Are you *sick* or something?' Ji-Ah said, pulling delicately away from him.

'Just – half asleep still,' Ben said. 'Weird dreams.'

'It was a really muggy night,' Niamh said. 'I don't think anyone slept well.'

'Eomma did,' Ji-Ah said. 'She's already out weeding the flowerbeds.'

Niamh pushed herself to her feet. 'And here I am, like a *lady*, in my dressing gown,' she said. 'I suppose I'd better go and help her, only I have no eye for a weed. I'd be pulling up her flowers by mistake.'

Fin swallowed a mouthful of cereal. 'You're less like a lady and more like a bad fake tan in that dressing gown, Aunty Niamh,' he said.

'You absolute *gurrier*,' she replied, smacking him gently on the back of the head, though her grin –

and Fin's – was wide. 'You're one hundred per cent correct. So, I'm off to put my face on.'

Ben took his bowl of cereal outside. The morning was bright and cloudless – a proper summer's day. It wasn't hot, yet, but it felt like things would warm up soon. He spotted Eun-Kyung on her kneeling mat beside the flowerbed that ran along the driveway on the approach to the house. She was busy, humming a tune under her breath.

Ben stopped, enjoying the sensation of the cold bowl on his skin, and leaned against the house as he ate. The brickwork looked *ancient*, like something that had been built centuries ago, and the windows were old-fashioned too, the type that needed to be opened by pushing up the bottom pane. He couldn't remember what they were called. Everything around here seemed like it had been pulled out of an old story, like a fairy tale come to life. It was all so different from his house in Dublin, with its smooth walls and open-plan rooms. Here, things felt heavy, rooted in the earth, like they would never change or be anything different. He wondered how long his family had lived here, and whether anyone was still around who could tell him. The fresh air began to clear his head a little, and he closed his eyes as the sunlight bathed his face.

'You okay?' Eun-Kyung called, pausing her work to look at him. She shaded her eyes with one gloved hand.

'Yep,' he called back. 'Just enjoying the morning.'

Eun-Kyung nodded, turning back to her work. 'It's a good one,' she said. 'I can smell *wonder* in the air. Can't you?'

Ben sniffed. Mostly, he could smell grass. 'Not sure,' he said, and Eun-Kyung laughed. He pushed himself away from the wall and strolled towards his aunt, before sitting cross-legged on the ground beside her. 'Hey,' he said, when he was settled. 'How old's this house?'

Eun-Kyung rolled back onto her heels, pushing some hair out of her face with the back of her glove. 'Oh, that's a question. I'm not sure. At least a hundred years? Maybe a lot more. It's been here for a very long time.'

'So, my grandad didn't build it?'

'Your grandfather?' Eun-Kyung looked puzzled. 'No, it was here before him. Though, how long before, I can't say.'

Ben chewed thoughtfully as his aunt unzipped

the light jacket she'd been wearing. She had one of her work T-shirts on underneath, even though today was her day off. It had her name embroidered on the front – *Dr Eun-Kyung Kang, Karst Landscape Specialist*. As she turned to toss her jacket behind her, Ben saw the logo on the back of her shirt.

A bear. A huge one, loping towards a round-topped mountain, its head lifted in a roar.

He choked on his mouthful of breakfast and Eun-Kyung turned back. 'Ben, are you all right?'

'I'm fine,' he sputtered, getting his breath back. 'I'm okay, honestly. Just – it went down the wrong way.' Eun-Kyung smiled, but her eyes stayed worried. 'I got a surprise, I think. Your T-shirt, and the logo on it. I mean, I've seen it before.' It was also on her four-wheel drive, painted on the doors of the vehicle and on the bonnet too. 'But it's just – well, I've been dreaming about bears. And then, I see one on your shirt. It made me sort of forget whether I was supposed to be eating, or breathing, so I coughed instead.'

Eun-Kyung smiled, properly this time. 'The logo? I love it. There *were* bears here, you know, thousands of years ago. There were bears all over Ireland then, and lots of other species that are extinct now.

That's why we have the bear as our logo, as a way to pay tribute to it and keep its memory alive.'

Ben's eyes widened. 'No way,' he said. 'There really were bears here?'

Eun-Kyung nodded. 'The oldest bear bones found in the area are over ten thousand years old. So, the landscape was probably quite different then, maybe forested, as bears don't often thrive in landscapes that look like the *modern* Burren. But they did live here, and for a long time too. Other bear bones, some with marks on to suggest they were hunted and killed by human settlers, have been found and they're all several thousand years old. The bear is part of the tapestry of this land, without a doubt.'

Ben's head began to swim. 'That's amazing,' he said.

'And they're in your dreams?' Eun-Kyung asked, gently.

Ben nodded. 'Just since we moved,' he said. 'My dreams have been pretty weird ever since we started living here.' As he spoke, he felt something like relief, or recognition, as though his worries were glad he was finally speaking them aloud.

Eun-Kyung shrugged. 'Dreams are important,'

she told him. 'In Korea, we believe dreams are omens, and they have a lot of meaning.'

'So, why do you think I'm dreaming about a bear?' Ben asked. 'What does that mean?'

Eun-Kyung looked thoughtful. 'Maybe it's a sign the bears are coming back,' she said, after a few moments.

Ben stared at her. '*Really?*'

Eun-Kyung laughed, reaching out to take Ben's hand. She gave it a gentle squeeze. 'Or maybe it's just because you saw the logo on my car, or on my shirt, and it was a hot night where everyone's dreams got muddled up,' she said, kindly. 'I don't know, Ben. All I know is, bears are found in lots of belief systems, all over the world. In Korea, when you dream about a bear, it's a sign that something great is going to happen to your household. Bears are even part of the foundation myth of Korea. And they're so important here too. How about I tell you some of the folklore and legends of this area, including the bits about bears? Maybe that will help.'

Ben nodded. 'Okay,' he said, settling himself more comfortably on the tarmac. A sudden realisation made him stop. 'Unless this is all too much like your job, and you'd rather not talk about it on your day off,' he said.

Eun-Kyung smiled. 'I love talking about this stuff. Especially to someone who's interested.'

Ben grinned. 'So. The bears.'

'Well. Bears are usually seen as guardians, right? Like guardian spirits. So, they roam the land here, keeping things safe, looking after everything.'

'What about crows?' Ben said, feeling uneasy as the words left his mouth.

Eun-Kyung's forehead wrinkled a little. 'Ooh. Crows are associated with battle, mostly. Like, they're a warning of a battle to come? I think. In folklore, I mean, they'd have that association with death, and in Korea, they're often seen as bad luck. But in real life? They're just extremely intelligent and quite brilliant birds.'

'And what about that mountain? You know the one you were telling me about before. The one with the light on it.'

Eun-Kyung nodded. 'Mullaghmore. Yes. Well, legend has it that it's the home of the Cailleach. She's also called the Hag of the Hills, and she's a sort of goddess, I guess – one with the power to shape the landscape, raise or flatten mountains and control the wind and the weather, especially thunder and lightning – a bit like Thor, maybe. She's supposed to have given the Burren its particular shape – though, as a scientist, I can tell you that's not how it happened,' Eun-Kyung said, with a smile.

'How does she do it? The Cailleach. The Hag. How does she flatten mountains?'

'With her hammers,' Eun-Kyung said. 'She has two, I think, and she uses them to mould the landscape. And as well as that, she also forges things from metal. Some of the legends say that the lightning from her mountain is the sparks from her metalworking, which sort of makes sense, right? And she's a swordsmith. She's supposed to have made some of the most important swords in Irish mythology, including the most important one of all – the Claíomh Solais. The Sword of Light, or Sword of the Sun.'

'Was it made of *actual* light?' Ben asked. 'Like, a lightsaber?'

Eun-Kyung laughed. 'No! Not like that. It's a metal sword. But it carries the light of the sun in it. The light of goodness, and justice, and mercy. It's the greatest weapon ever made, one which gives its wielder ultimate power in battle, and it's one of the ancient treasures of the Tuatha Dé Danann.'

'Wow,' Ben breathed.

'You've heard of them?' Eun-Kyung asked.

Ben nodded. 'I think we did them in school, a few years ago. Weren't there four? The Sword, and then a Spear, and a Stone, and – I can't remember the last one.'

'The Cauldron,' Eun-Kyung said. 'Four really important and powerful objects, and we've got a link to one, right here.'

'You reckon it's actually *here*? The Sword? Like, in the Burren?'

Eun-Kyung shrugged. 'Nobody knows. It's only a legend, anyway. The Sword has been lost since the Second Battle of Moytura, when its wielder, Nuada, was defeated by Balor of the Evil Eye.' She shuddered dramatically, her eyes shining as she got lost in her tale. 'Nuada lost an arm in a previous battle, against a Fir Bolg warrior named Sreng, but he had a marvellous silver one forged instead. They called him Nuada Airgeadlám, or Nuada Silverarm, from then on. The Arm has also been lost, but it's nearly as important as the Sword itself. Your grandfather wrote, in one of his books, that only someone of Nuada's blood, or the person who had the Arm of Nuada, could wield the Sword of the Sun.'

Ben jerked in surprise. 'Wait – my grandad wrote *books*?'

Eun-Kyung suddenly looked uncomfortable. She blinked, and the light in her eyes dimmed. 'Maybe this is something you should discuss with your parents.'

'But my mam won't talk about her dad,' Ben said.

Eun-Kyung took a deep breath and seemed to be thinking hard. Finally she spoke again, her voice low. 'Your grandfather was one of the foremost folklorists of this area, and he was obsessed with the Sword, and Nuada. He did a huge amount of scholarly work on them, and on the beliefs and magic and traditions of the region. I had read his work before I ever met and married Niamh. He's sort of the reason I even wanted to come and work here, so I have a lot to thank him for.' She tried to smile. 'I don't think there are copies here in the house, but I bet they'd have some of his books in the library.'

Ben did his best to return his aunt's smile. 'Thanks,' he told her.

'Don't be hard on your mam, or on Niamh,'

Eun-Kyung said. 'They missed out on a lot, as children.' She glanced down at his cereal bowl. The leftovers were starting to dry, cement-hard. 'You'd better get that into the kitchen, and fast! I don't want to listen to Niamh giving out as she tries to get it clean.'

Ben grabbed the bowl and got to his feet. 'Thanks, Eun-Kyung!' he called, as he ran for the kitchen door.

'You're welcome,' she whispered in response, trying to quell the fear that she'd done something wrong. A breeze blew in from the Burren, ruffling her hair, and she grimaced as she smelled the scent it carried – rottenness, like something hunted and left uneaten, allowed to go bad instead. She stared out onto the karst. Nothing stirred, but Eun-Kyung couldn't shake her sudden wariness at the expectant hush that seemed to fall over everything, as though something, somewhere out there, was *waiting*.

8

'You've got my seatbelt!' Ji-Ah's voice drilled into Ben's ear.

'No, I don't,' he muttered in reply, but Ji-Ah snatched it out of his hand anyway. After a few seconds of trying to make it click in, she shoved it back at him. 'Told you,' Ben couldn't help responding, which prompted her to throw him an acidic look.

'Eomma –' she began, but Eun-Kyung responded by starting the engine, which was loud enough to drown her out. She threw the vehicle into reverse.

'Children, children,' came John's voice from the middle seats. 'Calm yourselves.'

'I'm not listening to squabbling all the way to Ennis,' Aisling said. 'If you pair can't behave, you can forget about pizza night this week. Right?'

Ben sighed, pressing the palm of his hand against his mouth as he stared out of the window of Eun-Kyung's work vehicle. It was the only one big enough to bring him, Ji-Ah, Eun-Kyung, Niamh and his parents into town all at once. Eun-Kyung and Niamh sat in front, his parents were in the middle seats and he and Ji-Ah were stuck at the back. Fin got to stay at home and 'practise' – he and the other members of Eddie Ate Dynamite were trying to hold a session via videocall – but Ben had been deemed too young to stay without supervision. So, he'd been packed into the car along with everyone else.

'They'd better have a good selection of frames,' Ji-Ah grouched. 'Last time, they were *manky*. I wish we could go to a bigger opticians, where there might actually be a choice between *bleugh* and even more *bleugh*.'

'Lookit, you,' Niamh said, turning in her seat to meet Ji-Ah's eye. 'Cassidy's are brilliant, and it's where I used to go when I was your age. So cut it out.'

'Exactly my point,' Ji-Ah continued, as her mam settled in her seat once more. 'They've been in business since the Stone Age, so how could they possibly have heard of things like fashion?'

'Is she still talking?' Niamh called from the front seat, and Ji-Ah finally settled into glowering silence. 'What time's the appointment, again?' Niamh asked her wife.

'Ten thirty,' Eun-Kyung replied, straightening her wheel to point the vehicle down the driveway. 'Everyone strapped in?' she called, and got chorus of *yeses* in response.

'Anyone need the loo?' Eun-Kyung called, with a grin in her voice.

'*Eomma!*' Ji-Ah shouted, in disgust. Everyone else laughed and Ben grinned, though it was mostly hidden by his hand.

'Then we're off!' Eun-Kyung drove slowly down the bumpy driveway, and out onto the main road.

Ben watched fields and ditches whip past as Eun-Kyung drove, and they quickly reached the outskirts of Ennis, passing rows of neat houses. A lake – one of several, in this rugged, beautiful place – sparkled to their right as they joined a larger road which led into the town proper. It was busy, as usual, and Ben tried to find similarities between this bustling place, still so new to him, and Dublin, the city he'd been so familiar with. There weren't many.

They passed signs for a hospital, and then Niamh pointed to the right. 'There's your school, Ben,' she said. He looked, but they passed by too quickly for him to take it in. It looked a bit newer than the school he had been going to in Dublin. 'Don't worry,' his aunt said, turning to give him a smile. 'We'll pay a visit before term starts, and I'll give you the guided tour. You'll be grand.'

Ben nodded, but his anxiety was like cold mud around his heart. The kids whose class he'd be joining would probably have known one another since they were four or five, so would they be bothered to try and help him fit in? They only had one more year of primary left before they'd be splitting up to go to different secondary schools anyway, so would anyone care about the new kid? He sighed heavily. He missed his mates from Raheny. Mostly, they'd been kids he'd met in the coding group at the library, but he thought about his old class with a longing that felt painful, like part of him was stretching out across the country, trying to reach all the things he'd had to leave behind. While he'd actually *been* there, he hadn't been a huge fan of school, but now it was gone he felt like he'd do anything to get it all back.

While he'd been thinking, Eun-Kyung had found a place to park. 'Okay, team,' she said, turning to look at them. She held up her phone with the time displayed on it. 'It's ten-oh-eight. Niamh, Ji-Ah and I will make our way to the opticians, and we'll meet you all at about noon. Okay? Does that give you enough time in the library?' She looked at Aisling and John.

Aisling shrugged. 'It'll do,' she said. 'There either are jobs and houses here, or there aren't. I'm sure I'll know fairly quickly.'

The group split up, but as Ben and his parents began to walk he found himself dragging back. Aisling and John stopped, looking back at him quizzically. 'I was thinking,' Ben said. 'Can we go for a walk, or something, before we have to go the library? I'm just, sort of, not in the mood for spending all morning there.'

His parents shared a look, and Aisling nodded. She turned to Ben. 'Dad'll go with you,' she said. 'I'm quicker looking for stuff on my own anyway. Is that okay?'

John pretended to wipe his forehead with relief. 'Your mam is the computer whiz,' he said. 'I'm here hunting and pecking at the keyboard, while she's clattering away beside me like nobody's business.'

Aisling chuckled, shaking her head a little, as she gazed at her husband. 'Right,' she said. 'Don't go far. Do you have money for a cup of tea, or whatever?'

John patted his pockets. 'Wallet – check. Phone – check. Marbles? AWOL.'

'Fantastic. I'll ring you when I'm ready, or if I need you. Maybe you could stroll down towards the river? There's ruins of an old abbey you could look at, and a park not too far beyond.' John leaned in to kiss her on the cheek, Ben gave her a hug and then she was gone, into the old stone library building.

John looked down at his son, offering him a hand to hold. Ben raised his eyebrows and stared up at him. 'Right, right,' John said, sticking his hand into his pocket. 'Just thought I'd give it a go, for old times' sake.'

They walked away from the library, in the direction Aisling had suggested. Soon, they found themselves crossing the river, joining the flow of people across the bridge. The ruined abbey was right in front of them, just as Aisling had said it would be, and they wandered towards it. An information sign on the street outside proclaimed it was actually a friary, not an abbey.

'I must tell Mam that later,' he said.

'I'm sure she'll be thrilled to be corrected,' John replied, and they shared a grin. 'Will we go in?'

John got the fee ready, and they paid for two tickets. 'Go on and explore,' he said. 'I'm going to check out the museum bit, but I'll see you back here in ten. Okay?'

Ben nodded and made a run for it. The site wasn't huge, but the ruins were impressive – tall, pointed windows which seemed to float in space, without a wall around them. Carved tombs, with carefully worded signs nearby telling people not to climb on them. Weird little stone faces popping out of unexpected places, beneath lintels and on the tops of pillars. Ben found he was actually enjoying himself.

Then the peace was shattered by a loud caw. The other visitors to the friary didn't seem to hear it – certainly none of them jumped in surprise, like Ben. It was an ordinary noise for them, part of the tapestry of this ancient place, and no cause for alarm. For Ben, it was like someone blasting an air-horn right in his ear. He spun on the spot, looking for what he knew he'd inevitably see.

'There you are,' he whispered. The crows were back. They sat on top of some ruined windows, the glass long gone. All that remained was the stone surround and part of the wall they'd once been built into. The crows looked like they were waiting for a bus, Ben thought, the image so strange inside his head that he almost felt like laughing. They were settling themselves, trimming their feathers and adjusting their grip, looking at one another and all around as though they were old folk, chatting about the weather while trying to keep hold of their shopping.

And then, down below, a shape flickered past the empty window frames. Ben blinked, taken by surprise, not sure what he'd seen – but a moment later the shape passed the next window, and he saw it more clearly. It was a person, on the other side of the wall. He stared, willing the figure to pass the third empty pane – and then, there they were. This time, the person stopped. Their back was to Ben, and there was nothing really remarkable about them . . . but somehow, Ben found he couldn't look away.

The person turned a little, and part of their face became visible. It was a woman, Ben saw, with long black hair, thick as a horse's tail but shiny as obsidian. She wore some sort of robe – Ben had thought it was a coat – and when she turned fully, he was transfixed by the icy brightness of her eyes, an iridescent violet-blue, and the thick black lashes that surrounded them. Her lips and cheeks were weirdly bright, not with makeup, but instead like some kid had taken their most garish crayon and coloured her in. She fixed her eyes on Ben. A strange little smile lifted the corners of her scarlet lips. She raised her hands and the crows fluttered down to sit, one on each of her palms, their beady-eyed gazes feeling like pinpricks on Ben's skin.

'I don't like this,' Ben muttered, just as the woman's gaze flicked away from him and landed somewhere to his right. Ben could've sworn her eyes turned from deep purple-blue to a flashing red at the same moment, and something about the urgency in her expression made him turn, to see what she was looking at.

Another woman stood there, about five metres away from Ben but paying him no attention whatsoever. She was tallish, with a purple beanie. She wore a black-and-white patterned scarf around her neck and a short, bottle-green jacket. Her jeans were baggy. She stood, staring at the woman with the crows, her face set like stone. Her eyes, what Ben could see of them, looked extraordinarily blue, almost silver.

Ben became aware of a buzzing tightness in the air, like how it must feel inside a balloon when it's overfilled and just about to pop –

Something knocked him to one side, throwing him off balance. He turned to see a woman with a baby strapped to her front, and a large rucksack on her back. This bag was what had bumped into Ben.

'I'm so sorry,' the lady began, her eyes wide with apology. 'I didn't see you there, love!'

Ben shook his head. 'No problem,' he said, and the harried-looking woman gave him a grateful look before picking her way carefully onwards. Her baby grinned at Ben as they passed, and Ben couldn't help but grin back – but when he turned to the window again, he found it was completely empty. No sign of the crow-woman, and not even a leftover feather to suggest the crows had ever been there. He turned to look for the other woman, but she was gone too.

Quickly, Ben made his way to the windows. Once, the wall they'd originally been set into had run along the whole length of a now-vanished room, but all that was left of it were some tumbled stones. Ben hurried around to the windows' far side – and stopped dead. The ground here – where, he told himself, he'd just seen someone walking – was much lower than the ground he'd been standing on. There was a ditch, or a moat, outside the old friary wall, filled with long grass and strings of briar – it wouldn't be much fun to wade through that.

So there's no way I saw someone standing out here, Ben told himself. *Unless they were, like, as tall as a house.*

Unless, he realised with a judder of horror, they weren't standing on the ground at all.

9

Ben hurried to the museum display, where he knew
he'd find his dad. His feet slapped on the stone floor
as he ran, loud enough to make Dad turn round as he
drew near – and for a member of staff to call out, 'No
running, please!'

Ben slowed to a stop as he approached his dad.
'What's up, buddy? You haven't had your ten minutes
yet.'

'Saw it all,' Ben said. 'Got bored.'

John's eyebrows rose. 'Fair enough,' he said. 'Will
we head into the town, and see what's what? There
have to be doughnuts here somewhere. Or ice cream.'

Ben tried to smile. 'Two scoops.'

'Ooh,' John said. 'That sounds like a plan.'

They followed the narrow street, thronged with

people, towards the town centre. As they walked, Ben slipped his hand into his dad's. John looked down, happy surprise on his face, and gave his son's fingers a squeeze. Ben wrapped his fingers tight around his dad's, looking around at all the ordinary, normal people, coming and going from ordinary, normal shops, doing absolutely ordinary, normal things.

No floating *levitate-y people here*, Ben thought, focusing on the sounds and sights and the feeling of his hand in his dad's. *Absolutely nothing weird going on.*

They paused outside a bookshop to have a look in the window, and as Ben stood there he felt sure there was someone – or something – beside him. But when he whipped his head around to look, he saw it was just a pavement sign advertising the shop next door and he breathed a sigh of relief. Then, his eye was caught by an odd shadow in the glass of the bookshop window; a dark shape, that didn't seem to be cast by anything. It was just *there*, like a blot of ink. He turned his head again to look down the street and saw someone walking around the corner a few shops away – a tall woman, with ebony-black hair, wearing a billowing dark cloak. Barely a moment after Ben spotted her, one long stride took her right around the corner and out of his sight, but her presence lingered.

It was a warm day, but Ben felt like he'd just swallowed a snowball.

A jet-black feather came fluttering back round the corner, skittering down the pavement. As he watched it, Ben felt like things were moving in slow motion. He could see the feather dancing its way between the people on the crowded pavement, who seemed to move to avoid it without realising. *It's coming for me*, Ben thought, the words ringing in his head like a dulled bell.

The feather landed on his arm, right below the sleeve of his T-shirt. It stayed there for a moment or two, just long enough for Ben to realise that his skin was stinging, like the feather was coated in something that was making him itch. The sensation grew until it felt like he was burning, right where the feather was touching him. He grimaced and shook it off, and the feather continued its swirling journey. A hot gust of wind brought more feathers with it, some with their shafts pointed at Ben, like darts or arrows, and more with their shining black barbs like oil in the sunlight. One billowed around his dad's head, seemingly about to touch him and then pulling away at the last moment, almost like it was teasing Ben, who was staring at it in fear. Eventually, it fluttered away.

'Dad, come on,' Ben said, pulling at John's hand. 'I want to get out of here.'

Speaking aloud seemed to break whatever spell had been wrapping itself around him, and Ben was glad to see his dad react normally, looking down at him curiously. 'The call of the ice cream is strong, then? Even stronger than the call of the books?'

Ben tried to look unconcerned. 'Actually, I thought maybe we'd just head back and find Mam. I think I've had enough outdoors-ness. Maybe we could all get ice cream together instead,' he said. 'Okay?'

'Okey-dokey,' John sang, good-naturedly, as they turned away from the bookshop window.

Ben focused on his feet as they walked, something he often did when the world seemed too much to take. It helped him to block things out, to steady himself and know: your feet are on the ground, and that's all you need to worry about. *There is nothing freaky going on here, and I am* not *living in a daydream – not today!*

'Head up, son,' John said, jiggling his hand to get his attention. 'You know I hate when you walk like

that, all hunched over and staring at your shoes.'

'Sorry,' Ben muttered, trying to push his shoulders back. The world rushed in again, crowded and colourful and loud, and Ben started to scrunch his eyes shut to block it out – but just as he did, something caught his attention. A crow, though it seemed like an ordinary one this time, busy pulling some rubbish out of a street bin. It didn't even look his way as they passed, and Ben heaved a sigh of relief.

It didn't take long to get back to the library, and Ben was glad of the dim, cool, quiet interior. It was small, but neat and ordered and clean, and Ben saw his mam sitting at one of the computer terminals, squinting bad-temperedly at the screen. His dad let go of his hand before ruffling his hair. 'I'll go and see how your mam's doing. You'll be all right in here, won't you?' he whispered. 'Come and get me if you need anything. The toilets are over there. Okay?'

As soon as his dad was gone, Ben wrapped his arms tight around himself. His whole body was trembling. It felt like his veins were full of something that fizzed and bubbled, and as he found a cushion in the children's section to sit on, his fingers were itching to move. Whenever things got too much, sometimes he wiggled his fingers as fast as he could, and sometimes he found himself tracing words or letters either in the air or on his legs, over and over until the overwhelm began to settle. This was another thing his parents thought looked weird, but Ben knew there was nobody here to see him.

Help, he traced with his fingers. *Help. Help.*

'Are you all right?' came a gentle voice, and Ben looked up. There was a librarian nearby, crouched so her face was level with Ben's. She wasn't crowding him and she didn't try to reach out, but her expression was kind. For a second Ben stared at her, wondering how it felt like he'd seen her before.

Finally he nodded, and then shook his head, and the librarian smiled. 'Are your grown-ups with you?'

'They're at the computers,' Ben replied, and the librarian looked relieved.

'Can I help you with anything?'

'Do – do you know anything about crows? Or, not *crows*, but, like, a woman. Who's connected with crows.' Ben paused to swallow. 'And she's scary,' he continued.

'Ooh, a mystery,' the librarian said, getting down on the floor across from Ben. She wore a rainbow-striped jumper, baggy jeans, bright purple runners and a lanyard around her neck with her name – Dani. The final letter looked a little scuffed, as though it could have been 'u' or 'i'. 'Do you mean in a story? Because she sounds a lot like a mythological character called the Morrígan. Have you heard of her?'

When Ben shook his head, Dani continued. 'So, the Morrígan is a goddess, in Irish folklore. She's associated with crows, and she's a goddess of war and destruction and death, things like that. One of her names is Battle Crow.' Dani looked at Ben, her eyes wide. 'She's a pretty scary customer, but funnily enough in the original stories about her, she's not *always* bad. Sometimes, she fights for the "goodies".' She wiggled her fingers around the word "goodies", smiling at Ben at the same time. 'But usually she's seen as a baddie, or a figure of fear, probably because she's associated with frightening things. And she's super powerful. She's actually made up of three separate people – isn't that weird?' Dani smiled more widely, her nose crinkling, and Ben tried to smile back. 'Two other goddesses, her sisters Macha and Badhbh, are sort of part of her, and they can separate if they like or stay part of one body. So, she's called a triple-aspect goddess, because she has three "aspects", or three different appearances. It's a bit hard to understand.'

'Does she have dark hair?' Ben asked. 'And, like, red cheeks? And a cloak made of feathers?'

'I'm not sure about the cloak,' Dani said. 'But whenever I think of her, I imagine her with dark hair. Black, like a crow's wing.'

'Yeah,' Ben said. 'Pretty much.'

Dani stretched her legs out and crossed her feet at the ankle. Her head tilted to one side. 'Did someone scare you? Or did you see something on TV that made you frightened?'

Ben shook his head quickly. 'No – no, I'm okay. I just, do you have any books about her? About the . . .' Ben racked his brain, but couldn't recall the name Dani had just told him.

'The Morrígan?' Dani said. 'Sure – we've loads. And I can get you set up on a monitor, with your grown-ups' permission, if you want to have a look at some pictures of her.' She pushed herself up off the floor and held out a hand to Ben. 'You ready?'

Dani found Ben a chair, and piled some books in front of him while she went to speak to his parents. A few minutes later she came back with a library

101

card and an access code for a computer terminal. She helped him pick up his pile of books, and he followed behind her as she strode to a computer desk set up by itself in the corner.

'Right,' she said, stacking the books carefully on a windowsill before waking up the computer and entering the details from Ben's library card. Dani turned to Ben, still smiling. 'Let the research begin! This machine's set up to be safe for kids to use, but I'll be floating about if you need anything. Okay? And I've put these books through on your new card, so they're yours for three weeks.'

Ben gave her a proper smile, relief flooding his chest. 'Thank you,' he said.

'That's what I'm here for,' Dani said, with a wink, and then she was gone.

Ben looked through the books first. At the top of the pile was a slim old book, *Old Irish Myths and Legends*, with a picture of Cúchulainn, he guessed, on the cover. Cúchulainn was drawn with his hurl in his hand and a huge dog beside him, and Ben guessed this was the dog he'd killed by mistake, in the legend about how he got his name. He'd never owned it as a pet, so why was it there? Ben frowned, irritated by the lack of logic, as he opened the book. He flicked quickly through the pages, and his eye was caught by a story called 'The Queen of Crows and the Greatest of Heroes' – it looked like it was about the Morrígan, but there were no illustrations for it, so he put it aside to read later. Next was a green-covered book with drawings of harps and shamrocks and a fish on the cover – *the Salmon of Knowledge*, Ben thought, remembering how he'd heard about it from his teacher the year before – and he flicked to the contents page. He felt a chill as he saw the name – *The Morrígan* – written in black and white. He found the page, and on it was a picture.

A scary-eyed woman, with long black hair and sharp fingernails, a crow on each shoulder.

It didn't look exactly like the person he'd seen, but it had all the important things right. Ben put his hands under the desk and made two tight fists, fighting the urge to wiggle his fingers for comfort until he couldn't, any more. He let them flick until finally, he was ready.

The cursor blinked in the search box. Ben pulled the keyboard close, and began.

10

The Morrigan, he typed, slowly. He couldn't find the key to make the fada over the 'i', but he hoped it wouldn't matter.

A second later, the screen was filled with results.

He clicked on the first one. *The Morrígan*, it read. *The Phantom Queen, or the Great Queen (from the Early Irish 'mór', meaning 'great' and 'rígan', meaning 'queen'). A triple-aspect goddess connected with warfare, destruction, death and fate, she is thought to take pleasure in influencing the movement and outcome of battle, in having a role in deciding which warriors fall and which survive, and in foretelling death. She may also have a role as a sovereignty goddess, connected with the land and all that live on it, as she is a shape-shifter with an affinity* for animals. The three goddesses who together make up the Morrígan are usually thought to be Macha (known as the 'scald crow'), associated with war, bloodshed and the land; Badhbh (also known as 'badhbh catha' or 'battle crow'), who could influence the direction of a battle through the use of piercing, terror-inducing cries (see also: THE BANSHEE), and Anand, or the Morrígan herself, the third sister in the triumvirate.

Ben blinked and clicked the next link. *The Morrígan was a member of the TUATHA DÉ DANANN (see entry for DANU, mother goddess), and was a sister of the other triple-aspect goddesses Eriú (from whom Ireland, or Erin, gets its name), Banba and Fodla. She is, in some versions of her legend, the jealous and unhappy wife of THE DAGDA (the greatest of all Irish gods). In the stories of the ULSTER CYCLE of Irish mythology, we find the Morrígan interacting with CÚCHULAINN, the great hero, and in the MYTHOLOGICAL CYCLE of Irish mythology, the Morrígan is named as ANAND (who, along with her sister-goddesses BAHDBH and MACHA, make up the Morrígan). In this Cycle she is shown to help the Tuatha Dé Danann defeat the FOMORIAN army, and to prophesy the end of the world. She derives joy from battle; she loves the gathering of armies. She is an unpredictable, and largely malign, force in Irish folklore and story.*

Ben felt a weird combination of sickness and relief – sickness due to nerves, and relief that he was finally on to something. This was definitely the right person. The crows; the scary feeling that seemed to surround her like a forcefield; the feathers that felt like weapons . . . He looked down at his arm, which was still a little red where the black crow feather had touched his skin. He scratched at it, thinking hard. *But she's not real*, he told himself, staring at the screen. He clicked a third link, which brought him to a painting, and he held his breath as he took it in. The cold expression, the cruel eyes, the thick dark hair – and the crows whose beaks dripped with blood. Like the picture in the book, she didn't look exactly like the woman who had passed him on the street, and who had smirked at him through the ruined window of the friary, but she was close enough. Ben shuddered as he started to breathe again. *She is real*, he told himself. *She is real, because I've seen her.*

He closed his eyes and let the sounds of the library

soothe him while he thought. There was a low buzz of conversation in the large room, and from it he could pick out threads of sound – his parents' voices, low and worried; Dani's voice as she helped another library user, bright and upbeat; a mother, trying to shush her boisterous toddler in the children's section. His thoughts began to settle, like the flakes in a snow globe after it had been shaken, and something landed in his mind that he couldn't ignore.

He remembered his conversation with Eun-Kyung, where they'd talked about the light on the mountain, and how she'd told him about the Cailleach, and her hammers, and her skill as a swordsmith. And how the Cailleach had made the special sword, the one with the power of the sun in its blade – the strongest weapon ever made . . .

This Morrígan's a battle goddess, Ben thought. *So, maybe she's interested in weapons.* He felt his heart kick up a gear as he put the puzzle together. His fingers buzzed with energy and he couldn't help letting them flick while he thought. *And maybe the weapon she's most interested in is the big one – the Sword the Cailleach forged.*

He couldn't remember the Irish words that Eun-

Kyung had used, but he remembered the English translation. His fingers trembled as he reached for the computer mouse and clicked into the search bar. He put a space after *The Morrígan* and added *Sword of the Sun*.

This time, when he clicked, there weren't as many relevant results – but there were some. Before he could talk himself out of it, he clicked the first one.

It brought him to a screenshot of an old book. He enlarged it, to make it easier to read.

The Claíomh Solais (or Claidheamh Soluis), or the Sword of Light (alternatively called 'Sword of the Sun'), is the Irish form of the 'shining sword' trope found in many European folktales. Sometimes considered 'god-slaying' weapons (compare: the tathlum, *which slew the god Balor), they are also seen in stories where the hero must perform a ritual anointing him in his role, and the Sword is at once a helpful object and the prize he wins (along with a wife, in most cases). In almost every instance, the Sword of Light is an exceptional weapon; the only weapon which can kill the enemy which must be faced, and the one weapon the hero must win.*

Ben skimmed the next paragraph, which seemed to

be about stories from a different culture, and then his eye was caught by something interesting just below. The computer had highlighted a word, as it had appeared in his search term, and he sucked hard on his lips as he read.

The Sword of the Sun is a formidable weapon, granting its wielder supremacy in battle, and can only be claimed by an enemy if the sword-arm (holding the weapon) is severed. Nuada, king of the Tuatha Dé Danann, lost not only his arm but also his status as king when Sreng, the Fir Bolg warrior, wounded him in exactly this fashion; Nuada was unable to wield the Sword again until his magical silver Arm was forged by the Cailleach of Mullaghmore – Ben blinked at this and kept reading, remembering how Eun-Kyung had told him exactly the same thing – *and given its healing power by Dian Cecht. Nuada's silver Arm, as well as the Sword itself, has long been lost. Theoretically, the Arm (still in possession of the magic that was used to forge and animate it) should allow the wearer the power to wield the Sword, and the text in question here (*The Battle Crow's Revenge*) describes how it has been sought by several unsavoury figures, of which the Morrígan is top of the list.*

The Battle Crow's Revenge *survives only in a partial copy, made in the late nineteenth century. It describes the Morrígan's attempts to sully the bloodline of Nuada, to force one with the power to wield the Sword to fall under her will, with the aim of taking control of the weapon herself, and names that individual as Nimhfola, meaning 'poison blood'. This individual does not appear anywhere else in the literary sources.*

The text of The Battle Crow's Revenge *is unfinished, but its second half describes the Morrígan's plan (I quote from the text here, in my own translation; the original Old Irish can be found in Appendix D):*

The darkness will swallow it.

Its brightness will die.

With blood I shall hallow it.

With strength of my eye,

I shall watch its light dying

And my darkness live.

All shall echo with crying.

I do not forgive.

The Sword of Darkness will rise.

A curse on your eyes!

Ben felt his heart racing. *The Sword of Darkness?* He read the first two lines again. *The darkness will swallow it. Its brightness will die.* Was this 'it' the Sword of the Sun?

'Maybe it'll only do what she wants it to do if she destroys the light and makes the Sword dark instead,' Ben whispered to himself. He kept reading.

The text makes one single reference to an object called 'An Claíomh Dorchadas', which is found nowhere else in the corpus of Irish mythological literature. It is my opinion, based on my reading of The Battle Crow's Revenge, *that this object – the name of which translates to 'the Sword of Darkness' – is the same weapon as the Sword of Light, but transmuted, or adulterated, turned from light to darkness by foul magic. In all likelihood, this was blood magic, through the use of the blood of Nuada's 'line' (probably stolen from his descendant, Nimhfola, whose very name,* poison blood, *may be a clue to his significance in the Morrígan's plot). It is possible that the mingling of Nimhfola's blood with that of the spell-caster, presumably the Morrígan herself, would seal the magic, but as the text is incomplete, it is impossible to say what, exactly, the procedure entails.*

Ben stared at the screen. He'd guessed right. Whoever had written this book – he began to scroll the pages up, and up, and up, the text flashing by, to get to the start of the book so he could check who the author was – had agreed with him. *And this person sounds like they know what they're talking about,* Ben told himself, excitement building as he allowed himself to be pleased at how he'd put things together so well. Finally, the pages stopped scrolling; he'd reached the start of the book and he found himself looking at the title page.

A Reading of The Battle Crow's Revenge: *Some Clare Connections to the Ancient Mythology of Ireland* read the title.

And the author? *Brendan F. O'Donnell.*

Ben blinked at the screen. His stomach threatened to heave up and over and out of his mouth, but he swallowed hard against it and tried to think straight.

'Grandad,' he whispered.

'Hey, bud,' came his dad's voice, accompanied by his hand on Ben's shoulder. It took him so much by surprise that he yelled. 'Ben!' his dad whispered, loudly. 'You can't be shouting in the library, son. Calm down!'

'You gave me a fright, Dad!' Ben rubbed his shoulder where his dad's hand had landed. It hadn't been a hard blow, but somehow it stung.

'For God's sake,' his dad muttered, rubbing his hand through his hair. 'Look, Mam and me are finished, and we were going to go and grab that ice cream before we meet the others for lunch. Sound good?'

Aisling arrived to stand beside John, shoving a sheaf of printed pages into her bag as she walked. 'Are we ready, fellas?' she said, winking at Ben. He tried to smile back, but found he couldn't.

'Mam – look. Look what I found,' he said, pushing his chair back a bit so his mam could lean down and see his screen. He watched her face as she took in the title of the book, and then her eyes flicked briefly to the author's name.

'Sometimes I'm sorry I named you after him,' she said, stiffly, standing up and settling her bag around herself. She began to walk away. 'Are you coming? I'm not hanging around for you, Ben.'

John leaned in and looked at the screen – and then, wide-eyed, at his son. 'What are you *thinking*, buddy?' he muttered. 'You had to know your mam wouldn't be happy to see that.'

Ben grabbed his new library card and his stack of books before yanking his jacket off the back of his chair, and ran after his mam. His dad followed close behind. He caught up with her just as she stepped out of the library lobby, back into the daylight again.

'Mam!' Ben called. She turned to him, sliding her sunglasses down over her eyes. He could see his own reflection in their dark lenses. 'Wait up.'

Aisling turned to him. She wiped her cheek quickly, but not quickly enough to hide that she was crying. 'Come on,' she said. 'I really need that ice cream.'

'Mam, I'm sorry,' Ben said. His chest began to ache, and he clenched his free hand hard to stop his fingers twitching. 'I really am. I didn't mean to upset you.'

His mam opened her arms wide and Ben stepped into her hug. 'You didn't upset me, you turnip,' she said, affectionately. 'Your grandad's the one who upset me, a long time ago, long before you were even a dream of mine. It's not your fault, pet.'

'His book is good, Mam,' Ben said, stepping back a bit to look his mother in the face. 'I read some, and –'

'Look, love,' Aisling said. 'I'm sure your grandfather's book is excellent. But I haven't read it, nor has Niamh, and nor did your granny, God rest her, while she was alive.' Her lips tightened, and Ben wondered if she was going to speak again. Eventually, she managed it. 'His books took Grandad from us while we had him. He ignored everything except his work, and finally, his work took him. Granny found him one morning when she went into his study with his breakfast on a tray, like she did every day – but this particular morning he wasn't sitting with his head in a book or his fingers stained with ink or his thoughts halfway across the world or his eyes staring out of the window.' She looked down at Ben.

'That morning, your granny found her husband dead, sitting at his worktable, with his papers scattered all around him. Dead as a doornail, at forty-four years old. He'd probably been there all night, alone. That's what his work did for him. So, son, if I don't want to read his books, I'm not going to apologise to you or anyone else.' She gave him one last squeeze and then let him go, turning away while she fumbled in her bag for a tissue. As she started walking away, Ben heard her blowing her nose.

'Come on, pal,' John said, coming up behind Ben and placing a hand – more gently, this time – on his shoulder again. He lifted the books out of Ben's hands and tucked them into the crook of one arm, fishing a reusable shopping bag out of his pocket with his free hand. 'Mam needs us now. So, no more talk of your grandad or whatever he was up to, yeah? Let's try to make things as easy as we can for her. We've got to pull together as a family and get through this. And it's hard enough for her being back here, where she grew up, where she was so unhappy and where her da died long before he should have.' He dumped the books into the bag and tested the weight, settling his grip on the handles.

Ben nodded, but as he opened his mouth to speak, his dad raised a finger. 'And you are *not* to say you're sorry,' he said, reaching down to tickle Ben on the side of the neck, which always made him laugh.

'Are you pair *coming*? There'll be no ice cream left at this rate!' Aisling's voice rang out down the street, and John and Ben gave one another a look that said *whoops!* before hurrying to join her.

11

As soon as they got home, Ben grabbed his library books from his dad's bag and tried to find a quiet place to read. It was a big house, but there were a lot of people living in it, and there never seemed to be a quiet corner that wasn't immediately discovered by someone else, or turned into a spot where one of the adults desperately needed to do something urgent, like put on a load of washing, or scrub a floor, or look for a spare pair of shoelaces.

Eventually, he headed to the garden. The day was hot and humid, and it felt like there was thunder in the air. He turned to look at the slopes of Mullaghmore, thinking about the Cailleach and her hammers. It was weird, he thought, that someone could use their hammers for things like forging magical metal arms and fashioning powerful swords, and also to flatten hills and raise mountains and bring thunder and lightning down, to batter the earth and the people below . . . Ben sighed. *This is all too much*. It was like the bones of his skull were creaking, shifting like tectonic plates, and inside his brain felt a bit like an electrical storm – chaotic and scary and full of sudden sharp jabs of light and sound.

He settled beneath the shade of one of the trees. It had several small trunks which seemed to weave around one another, and the bark was dark and ridged, with long fissures running down through it. The tree had been covered with thousands of whitish-pink blossoms when they'd first arrived to live here, but they were beginning to fade, now, like the heat of summer was burning them away. Something about the tree made Ben calm, despite its profusion of long, sharp thorns, and he sat, cross-legged, with the books around him.

He tried the oldest-looking of the books first, the one called *Old Irish Myths and Legends*. It had a map of the country on the flyleaf, where places like the Hill of Tara and the Giant's Causeway were marked. He glanced at Clare, seeing a shaded area which looked like it was supposed to represent the karst landscape of the Burren, and written on it, in tiny letters, was *THE FORGE OF THE CAILLEACH*. Something made him happy to see it, like it was already familiar, even though he'd only just learned about it, but that feeling drained away as he flicked to the contents page and found the story he was looking for. 'The Queen of Crows and the Greatest of Heroes'. He flicked to the page, closed his eyes while he took a deep breath, and started to read.

The Queen of Crows is but one of her names; others have called her She-Who-Is-Three, the Shadesinger, the Battle Crow and more. But you might know her as the Morrígan, the Great Queen, whose voice has the power to shape and dictate who will live and who will die, by sword and by arrow. The mustering of armies is her nourishment; the call of war is her joy. And this tale is told of how, one day, she met Cúchulainn, and of the words they spoke to one another.

As the old stories tell us, one day as the Morrígan walked through a fragrant wood, she found a cow, young and strong and lively of step, with a fine twist to her horns and a pleasing pattern of dun and gold on her flank. 'Ah,' said the Queen of Crows, 'this cow will come home with me.' And with a 'hup' from her lips, the cow was bewitched, and began to follow the Queen of Crows out of the wood, and away from the land she was born and reared on, away from the rivers she drank from as a calf, and into foreign territory – the Morrígan's own land.

Before they reached the end of the cow's native country, a voice was heard. 'Hold!' it shouted, loud and deep. 'You will stop, before I draw my next breath, on pain of being split in half with a blow from my fist.'

The Queen of Crows turned to see a young man there, tall and broad and in every way pleasing, and his face was like golden sunlight, and his hair like honey and milk. She knew him to be Cúchulainn, the most stout-hearted man in Erin, but was sure he did not know her.

'Surely you would not deny me this beast,' she said, 'on your honour as a warrior?'

'My habit is not to give the best of my possessions to any hag who asks,' retorted the young man, and at this the Queen of Crows was angered. In a swirl of her dark magic, she changed from woman to crow, and landed on the branch of a yew tree. No sooner had she done this than Cúchulainn recognised his error.

'I did not know you, Great Queen,' he said, bowing his head. 'I would not have spoken so ill, had I recognised you.'

'It matters not,' replied the Queen of Crows, 'for whatever your actions were this day, your doom would have been foretold.'

Cúchulainn laughed, and at the sound the leaves rained from the trees, so that the branches were bare as winter despite the burning sunshine overhead. 'What harm can you do to me? In battle, I would slay you without a thought.'

'That may be true,' she replied. 'But an enemy is coming, direr than your imagining; an enemy armed with a weapon that is death itself; an enemy as unstoppable as lightning, as the waves, as time. That enemy is your enemy. That enemy is the enemy of all. And I tell you now, that enemy is –'

'All right, puke-face,' came a voice, shattering Ben's concentration. Fin flopped down beside him, smelling overwhelmingly of the body spray he liked to fill their bedroom with each morning, his hair covering his eyes.

Ben shifted over to make room. 'What are you doing out here?'

Fin growled quietly before answering. 'Ji-Ah's wrecking my head with her new glasses,' he said. 'She keeps going around the house posing for selfies, making these ridiculous faces,' Ben looked up to see Fin tossing his hair back and pouting, making a peace sign with his fingers, 'and she was always trying to get me in the background, even though I asked her very nicely to give it a rest. So I eventually told her where to go, and I cleared out.'

Ben sighed, closing the book and putting it on top of the pile. 'Fair enough,' he said.

'You up to anything?' Fin pulled a handful of grass out of the lawn and let it scatter in the breeze. Ben watched as the blades fluttered away, his gaze being pulled to the garden fence, and to the vastness that lay beyond it. After a second or two he realised he was straining his eyes, trying to catch a glimpse of the forbidden cave . . . He cleared his throat, pulling himself out of a half-daze.

'Just – reading.' Ben glanced at the books. 'How did your band practice go?'

Fin shook his head. 'The broadband here is so

rubbish, we couldn't connect properly. It didn't really work.' He paused for a moment, ripping up another handful of grass and throwing it this time. 'I reckon they're going to ask Jayo to replace me. He was always angling for a way in, anyhow.'

Ben stared at the side of his brother's face in disbelief. 'But it wouldn't be Eddie Ate Dynamite without you,' he said.

Fin shrugged. 'That's rock and roll, man.'

'So, what did you do while we were away?'

Fin was silent for a moment. 'I did a bit of drawing, and then – I fell asleep,' he said, almost like he was embarrassed. 'It was weird, right? I wasn't even tired. But it was like I switched off, or something.'

Ben tried to radiate silent sympathy. 'Maybe you were tired, and just didn't realise.' He sighed, deeply. 'Happens to me all the time.'

'I had this intense dream though. *Super* metal. I want to try to write a song about it, maybe,' Fin mumbled, his words quick and so low Ben could hardly hear him.

'What was it about?'

Fin started and looked at him properly, parting his hair to peer out through it. 'What? Nothing. I mean, never mind.'

Ben pressed his lips tight. 'I've been having them too, you know. Dreams, I mean. Weird ones.'

Fin's gaze darted towards him, briefly. 'Yeah?'

'About – bears and stuff. And crows.' Ben cleared his throat. 'They're scary.'

'Mine was like, I was flying over a battlefield,' Fin began. 'But, like, a *medieval* one or something – all swords and axes and armour – and I was just, y'know, *looking*. Or hunting, maybe. Or – I dunno. Like, checking everything out. And I felt this weird *power* in me, you know, like I'd been behind the whole thing. The – the battle, and all the death, and stuff.' He coughed, blinking out of his memory. 'I felt like some sort of god. Anyway, who cares – it was a dream, right?'

Ben shrugged. 'Dreams are important, y'know.'

'Just your brain dumping stuff out, isn't it?' Fin scratched at his chin. 'Nothing major.'

'Eun-Kyung doesn't think so,' Ben said. 'She told me about dreams in Korea. Like, how they mean something. She said they were omens.'

Fin shrugged. 'I'm probably just remembering a movie, or whatever. I mean, how could a dream like that be an omen?' He looked at Ben, trying to smile.

'Unless I'm going to sprout wings.'

Ben half-grinned back. 'You were probably floating on a cushion of your own farts, anyway,' he said.

Fin laughed, leaning over to bump Ben with his shoulder. 'At least I might get a good sketch or two out of it.'

'Hey, can I see your drawings?' Ben looked up at his brother.

Fin jerked awkwardly, his laugh fading. 'Nope. And no snooping to find them either.'

'Sorry,' Ben said, automatically.

'Cut it out,' Fin said. 'And listen to Dad! You don't have to apologise, like, all the time, just for existing.'

Overhead, there was an ominous rumble and rain began to fall, so suddenly it was like someone had turned on a tap. Large, fat drops, slowly at first but quickly growing heavier.

'The library books!' Ben gasped, scrambling to his feet.

'I'll give you a hand,' Fin said, bending to scoop some up. 'Does Mam know you're reading this stuff?' he said, as they ran for the house.

Ben cradled the books to his front, hoping to shield them from the worst of the weather. 'I dunno,' he said.

'Well,' Fin replied, once they'd reached the safety of the back hallway, 'I wouldn't let her see you with them, just in case.' He began to dump the slightly soggy books into his brother's arms, before slicking his wet hair back off his face to stare at Ben. 'This is the woo-woo stuff that basically *killed* Grandad, right? She's hardly going to be happy seeing you get into it too.'

'It's not woo-woo,' Ben said, suddenly defensive. 'It's *myths*. It's basically like history. And some of it is really interesting.'

Fin scoffed. 'No, it isn't,' he said. 'It's rubbish, and the harder you try to make it make sense, the more complicated it's going to get. So, don't get lost down any rabbit holes, little brother.' Something like a spasm of pain passed over Fin's face, but it was gone so quickly that Ben wasn't sure he hadn't imagined it. 'We've got to keep it together, for Mam and Dad, right? They need us. We can't be crashing out on them.' Ben wondered if his brother was talking to him, or to himself.

'Yeah. Sure,' he said.

Lightning flashed, and Fin pushed the door closed. 'Great. Good talk,' he muttered, before turning and disappearing into the house.

12

The weather stayed bad for the next three days, with bursts of intensely hot sunshine interspersed with equally intense storms. Everyone had a headache, nobody had been food shopping, the house just felt too small – and tempers were short.

'All I want is a *biscuit*! Seriously!' Ji-Ah slammed the cupboard shut, so hard that it rattled on its hinges. 'Why is there *nothing* to eat in this house?'

'All right, all right!' Niamh shouted. 'I'm going to the shops! Even if it's just to buy painkillers for the *brain-ache* you're giving me.' She grabbed her car keys. 'Anyone who wants to come had better hop to it,' she said. 'This train's leaving in five!'

'I bagsy shotgun,' Aisling shouted, from the living room. 'John, you're staying with the kids.'

'Mam, for God's sake, I'm nearly *fifteen*,' Fin yelled from upstairs. 'I don't need a babysitter!'

John walked out of the sunroom, his eyebrows raised. Aisling strode into the front hallway, glowering, her jacket already on. 'I was working my first job at fifteen,' he told his wife, mildly. 'I'm sure Fin can handle a bit of childminding.'

Aisling rolled her eyes, before regaining her composure. 'We'll be two hours, max, because we've got to get dinner ready before Eun-Kyung's home from work,' she shouted. 'Nobody had better be dead, missing, or on fire by the time we get back. All right?'

A chorus of agreement rang out from all over the house until – finally – the front door banged closed and everything fell still. Ben, in the corner of his bedroom with his notebook on his lap, breathed a sigh of relief.

'About time,' Fin muttered. He was working at the desk in the other corner of the room. Ben could hear his pencil scritch-scritching over the paper as he drew. He was still being secretive about whatever he was working on, but that wasn't unusual. It was just good to see him drawing again – before they left Dublin, Fin hadn't picked up his pencils for ages.

Ben looked away from his brother and leaned his head back against the wall, closing his eyes. If only, he caught himself thinking, his own efforts could be so productive. His head swirled with questions, but also with half-remembered dreams. They'd been bad, the past few days, pressing on him like the heavy, inescapable weather. Flocks of crows, flying in formation, and suddenly they'd all turn and swoop towards him like a squadron of fighter pilots . . . And the bear was back, its blue eyes shining in the dark, its growl low but ever-present, and its shadow stalking his days. Eun-Kyung might believe bears were a good omen, but Ben wasn't sure he agreed. He'd never felt so tired. He was sleeping all right, but there was no rest to be had in his dreams. Every sleeping moment seemed to be taken up with being afraid – a bit too much like his waking moments, sometimes.

He opened his eyes and looked down at the open notebook balanced across his knees. He'd written some questions, based on the stuff he was reading, but all his work had amounted to nothing. He'd started out confused, and he was growing more confused by the day.

The Morrígan – the Sword of the Sun changed

to the *Sword of Darkness. Why?* He had no answer for this.

The Cailleach – forger of the Sword and Nuada's Arm – where are they?

The Cailleach and the Morrígan – what's the link? Ben sighed and chewed on the lid of his pen. He wished he knew. None of the stories had even mentioned the two of them together. In fact, the stories were often contradictory or confusing – in some versions, the Morrígan was Nuada Silverarm's granddaughter, and in others there was no connection between them. *Maybe it is all woo-woo, like Fin says,* Ben thought, despairingly. *And maybe there's just no way of knowing what's true, or real, or if any of it means anything.*

He picked up one of the books from his pile and flipped to a chapter that had been written by someone who'd read his grandad's work. It was the closest he could get to actually reading Grandad O'Donnell's writing without going back to the library, but he felt like he was betraying his mam by even looking at this book. He tried to push his guilt aside and focus on the words.

Rathcroghan, known as Ráth Cruachán in Irish –

which means 'the fort of Cruachán' – is located in present-day County Roscommon, and has long been seen as the entrance to the Irish otherworld. The cave of Oweynagat (the Cave of the Cats) in Rathcroghan was associated most closely with the Morrígan, and other tales of this underground realm tell of hordes of destructive beasts, or monsters, which emerge from it to lay waste to the land all around before being hunted or vanquished by a hero.

Ben slapped his book shut in frustration. His head pounded. None of this stuff made sense, and the more work he tried to do, the more confusing it all seemed. For one horrible moment he wondered if this was how it had started for his grandad – had it all seemed simple at first, and then the twists and turns of the unfathomable stories made him so confused he couldn't find his way out? He thought about what he'd just read. Maybe getting too into all this stuff was like getting lost underground, without any way of finding your path back to the surface.

Ben began to shove the books back into his rucksack, ready for return to the library. This was all rubbish – he could see that now. Fin had been right all along. He was seeing connections when none actually existed, and he was putting things together and coming up with the wrong answers. What he needed was to step right back from everything and get some perspective. He huffed out a laugh, but there was no joy in it – he felt like he was laughing at his own stupidity. 'Witches hammering mountains. I mean, come on. Of *course* it's nonsense,' he muttered to himself.

'Did you say something?' Fin asked, suddenly enough to make Ben jump.

He zipped the bag closed and tossed it into the corner. 'I was just talking to myself,' Ben said. 'Or, I guess, I was agreeing with something you said. About how pointless all this folklore stuff is.'

'Mmm,' Fin said, half-listening.

Ben pushed himself up. His legs were wobbly and half-asleep as he walked across the room to the window. He leaned on the sill, staring out through the slightly warped glass at the countryside below. Mullaghmore was there, on the horizon, ever watchful and ever quiet. The eerie, flat landscape all around seemed full of some strange power. He found himself wanting to look towards the cave entrance, again, and tried to block it out, but it was there, sucking at his attention, pulling him towards the window, urging him to look and see.

'Fin,' he began, closing his eyes against the call of the karst. 'You know how we were talking about dreams? And you said they didn't really *mean* anything.' He glanced around. His brother didn't answer – he was completely absorbed in what he was doing. Ben turned back to the view. 'I mean, I think they do mean something. But I'm still having so many weird ones. And when we lived in Dublin, I didn't dream like this. I'm a bit scared, you know? It's like something down here is messing with my head, but that's impossible. Isn't it?'

The only answer was a continued *scritch-scritch-scritch* from Fin's side of the room. Ben wondered if Fin was trying to etch his way through the paper.

'I can't help but think Grandad was on to something,' he continued. 'I mean – he *can't* have been. I *know* that! My head knows that, for sure. It's impossible to tell what's true, or if any of it is, or ever was. But something about it *feels* true. Like, in my bones. That all this stuff happened.' He paused, swallowing hard. 'That there really is a witch out there. A Cailleach, with hammers that can shape mountains and control weather. And that there really is a war goddess on the loose, with crows and – I dunno. Ballistic feathers, or whatever.' He rubbed absent-mindedly at his arm. 'I felt it. That feather *burned* me, Fin. I didn't imagine that.'

Scritch-scritch-scritchscritchscritch.

A dark rage boiled up in Ben. 'Fin!' he shouted, turning to his brother. 'Are you even *listening*?'

Fin stared at him, his eyes somehow empty, and then he blinked and he was Fin again. '*What?*' he shouted back. 'I told you, I don't want to talk about any of this stuff. Okay? It's all *nonsense* and Grandad was a crackpot, and I *do not want it*. So, back off! It's hard enough having to share a room, but if you can't shut up, Ben, I'm going to ask Mam and Dad if one of us can sleep in the shed.'

'You're honestly telling me you can't feel it?' Ben said, taking a step towards Fin. Quickly, Fin flipped his sketchbook closed. 'You're telling me you're not having dreams that wake you up in a cold sweat? Or that you're not wondering, even a little bit, if what Grandad was working on *meant* something? If it was important?' He stared his brother down. 'I hear you whimpering in your sleep, Fin. I know you're having scary dreams too. So stop lying!'

'I'm not *lying*!' Fin stood, red-faced. 'You're just *full* of it. So full of it, you can't listen to – or *hear* – what anyone else wants. Dreams are just dreams, all right? They're not *real* – they can't be. So who cares about them?' Fin's face was tight with fear as he spoke. 'All I know is, I do not want any of this, and that is it. So, *hear* me this time! And just – shut up about your stupid theories!'

'They're not stupid!' Ben shouted. He strode to the door and yanked it open, before standing back in surprise as Ji-Ah almost fell into the room. She stumbled as she tried to get her balance, looking from Ben to Fin, her cheeks pink. Her phone was in her hand. 'I – I – I didn't hear anything,' she said.

'Were you literally *leaning* on the door?' Ben asked.

'Not – really,' Ji-Ah said. 'I mean, not technically leaning? Sort of, I was door-adjacent. With my ear pressed to the wood, I mean. But the rest of me wasn't pressed against it. I wasn't putting my weight on it.' She grinned nervously. 'Honest.'

'So you heard all of that?' Fin asked, tossing his hair out of his face as he spoke.

Ji-Ah shrugged. 'Most of it.'

Fin flopped down on his bed. 'Brilliant,' he muttered. 'So I guess you'll be straight on to our parents, full of *Ben said this* and *Fin said that* and *they're talking about Grandad*, and all that stuff.'

'No!' Ji-Ah protested. 'I won't, I promise! I don't care what you're fighting about.'

'Wait,' Ben said. He looked at the phone in Ji-Ah's hand. 'You weren't *recording* us, were you?'

Ji-Ah went pale. She pushed the phone into her back pocket. 'No way! Why would I *even*?'

'You'd better be telling the truth,' Ben said, pushing his way past her.

'I am!' Ji-Ah shouted. Ben turned back; she looked genuinely upset. 'I don't lie. But it's like what Fin said. You never listen, Ben. You're too busy focusing on *yourself* to even care about anyone else.'

Ben stared at her, his head boiling with thoughts and his body fizzing with strange energy. He looked at his brother, who was rubbing his face with his hands, which were covered with graphite from his drawing. Then Ben spun on his heel and strode away, leaving them both behind.

13

Ben paused in the hallway. He'd been about to burst out through the front door and keep walking, on and on to who knew where, so long as it was far away from everyone he was being forced to live with – but instead, his attention was caught by the plain wooden door he'd seen on his first day in this house.

The door with the faded rectangle which had probably once been a brass plate, screwed into the wood. The place where his grandfather had lived and worked – and where he had died.

Ben squeezed his eyes shut. He *knew* his mother would go thermonuclear if she sensed he was even thinking about poking around in there, but he also knew he had to do it. He had to see if Granny had kept anything of Grandad's which might be useful, or if there were *any* clues to why, ever since he'd moved here, Ben's dreams had gone bear-shaped and he was being followed around by crows. He had no choice. And right now was the only opportunity he was going to get. Ji-Ah's voice whispered in his memory: *She keeps the key in the kitchen somewhere . . .*

First, he tried the office door, but as he'd expected it was locked. He hurried to the kitchen, hoping the others wouldn't come looking for him, and glanced around at the presses, the neat worktop, the appliances and the busy pinboard covered with detritus and takeaway menus. He tried to figure out where something might be hidden in a kitchen like this. His aunt kept her Credit Union book, her house keys, her car keys and her supermarket loyalty card in one of the cupboards, tucked in beside an old crockery set that had probably been in the house since before the Famine. Ben wondered if that was the logical place to start his search for the key to Grandad's office.

Three paces had him in front of the cupboard and he carefully removed his aunt's possessions. Her Credit Union book was there, but she had her keys and loyalty cards with her. There was nothing else to be seen.

For a long moment, Ben stared at the gap beside the stacked plates, feeling empty. He'd been sure this was it. It made *sense*. And he hated it when things that made sense didn't . . .

His thoughts trailed off as he looked at the plates. They were old, unused, covered in dust, heavy and thickly painted with a horrible pattern. He had no idea who they'd belonged to, once. *But*, a little thought whispered, *wouldn't they make a great place to hide something? Especially something small, like a key . . .*

Quickly, he began to lift the crockery from the press. There were dessert dishes, then soup-bowls and beneath them the stack of plates. Carefully, he lifted each piece, checking inside the bowls and between each dish, and when he lifted the very last plate, there it was.

A key, flat and dull, with a piece of old brown string tied around the loop.

Now that it was actually *happening*, Ben's nerve began to fail. He picked up the key with fingers that felt numb and floppy, like they didn't belong to him. *Come on*, he berated himself, shaking off his misgivings. Wrapping his fist around the key, he hurried back to his grandfather's office door. The key went in and turned as smoothly as if his grandad was just returning after his tea break. The lock gave no resistance.

And then, Ben was inside.

He closed the door behind him before fumbling for the light switch. The bulb overhead was weak, hanging from a plain white wire in the middle of the ceiling, with no shade around it. The heavy curtains were drawn across the tall window at the back of the room. There was stuff piled up everywhere – old clothes, broken toys, a TV set from a million years ago, its screen black and silent. Boxes filled with more old crockery, an ancient pair of over-patterned curtains, information leaflets from the visitors' centre where Eun-Kyung worked. One entire box was filled with shoes. A large fireplace took up most of the right-hand wall, its mantelpiece almost as high as Ben was tall, and a huge, age-spotted mirror hung over it.

Behind an old sofa shoved almost all the way up into the corner, Ben noticed something. A tiny door, built into the wall, so neatly made that his eye almost skipped right over it. With a grunt of effort – followed by a fit of coughing, as the air filled with dust – Ben pulled the sofa out just far enough to examine the door.

It was a storage cubby, kept shut by a thin wedge of wood shoved in at the bottom of the door, which took some wiggling to work free. Finally, the cupboard door popped open a little, and Ben pulled it even further.

It was dark as a cave inside the tiny space. Ben fumbled with the musty curtains behind him, pulling them apart just enough to let in some light. His hand shook a little as he took in what he saw. A cardboard box with a lid, furry with dust, stuffed right back into the cubby as though someone had wanted to force it away.

Ben heaved and tugged for all he was worth, sneezing as the dust billowed up into his face. Eventually, his heart hammering like he was running a race, he gave one final haul and the box was out of the cubby and in front of him. He shifted position slightly, trying not to block the light from the window, as he used both hands to pull off the lid.

The first thing he saw was a large black feather, left lying across the top of the box's contents. It shone like freshly spilled oil, the barbs gleaming weirdly, looking as though it had just been plucked from the wing of a crow. Ben felt his skin prickle all over at the sight of it. For a long moment he just stared at it, before pulling his sleeve down over his hand and knocking it to one side. It fell to the floor, and he tried to ignore it.

Ben looked back into the box. He could see books. Papers. A paperweight. An old metal ashtray, empty except for a clinging haze of something ancient and whitish-grey. He lifted some sheets and was met with a glass-framed photograph of two very small children, one a tiny baby and the other about two or three. They could be girls? It was hard to be sure. He put it gently aside and kept digging.

A bundle of old, long-dried biros tied together with an almost perished rubber band. Books, more books and sheafs of loose papers that would take forever to go through. And just as he thought he'd reached the bottom of the box, Ben found a book that was larger than the others, heavy and leather-bound. He lifted it, one-handed, onto its spine, noticing a wedge of pages which had become tucked in, dog-eared. He set his teeth – nothing bothered him more than people bending pages in books.

Ben hauled the book out properly and opened it at the dog-eared pages. Carefully, he folded the long-bent sheets back and ran his hand across one of the pages. There was something on it – a drawing, he thought. He angled the book towards the daylight, and right away his whole body was pulled to attention. It was an illustration in black and white, very finely drawn, showing a hugely tall man, his legs and arms too thin to be human. He held a huge sword in one gigantic hand, and was surrounded by three women. One of them was the Morrígan, Ben was certain. The second was younger, her long hair swirling and her skirts billowing around bare legs and feet. She, too, carried a sword, which looked like it was dirty – she seemed to be wiping the blade on her skirt. The third was ancient, a hobbled crone, somehow perched on the tall man's shoulder – and when Ben squinted at the image, he saw something that made him pause.

The ancient lady also had a blade – and she was using it to cut off the man's sword-wielding arm. And when he peered closer, Ben could see a wound in the man's torso. He looked back at the younger woman, cleaning her sword, and shuddered.

Ben read the words beneath the drawing. *The Death of Nimhfola, of the line of Nuada Silverarm, by Anand, Badhbh and Macha, the three Aspects of the Morrígan, on the Night of the Big Wind, January 1839.*

Ben's heart was pounding so hard he could feel it shaking his whole body. The Night of the Big Wind. There it was again, cropping up. *Too many times to be a coincidence*, Ben thought. He read some of the text printed in small type beneath the picture.

Out across the water, lightning flashed. It drew the attention of both figures on the mountain. Seconds later thunder rolled, tearing the air into pieces. The wind whipped up, pushing so hard against the figures on the mountaintop that it forced them to take a step backward, their feet sinking deep into the snow. Around the woman, a whirlwind of black feathers blew, landing haphazardly all around.

'Clash your hammers, you old witch,' she spat. Her lips parted in a sneer. 'You are no match for the Morrígan, She-Who-Is-Three, and he who stands with me – Nimhfola, of the line of Nuada Airgeadlám, first bearer of the Sword.'

Nimhfola held up the Sword he carried in his hand. It shone brighter than the lightning they'd just seen, sending a bright beam high into the sky, and far out to sea the gathering storm roared an answer. The Morrígan blinked, looking out over the water with eyes that now shone blood-red, and in the midst of the darkening clouds she could see the immensity of the Cailleach. Bigger than a thunderhead and growing with every breath, her lips pulled back in fury, and in each of her huge hands was a mighty hammer. It was easy to believe that she had the power to shape the landscape, that her strength was enough to raise mountains – or fell them.

The Morrígan smelled battle on the air, and she threw back her head. Her cry of jubilation was an avalanche, a rockfall, a bursting dam. War was her lifeblood, anger her nourishment, destruction her joy. She knew no fear. 'The Sword is mine, you weakling!' she roared. 'You shall not have it, not you, nor any who bear the Seandraíocht in their veins!'

Nimhfola stared at his companion, sidelong. 'The Sword is ours, Great Queen,' he said. 'Without my help, you would never have laid eyes upon it.'

The Morrígan turned to him, her eyes cruelly violet

once more. 'Never trust One-Who-Is-Three,' she said, her voice a low cackle.

Ben turned the page, the heavy book wobbling a bit in his grip. Another illustration met his eye, this time of a gigantic woman with a hammer in each hand, unimaginably big. She looked like she was mostly made of storm and fury, her body formed from writhing clouds and her eyes like lightning.

The Cailleach of Mullaghmore engaging the Morrígan in battle; the latter bearing the Arm of Nimhfola, who was of the Blood of Nuada, the true bearer of the Sword of the Sun.

The facing page had another amazing drawing, this time of a man as tall as a mountain with a beard like seaweed and hair like a breaking wave. He rode on the back of a horse with a long mane, and they burst out of the sea, facing a tiny figure with its back to the viewer, standing on a clifftop. The huge rider had a sword, pointing right at the smaller person, drawn so skilfully it was like the point was about to come out through the page.

Manannán Mac Lir, god of the sea, facing the Morrígan with his Sword, the mighty Fragarach, *the Answerer, the Blade of Truth, which drove*

*the Morrígan's Sister-Aspects from her body and
imprisoned them in Earth and Sky.*

Ben's head felt fuzzy. He felt as though he'd missed
something – like when his teacher was trying really
hard to explain a concept, and he *almost* understood
it, but at the last second his brain just let it slip out
again, as though it lost its grip.

He flipped the book closed, and the movement
of the pages made some loose sheets spill out. Ben
carefully pulled them free. They were drawings, he
saw, done by a very young child – and they were old.
The paper was thin and fragile, the edges browned.
There were drawing-pin holes along the edges of each
sheet, surrounded by a circle of rust.

To Daddy from Niamh was written in huge,
childishly awkward letters along the bottom of one
picture, which showed a little girl holding the hand
of a grown-up with comically long legs and a tiny
box of body, a huge circular head plopped on top.
Ben turned the page over to see a grown-up's careful
handwriting, noting the date the picture was presented
to him. *A gift from my beautiful daughter Niamh* was
written beneath the date. 'Grandad,' he whispered.

Ben saw a crayon drawing of a stick-figure baby

being held like a trophy by an older stick-figure child. Quickly, he flipped it over. *My beloved Maura was safely delivered of a perfect baby girl at 3.10 a.m. – Aisling Dearbhail O'Donnell. My second dear daughter.* The date was his mam's birthday. He flipped the page over again, smiling at the drawing.

All thoughts of his grandfather fled his mind as he heard a sudden noise – the grumbling of a car engine. He peered out through the gap in the curtains. *They're back!*

Ben tasted panic as he slapped the book shut and shoved it, and all the papers and other books, haphazardly back into the box. He paused for a split second to look at the framed photo again, and realised it was his mother and his aunt, when they were tiny. His grandad must have looked at it every single day. Carefully, he put it away. Then, he pushed the box back in. At the last second his gaze fell on the feather, now sitting boldly on the carpet. He grabbed it, keeping it between his fingers for as brief a time as possible, and threw it into the darkness. He couldn't close the cubby properly, but there was no time. Ben vaulted the couch. With shaking fingers, he relocked the office and had just put away the dishes when he heard his mother's laughter in the hallway. Quickly, he filled a glass with water and took a huge swig, casually leaning against the worktop as the adults bundled into the room.

They paused, looking at him quizzically as he swallowed.

'What?' he said, staring back at them.

14

'Charmed as I am that none of you *expired* while we were away, I would like to ask if anything happened,' Niamh said, eyeballing her daughter and nephews across the dinner table. 'This peace and quiet is, admittedly, welcome, but,' she paused to give a dramatic shudder, 'it's beginning to make my insides itch.'

Ben looked up at her, his mouth full of mashed potato, and didn't answer. Ji-Ah, to his right, picked at her vegetables. Fin, to his left, sat with his arms folded, staring at the kitchen ceiling.

'Right,' said Niamh, with a sigh. 'Whoever did whatever, say sorry. Whoever took whoever else's stuff, give it back. And if something got broken, just tell us, and we'll look at you sympathetically and say "tough luck – you can get yourself a replacement when you're earning".' The only response was the *whirr* of the oven fan.

'Lads,' John said, frowning at his sons. 'Will one of you answer your Aunt Niamh, please? What's got into you?'

'Can I leave?' Fin said, looking at his dad.

'The country? Or, like, the house? I mean, you'll have to be more specific,' Aisling said, spearing a forkful of mash.

'The table,' Fin said, already pushing his chair out.

'You haven't eaten anything,' his mother pointed out, mildly.

'I'll live,' Fin grunted, standing up.

'If I come down here tomorrow and the Chocko Pops, the brand-new box I just spent a *ridiculous* amount of money on, is gone, I will fully do a roundhouse kick to your bottom, young man.' Aisling's words were muffled through her mouthful of food.

'Whatever, Mother,' Fin retorted, stalking away from the table.

'I'm serious, Finian!' Aisling shouted, as he left the room. 'He's *notorious* for midnight cereal robbery, that fella,' she continued, before taking another mouthful of dinner.

A clattering at the front door let everyone know that Eun-Kyung was home from work. Niamh rose to take a plate from the oven, where it had been keeping warm. 'Good day, love?' she asked, as Eun-Kyung joined them in the kitchen. Eun-Kyung looked exhausted, but she smiled at Niamh as she took her seat.

'Busy!' she said. 'Summer is like that though – everyone descends on us at once. I'm not complaining! It's wonderful. But, yes. It can make for tough days.' She leaned forward to look at Ji-Ah. 'Everything okay?' she asked.

Ji-Ah didn't meet her mother's eye. 'Fine,' she said, quietly.

'The children had a row,' Aisling said. 'We don't know what about yet, but we're all sincerely hoping they snap out of it quickly – aren't we?'

Ji-Ah tried to smile at her mother. 'May I leave the table, please, Eomma?' she asked.

Eun-Kyung looked confused, but nodded. As Ji-Ah stood to leave, she bowed her head a little towards her mother and then left the room.

Eun-Kyung raised her eyebrows. 'Ji-Ah *never* bows,' she said, looking up at Niamh as she placed a plate of food in front of her. 'Something's definitely not right with that girl.'

'Sort it out tomorrow, love,' Niamh said. 'You've had enough to do today.'

'Mam, what did Grandad die from?' Ben asked, so suddenly that it made Aisling cough on her dinner. She grabbed her glass of water and took a mouthful, her wide eyes on her son all the time.

'Brendan!' Niamh said.

'Forget your grandad – are you trying to kill *me*?' Aisling asked, once she'd got her breath back. She took another mouthful of water.

'I'm just asking,' Ben mumbled.

'It was a massive heart attack, if you must know,' Niamh said, as Aisling composed herself. 'My mother told me it was as if Dad's heart had just *stopped*, like someone had switched it off. He was young, he wasn't in bad health and it was totally unexpected.' She fixed Ben with a look. 'So, are you happy now?'

'Weren't either of you ever curious, about the stuff he was working on?' Ben met his mother's eye, even though it felt like being skewered with a lance.

'About why it was so important? And why Granny never did anything with it?'

Aisling paused for a long moment before answering, as though she were trying to get her thoughts in a straight line. 'Imagine if your dad was never there for you, Ben,' she began, in a low voice. 'Imagine, every time you'd had a games demo in the library, that Dad didn't show. Or when it was time to display your Lego art and all the parents came to have a look. Or when it's time for the Christmas show at school, and you're up there singing, and there's no Dad in the audience.' She pressed her lips. 'My dad died when I was one and a half years old. Your Aunt Niamh was five. And almost exactly the same amount of time has passed since then as our father spent alive. This year, it will be forty-five years since he died.'

'Thanks for giving away my age, sis,' Niamh muttered.

Aisling gave her an affectionate elbow-nudge, before turning back to Ben. 'You have no idea how that feels, because your father has been there all your life, no questions asked, supporting you and caring for you the way a father should. I never had that. Niamh never had that, because even when our dad was alive, he was absent. Our mother raised us by herself, and I don't judge her for one single second for putting our dad's work away, once he didn't need it any more. All it meant to her was misery, and a reminder of everything that had been taken from her.' She paused again, piercing Ben with her gaze. 'So, no. I've never been curious. Not even for a minute. It's never crossed my mind to wonder what my father preferred to spend his time doing, or what was so interesting that it kept him from being a parent, or what was so *important* that it claimed his life when he was younger than both Niamh and I are now. Honestly, Ben? Nothing is important enough for that.'

Ben closed his eyes. They felt like hot marbles in his head. He *had* to get them to see the truth – that Grandad *had* loved them both, and that it must have been something *really* important that had kept him so busy – without revealing he'd been poking around in things he shouldn't be poking around in, and he didn't see how he could manage it. He was full of questions he wished he could ask his grandad. *Is the Morrígan real? Like,* really *real? And is she looking for me?*

'I think it is,' Ben said, his voice shaking as he

spoke. He opened his eyes again. 'I think Grandad's work is important.'

Niamh snorted softly, folding her arms on the tabletop. 'Well, we'll have to agree to disagree on that one.'

'But if you haven't read it –' Ben began.

'Brendan Donal O'Donnell-Mulhern,' his mother interrupted, her voice low and dangerous, and Ben got the message. Moodily, he attacked his mashed potatoes again, slopping them around his plate.

'Anyone have any *other* business for this family meeting?' Niamh said.

'When are we leaving here?' Ben said, looking back at his parents. 'Did you find anything, when you were searching online?'

John and Aisling shared a worried look. 'Nothing so far, bud,' John said. 'I have an interview for a job next week, which is great, and Mam's going to look properly for something once you lads are back in school. But no sign of a house, yet.'

'We'll get there,' Aisling said. 'I promise.'

Ben nodded, but he wasn't reassured. The weird dreams, the strange feeling of being watched, the visions of the scary dark-haired woman and the mark of her feather on his arm (which still stung, sometimes, especially in the middle of the night) – it had all started when they'd arrived here. Not in Clare, the county; not even in the Burren itself, as magical and strange as it may be. But in this *house*.

There was something building, and Ben had been aware of it for longer than he wanted to admit. It was like water filling a bath, and how it looks for the longest time like it's not going to overspill, until finally – that one drop is enough to cause a deluge.

His thoughts were interrupted by a sharp *bang*.  Everyone turned, startled, to see what had caused it, and Ben almost threw up at the sight of the huge black-and-grey crow on the patio. It had pecked the glass of the sliding door so hard with its beak, that Ben marvelled the pane hadn't shattered.

'Get out of it! Go on!' Niamh shouted, getting to her feet and picking up a tea-towel. She waved it at the bird, slapping her hand on the inside of the door, and the crow took to the air. It flapped away, leaving nothing behind but a single dark feather, which floated slowly to earth. Ben scratched at his arm. His own feather-mark was tingling.

'Horrible yokes,' Niamh said, shaking her head as

she resumed her seat. She tossed the tea-towel onto the table in front of her. 'I hate those big crows. They always look like they're up to something. Or that they'd like to pull the eyeballs out of you for their supper.'

'Niamh,' Aisling said, gesturing to her plate. 'Will you give it a rest?'

'Actually, do you remember what Mammy always said, Ash?' Niamh began. 'About the crows.'

Aisling frowned at her sister, swallowing some food.

'About the feathers?' Eun-Kyung said. Every hair on Ben's body seemed to stand on end. He remembered the feather in the box, the malevolent gleam of its barbs.

'What about the feathers?' he asked.

Niamh turned to him. 'My mother used to say that Dad was killed by the crows. She wondered if they'd come in through an open window, or if they'd bombarded him and frightened him enough to bring on the cardiac arrest. She hated them, anyway, from that day on. I suppose I've inherited it from her.'

'Why would she think that?' Ben asked, almost scared to know the answer.

'Oh yes – I remember now,' Aisling said. 'Didn't Mammy always say that when she came into the room and found Dad the whole place was covered in crow feathers?'

Niamh nodded. 'Hundreds of them, like drops of midnight, all over the room.'

Ben turned to the window again. Silhouetted against the evening sky, not far from the entrance to the forbidden cave, were three crows, flying in a zigzag around one another, almost like they were dancing.

15

Ben woke, choking. He sat up quickly, coughing hard enough to retch, trying to clear whatever was in his throat. It felt like fluff, or cotton wool – or featherdown. Finally, he got his breath back, and the clogged feeling passed. He pulled his knees up and wrapped his arms around them, trying to breathe calmly and steadily, hoping his heart would slow to a normal rhythm.

He tried to recall what he'd been dreaming about, but it was gone. All he was left with were fleeting impressions – speed, and air, and height, and the Burren from above. Freedom. Cold. Rain. He shivered, bone-deep, despite the clammy night.

Once he felt calmer, he realised that the room was completely silent. Fin wasn't snoring, which meant he must be awake, but he hadn't said anything either. He hadn't asked if Ben was okay, or even thrown a pillow, or a shoe, to get him to shut up.

He pushed the covers off and put his feet on the floor, scrunching his toes into the rug once, twice, three times – he always did this, even if he was in a hurry, as it felt like he was walking on an uneven surface otherwise. Then, he popped on his dim bedside light and tiptoed across the room. Fin's side was mostly in shadow. His bed was a dark nest, the blankets tossed and untidy.

'Fin,' Ben whispered. 'Fin, are you awake?'

There was no reply.

'Fin!' Ben whispered, more loudly this time. He leaned down to shake his brother by the shoulder – but his hand passed straight down into the pile of blankets, meeting no resistance. With a jerk of shock, Ben realised: *Fin's not here.*

Breathing quickly, Ben pulled the string to turn on the light over Fin's bed. It was much brighter than his own, and showed him the truth he already knew: his brother's bed was empty. Ben scanned the room for clues, his eyes hopping around his brother's things, trying to see if anything was missing. Fin was so messy that it was hard to be sure, but Ben was almost certain stuff wasn't exactly how it had been earlier, when Fin had turned out his light and gone to bed.

And then Ben's gaze fell on Fin's sketchpad, which still lay on his desk. It was closed, but some of the sheets had come loose. They seemed to be covered in vicious black strokes, wide and deep gouges into the paper, made with a pencil wielded by an angry hand. For a few very long seconds, Ben stood, his eyes glued to the cover of the sketchpad. Fin's name was drawn on it in three-dimensional letters, along with the names and logos of some of his favourite bands. With a pang, Ben noticed how carefully Fin had drawn the logo for Eddie Ate Dynamite, and he realised how much his brother must really be missing his band. Being a musician was all he'd ever dreamed of, and he'd had to leave it all behind. *They're right*, Ben realised, thinking miserably about what Ji-Ah and Fin had said, earlier. *I do only think about myself. Fin's had a hard time too. And Ji-Ah – her dad's so far away, and she must miss him, and her little sisters. None of us have it easy here.*

He swallowed his feelings of guilt and looked

towards the door of their room, half-expecting to see his brother standing there, but there was no sign. Was Fin just in the bathroom? Or maybe, in the kitchen stealing cereal? If Fin came back and found Ben standing here, on his side of the room, all up in his things, Ben knew it wouldn't go well for him. His brother was already angry enough – this would be the final straw.

'Where have you gone, Fin?' he whispered, standing back to properly take in what he was seeing. He spotted it right away – Fin's trainers, which had been lying on the striped rug, were missing. His phone was gone from its charging pad. His jeans and T-shirt, which he'd draped across the back of his chair, were gone too. So, wherever Fin had gone, he wasn't in the house. He'd dressed, which meant he'd gone outside. But how long ago? And what for? And *where*?

Ben turned to his own side of the room and pulled on whatever clothes he could see. Tracksuit bottoms, an old *Puppy Rangers* T-shirt that he'd been meaning to put in the 'throw away' pile but had never quite managed to, and his trainers, which were neatly placed beneath his bedside table, as usual. He was about to make for the door when something pulled him back. He crouched beside his wardrobe, pulling out the box of camping stuff that had been thrown in there, haphazardly, when they'd moved in. A few seconds of rooting in the box brought forth his old torch, which he hadn't used in longer than he could remember, but a quick check showed that the batteries were still working. He looked at his bedside clock. The digital hands were luminous and he could see them from anywhere in the room. 11.40 p.m. Almost the witching hour.

Ben stuck the torch in his pocket and stood in the middle of the room. His fingers twitched as thoughts buffeted their way through his head. *Should I wake Mam and Dad? Or should I just find him, get him back home, and let it be a secret? Where should I start looking? Has he gone to town, or into the garden, or out across the karst?*

He made fists and released them again, over and over, and eventually his thoughts settled into something like a plan. *Go and find him. Bring him back. Say nothing to Mam and Dad.* And he was pretty sure Fin hadn't gone towards the town. He closed his eyes. The karst was calling, he could feel it.

And he was positive that Fin had felt it too.

Just as he started to walk towards the door, Ben glanced at Fin's sketchbook once more. He knew Fin would be upset if he caught Ben looking in it. He knew it was private, and he struggled with the idea that he was going to have to look in it anyway, despite knowing all that. *Maybe there's a clue*, he told himself, *or some sort of hint about how he was feeling, or what he was thinking, right before he left*. He swallowed his misgivings, and quickly made his way around the end of Fin's bed until he was standing at the desk.

Before he could stop himself, Ben reached out and flipped the sketchbook open. The first fifteen or twenty pages were old drawings, and he didn't linger over those – mostly rock stars, in rock-star poses, or band logos, or instruments. But then, Fin's drawings changed. The last four or five sketches he'd made were all of the same thing, and Ben's legs went wobbly as he looked at them. He sat on the end of Fin's bed, the sketchbook in his hands, and stared at the images.

They were of a woman with long dark hair, wearing a feathered cloak, her eyes cruel and beautiful, her lips drawn back from sharp teeth, her fingernails like talons. Fin had drawn her over and over, sometimes several times on the same page, lots of little thumbnails of her in different poses or from different angles. If you didn't know better, you'd assume she was the lead singer of some rock band or other – one of the bands Fin devoted his heart to, perhaps one that was obsessed with crows. But Ben did know better.

'The Morrígan,' he whispered, staring at his brother's work. He ran his fingers lightly over one of the sketches of her face. It was exactly the face he'd seen in Ennis, exactly the same slope to the forehead, the same delicate sweep to the nose, the same shape to her eyes. It was the same person. None of the other drawings he'd seen of her had come anywhere close – he was sure Fin had seen the same woman he'd seen. But he'd never said anything. *No wonder he was whimpering in his sleep*, Ben thought, wishing he'd really talked to Fin about it, and really listened, instead of letting things end up in a fight instead. Something in the background of one of the sketches caught his eye; it looked like a dark hole in the ground, or a shadowy doorway. It seemed familiar, though Ben wasn't sure why.

He quickly put the sketchbook back as he'd found

it, hoping it wasn't obvious that he'd peeked. Then, he turned off Fin's light. He left his own small reading lamp on, because somehow knowing it was waiting for him to come back and switch it off made it feel more likely that he *would* be coming back, and made his way quietly to the door. He crept downstairs on silent feet, hoping against hope he'd find his brother slouched against the kitchen cupboards, a bowl of milky Chocko Pops in his hand.

But the kitchen was silent and empty, full of shadows. Ben stood just inside the door and blinked, waiting for his eyes to adjust to the darkness, and as he walked into the room he felt something unexpected – a cool breeze that shouldn't be there. He looked towards the sliding doors that led from the kitchen into the garden, right at the spot where he'd seen the crow at dinnertime, and realised they were open. As he watched, the curtains billowed in the night air, spookily graceful, just about visible in the moonlight. And then, like a cog turning, the reality of what Fin had drawn in his sketchbook clicked into place in Ben's mind. The dark doorway. The opening into shadows. *Grandad's cave.* His heart started to pound.

He made his way over to the doors, leaning out

into the night. 'Fin!' he called, in a hoarse whisper. He didn't dare shout. '*Fin!*'

There was no answer. Ben stepped out onto the patio before turning to pull the sliding door closed behind him – but not all the way. He didn't want the door to lock and leave him and Fin stranded outside. Eun-Kyung's solar lights were glowing gently all along the bottom of the wall that bounded the edge of their property, so he used them to make his way across the lawn and right down to the end of the garden. He stopped at the fence, feeling like he was safe enough to shout now – there was enough distance between him and the house.

'Fin!' he called. 'Where are you?'

The only answer was the sighing of the breeze across the karst. Ben climbed onto the second plank of the garden fence, afraid to put his leg over the top and push himself off into the unknown on the far side. If he did, something told him he might not come back. 'Come on, Fin,' he pleaded, quietly. 'Just come out, so we can go back inside. Please!'

He stood there, staring into the darkness, for as long as he could bear, before swinging himself over the top of the gate. He held his breath as he dropped over the other side, landing heavily on the stony soil. Now, he was in the grip of the dark. The solar lights couldn't reach here. It was like the night swallowed all sources of illumination on this side of the fence.

With trembling hands, Ben pulled his torch out of his back pocket and flicked it on. The beam was weak at first but quickly grew stronger, though it still didn't seem to reach far. He pointed it at the ground, checking where he put his feet before each step, and every few yards he'd stop and swing the light from side to side, just searching. 'Fin!' he shouted again, into the emptiness. 'Come on!'

Ben realised he was coming close to the cave, the one his grandfather had gated off and insisted nobody ever enter. He swallowed his fear as he realised: he'd known, all along, that this was where Fin would be. There was simply nowhere else he could have gone. *And he's been dreaming about it*, Ben told himself. His steps stumbling a little on the unfamiliar surface, Ben shone the torch at the cave entrance and saw the gate his grandfather had put up was open now. Its rusted old padlock must have offered no resistance to Fin's strong hands. It looked like he'd simply yanked at it until it slid undone, the fifty-year old metal weakened and crumbling, falling apart and flaking into brownish-orange dust. Its warning unheeded, its danger loosed, the cave was finally open.

Nothing met Ben's eye inside the cave mouth besides darkness, and all he could hear was the distant *drip-drip* of moisture falling from the rocky roof. He tried to shout Fin's name, but he couldn't gather his voice enough to get it to work. Instead, he pointed his weak light at the cave floor, tried to suppress his shudder of fear and stepped inside.

16

Almost immediately, Ben felt his feet starting to slide. The cave floor was sloped just beyond the entrance, and also quite wet. He almost dropped the torch as he reached out to grab something – anything – that could keep him upright, but as soon as his hand made contact with the cool, damp cave wall, he managed to steady his balance.

'Idiot,' he muttered to himself, setting his next steps carefully. The cave was completely still. There was a mouldy smell in the air, damp and earthy and faintly sweet, and he could feel a gentle but insistent draught moving over his skin. The only noise, besides his own breathing, was the constant *plink-plink* of moisture dripping somewhere. *Does that form stalactites or stalagmites?* he found himself thinking, his brain a desperate whirl. *C for ceiling; g for ground. Isn't that it?*

'Fin!' he called out, his voice little more than a strangled gasp. 'Fin, are you in here? Come on! This isn't funny. Mam is going to kill us!'

The floor began to level out. Ben swung the torch slowly, watching the weak light dance on the uneven walls, which sparkled as the beam touched them. He began to shiver; it was a lot colder in here than it had been outside, and his thin T-shirt was no match for the conditions. He *had* to find Fin and get home, before someone noticed they weren't in bed – or he froze to death. *How far does this cave go?*

He filled his lungs to shout again but before he could, there was a terrifying sound right at the mouth of the cave. Ben spun on his heel, trying to wield his torch like some sort of club, but the thing that was pursuing him was out of his reach. All he could see was a weird, ill-defined shape, and he could hear its rough, loud breaths, like a hunting animal running its prey to ground. Panic took hold of his brain, and he threw his torch. It went spinning out of his hand to land, hard, against the rocky cave wall. With a *smash*, its light went out.

'Oh, brilliant,' said the shape. 'That was smart, huh?'

It fumbled with something for a second before a piercing white light emerged from it. Ben blinked in confusion, his terror beginning to drain away.

'Ji-Ah,' he whispered.

Ji-Ah held her phone light under her chin, illuminating her face with weird angles and shadows. 'I know you guys call me a cave troll,' she said. 'So, meh. I figured I'd live up to my reputation.'

Ben tried to get his breath back as he stared at her. 'What?' He shook his head. 'I mean – sorry about the cave troll stuff. That was a joke.' He wiped his damp face on his even damper forearm. 'What are you doing here?'

'I had to go to the bathroom,' Ji-Ah explained. 'I saw your light on – you left your bedroom door open and I realised you guys were gone. And when I found the sliding door unlocked, the rest put itself together from there. I mean,' she shrugged, 'where else would you go?'

Ben nodded, his breathing finally settled. He was grateful that the person who'd realised they were missing was Ji-Ah, and not one of their parents.

'I haven't found Fin yet,' Ben said. 'Does your phone have much battery?'

Ji-Ah peered at the screen. 'Eighty-six per cent,' she said. 'Should be fine for a while.'

'Okay. Come on.' Ben waited for her to make her slow, slippery way down the sloped cave entrance, and once she'd reached the flatter part he turned away, picking his way carefully over the ground. Ji-Ah followed, keeping her phone torch focused on the floor in front of their feet.

'So – um,' Ben began, after a minute. 'I'm sorry?'

'Are you, or aren't you?' Ji-Ah said. 'You don't sound sure.'

'Well – I am sorry. I'm just not sure what I did exactly.'

'I suppose you didn't do anything, really,' Ji-Ah said. 'It's just – Fin's having it tough too, you know? You're not the only one struggling with this whole "unwillingly blended family" thing. And it's like, whenever he tries to talk to you about it, it gets turned into this *other* thing, like an argument or you making it all about you, or whatever.'

Ben thought about Fin's sketchbook. 'I get it,' he said.

'But, hey!' Ji-Ah said, ducking to avoid a dripping

stalactite. 'Check us out. Venturing into a midnight cave with nothing but the *Puppy Rangers* shirts on our backs to keep us from mortal danger, all to rescue one of our own? We're a team!'

Ben was glad of the darkness, as he felt sure his cheeks were burning. 'I've had this T-shirt for ages,' he began, 'and I keep meaning to donate it. It was the first thing that I grabbed when I saw Fin was gone –'

'Oh, get over it,' Ji-Ah said. '*Puppy Rangers* were the best.'

Ben smiled. 'Yeah,' he said, quietly. 'They were.'

They walked on for another few steps, until Ji-Ah's torch caught something that didn't look like a cave wall. It looked like –

'Fin!' they shouted together. The cave was too narrow for them to run – and too dangerous underfoot – but they hurried forward as fast as they could, Ji-Ah doing her best to keep the light focused on Fin's back. He didn't turn around, not even when they landed on top of him in a jumble of arms and legs.

'Hey!' Ji-Ah said. 'Come on, bonehead! If we get caught in here, we'll be the first kids to be grounded so long that it becomes, like, *posthumous*.'

Fin didn't move. His eyes were wide, and he didn't blink, even when Ji-Ah shone the torch right in his face. 'What's wrong with him?' Ben said. His heart was thumping, not just with cold and exhilaration, but with fear.

'I – I don't know,' Ji-Ah said. Ben met her eyes. She looked just as worried as him.

'It's like he's frozen, or something,' Ben said. He put one hand on Fin's cheek. He wasn't icy – he felt alive. But he looked like he'd been switched off. 'It's like Grandad,' Ben said, his teeth beginning to chatter. 'Like how Niamh described it. When Granny found him, it was like someone had just pulled out his plug.'

Ji-Ah handed Ben the phone and quickly pressed her ear to Fin's chest. Immediately, she pulled a face, but she kept listening for a few seconds. 'His heart's beating,' she said, lifting her head again and taking the phone back. 'And he really needs to find himself some new deodorant, because whatever he's using right now? It should be declared a weapon of torture.'

Ben nodded. 'Okay. That's something. But how are we going to get him out of here?'

Ji-Ah frowned. Then her face lit up with inspiration. She turned to Fin and started shouting, right in his face. 'Hey! Fin! Girdle of Agony haven't made a good album since 1991's *Freakshow*. Right?' She glanced at Ben, waving a hand encouragingly, but he stared at her blankly. *What was she doing?*

'I'm trying to get through to him in the language he speaks best,' Ji-Ah said. Then, she turned towards Fin again and raised her voice. 'Really terrible music!'

Ben nodded. 'Yeah!' he began. 'Everything else they've released has been like nursery rhymes. Imagine spending money on their merch!'

Ji-Ah gave him a thumbs up. 'Atomic Eyeroll are the best band in the WORLD!' She shouted the last word, so loudly that it made Ben wince. Didn't things sometimes live in caves? He shuddered at the thought of being surrounded by a cloud of angry bats, disturbed by their yelling.

'Hey, maybe we shouldn't –' he began, but his words were cut off by a sound from deeper inside the cave; a sound that bypassed his brain and went straight to his belly. Ben felt his heart kick up yet another gear, and his muscles tense for running. His breaths were fast and shallow, his eyes scanning the cave for threats.

'What was that?' Ji-Ah whispered.

The noise sounded again: a low rumbling, like a rockfall.

'Come on,' Ben said, grabbing Fin under the armpit. 'If he can't walk, we're going to have to pull him out.'

'All that way?' Ji-Ah said, staring at Ben in panic.

'Just help me!'

Ji-Ah looked determined. 'I want to check something. All right? I won't go far. Promise.'

'Ji-Ah,' Ben whimpered. 'We have to get out of here.' The cave was beginning to feel oppressive, like they were in the stone fist of a giant, who could close their fingers tight at any time, crushing flat any unfortunate soft-bodied humans who happened to be inside. Ben looked back the way they'd come, desperately hoping to see some light, even if it meant his parents were on their way. He'd take their anger over whatever else was in here with them.

He looked back at Ji-Ah. She was crouched low, her phone torch shining ahead of her, carefully picking her way deeper into the cave.

'What are you *doing*?' he hissed.

'I want to see what's down here!' she whispered back. 'See if there's another way out, instead of having to go all the way back to where we entered this cave. Okay? Eomma told me about how this stuff works – these caves can often be connected, right, and there's more than one entrance into most of them. So, if there's a way out to the surface down here, and it's closer than the one we came in through, I'm taking it!'

Ben gave one quick nod, tightening his grip on his brother, and Ji-Ah gave him a grateful look before continuing into the cave. The further away Ji-Ah went, the darker everything was becoming – she had their only light, and if she lost it . . . Ben squeezed his eyes tight shut, forcing that thought from his mind.

'There's a cavern here!' she called, her voice echoing strangely. 'It's wide, and dry, and –'

Whatever Ji-Ah was going to say next was lost in a noise that turned Ben's bones to water – a growl, so loud and so deep that it rattled the cavern, shaking dust and debris from the ceiling and making it feel as though everything around them was about to collapse. Ben couldn't catch his breath – his panic was pushing all the air out of his body.

'Ji-Ah!' he finally managed to shout. '*Ji-Ah!*'

She came scuttling backwards, her phone torch skittering giddily along the walls and floor, before turning over and getting to her feet. She tried to run, but slipped and bashed her leg against the wall. It didn't stop her from getting up again. 'Hurry!' she shrieked, and Ben wasn't sure if it was at him or Fin. '*Get out!*'

She shoved her phone into a pocket as she took hold of Fin's other arm, dousing the entire cave in darkness – but only for a moment. Another light, a different one, trickled into the cave as they tried to drag Fin backwards and out. A bright bluish-silver light, one which Ben had seen in his dreams – the light that glowed from a pair of eyes, which belonged to the most terrifying creature he could imagine. A creature so huge, in this tiny underground space, that it was bigger than the world. A creature that could tear him apart without even thinking about it – which could end his puny life with one sweep of its massive paw.

And then the owner of those eyes appeared in front of them.

17

The bear was so petrifying that the sight of it turned Ben's brain to static. It was so huge that it filled the entire cave, pouring through it like smoke as it approached. It seemed to expand as it came, growing to choke out all light, all air, all space . . .

'*Ben!*' Ji-Ah's shriek of panic snapped him out of his trance. He scrambled towards her and Fin, digging his hand around his brother's arm as they tried to drag him backwards. There wasn't enough space for them to do it side by side, and they kept bashing into one another and stumbling as they went. Ji-Ah's breaths were coming fast, and she was crying.

'Eomma!' she shouted, over her shoulder. '*Mammy! Help us!*'

But there was no reply.

Ben could smell the bear. It stank of death, its breath hot and foul and meaty. Its fur crackled with blue and silver, like tiny flashes of lightning. Its claws were long and sharp and shiny, clicking mercilessly on the cave floor as it crept forward, ever forward, its head low and its shoulders high and tensed, ready to spring. And always its eyes – those eyes Ben had dreamed of. Those bright, electric-blue eyes, narrowing in anger.

A rumbling growl deep in its chest turned into a full-throated roar. Ben watched the strings of saliva rattling between the bear's teeth and felt its hot, putrid breath wash over him, pushing back his hair. There was nothing in the universe besides him and the bear now. Every part of him was focused on this threat, on getting away, on *surviving*.

And yet, a tiny part of his brain kept trying to tell him something. *Bears are guardian spirits . . . They are a part of the tapestry of this land . . . They roam around, keeping everything safe . . .* Surely, if this bear wanted to destroy him, Ben thought, he'd be a gently steaming pile of entrails on the cave floor by now. This animal meant business. But it hadn't attacked. Was it guarding something? If so, what?

Then he heard Ji-Ah scream, and he focused again on the task at hand. 'Come on,' he called, as he renewed his grip on Fin's arm and took the strain. How could his string-bean brother be so *heavy*? The slippery floor helped a little, but it also meant he and Ji-Ah had to fight to keep their balance – he lost count of how often one or both of them slid and landed painfully, usually bringing the other down with them.

He glanced towards the cave entrance. 'We're nearly there,' he gasped. 'Ji-Ah, we've nearly made it! But we've got to get him up the slope.' Ben remembered how he'd almost fallen flat as he'd entered; the first few metres just inside the cave angled steeply downwards, and the slope looked like the side of a mountain from here, like an obstacle too great to be overcome.

'I'll pull him,' Ji-Ah said. 'You go down and push him, okay? Push him up as hard as you can, Ben. And we've got to hope this bear's too big to make it out after us.'

Ben nodded, clambering down over Fin's still-unconscious form. He faced the bear, pushing backwards with his legs, his brother's feet draped over his shoulders. 'Please, please, please,' he begged, under his breath. 'Please let us make it.' His feet

183

slipped, his ankles cracking painfully against rock, but he didn't give up. He *couldn't*.

And still the bear came – though slower this time. Its blue eyes weren't so overwhelmingly bright. Ben could even have sworn they'd *dimmed* a little, like their power was running low – or like the creature was reconsidering. It was silent now, besides the billow of its breath as it walked.

Ji-Ah gave a roar of effort as she neared the top of the slope, Fin weighing heavily in her arms. 'Ben!' she shouted. 'Come on – push!'

Ben braced his feet and shoved, the effort tearing at his muscles. The bear was quiet, and it seemed *smaller* somehow, but he could still hear the click of its talons and the *huff-huff* of the air in its lungs. He shifted his foot, trying to get a better purchase on the rocky floor but as he pushed against Fin's weight, he felt himself slipping – and next thing he knew, he was sliding down the slope, out of control, right towards the bear.

'Ben!' Ji-Ah screamed.

He couldn't shout – he couldn't even talk. His breaths were galloping, one on top of the other, his eyes wide with terror. He felt his body curling into a ball as he lifted his hands over his head, trying to shield his face, trying to do *anything* to stop the bear's attack. He was going to land right *on* it, going to crash into its drool-stained muzzle, its crackling fur, its dinner-plate paws with their flesh-rending claws . . . It was game over!

But instead of leaping forward and sinking its talons into him, the bear took a step back. It gave a small whine before sniffing at Ben. He could feel the bear's nose, wet and slimy, as it rooted in his clothes and hair. Then it took another step back and Ben could hear the sound of its tongue, slapping and slithering, reaching up to lick its muzzle. The bear stopped, waiting, for Ben to unfurl. Slowly, bit by bit, he did just that.

'Are you alive?' Ji-Ah's panicked shout echoed strangely in the cave. 'Ben!'

'I – I'm okay,' he called back, his voice cracked and hoarse. 'How's Fin?'

'We're up,' Ji-Ah said. 'At the top of the slope. We're just inside the cave entrance.'

Ben kept his eyes on the bear as he crept backwards. The bear watched him too, its weird blue eyes wary and curious, but not afraid. 'It's okay,' he whispered to it. 'It's okay. Right? I'm just going to leave now, and we can forget all of this ever happened.' He kept his voice low and quiet, hoping it would soothe the bear, hoping that – maybe, if he was *super* lucky – he would get an extra life in this particular game, and live to play again.

'*Ben!*' came a shout from above – a different voice than before. *Fin!* The bear reared, startled by the sudden sound, and a low growl began in its chest. Its eyes glowed a little brighter, a little more menacing.

'It's okay!' Ben gasped, scrambling harder to push himself up the slope. 'It's all right, bear!'

'Come on, pal, we have you,' Fin said. Ben looked up to see Fin and Ji-Ah reaching down for him. He stretched as far as he could, finally feeling his brother's strong fingers wrapping around his own. Fin hauled him up a few feet until Ji-Ah could grab his other hand, and together they made short work of pulling him up the rest of the way. The three of them staggered out of the cave entrance all in a tangle, Ben being half-carried, half-dragged by the other two, until they eventually flopped to the ground, gasping for breath, staring up at the stars. From the cave, there was complete silence. Not only was the bear not pursuing them, but there was no sign of it whatsoever. *Almost*, Ben thought, *like it was never there at all*.

'What just happened?' Ji-Ah whispered, after a few minutes.

'Don't ask me,' Fin said.

Ben rolled over and whacked him. 'What was all that about? You were like someone in a coma, or something! Totally out of it. What *happened* to you?'

Fin pushed himself up on his elbow, running a hand through his hair. 'I was asleep, all right? Like, sleepwalking, or something. I – had a dream. There were crows. And something to do with the Cailleach?' Fin shook his head, as if trying to settle his tangled thoughts. 'I don't know. I can only half-remember it, now.'

'The Cailleach,' Ben repeated.

'Who *is* that?' Ji-Ah said, sitting up.

'Yeah,' Fin said, scratching behind one ear absent-mindedly. 'Who is that?'

'You're going to think I'm talking woo-woo,' Ben said, staring at his brother.

Fin raised his eyebrows. 'Dude. After all this? You can talk all the woo-woo you like.'

187

Ben licked his lips as he steadied himself. 'She's – like, a goddess. She can do magic. One of her jobs is shaping the landscape – like, making mountains, forming the karst, that sort of thing. She also makes weather, winter storms mostly. Wind, snow and all that. And she's also a smith.'

'A what?' Ji-Ah wrinkled her nose in confusion.

'Someone who makes stuff from metal,' Ben said.

'Like, forks and spoons?' Ji-Ah said. 'I thought all that would be done by machines.'

Ben blinked, very seriously. 'No – not like forks and spoons,' he said.

Ji-Ah rolled her eyes. 'Oh my God, Ben. I *know*. I'm not an idiot – it was a joke, okay?'

'Like what, then?' Fin said. 'What sort of metal things does this person make? Or *smith*, or whatever.'

'Swords,' Ben answered, meeting his brother's eye briefly.

'Right,' Fin said, pushing himself up onto his feet. 'I think we've all had enough – whatever this has been – for one night. Okay? Let's get home, and we can tell the olds tomorrow that there's something living in Grandad's pit, and that maybe they need to call, like, the exterminator or something.' He paused. 'Or the

Terminator, maybe. He might have more luck.'

Ben scrambled up beside him. 'Are you serious? An *exterminator*? That's a *bear* down there. There haven't been bears living here for thousands of years!'

Fin shrugged, but Ben knew he wasn't mistaking the panic in his eyes. 'So?'

'So it's important!' Ben stopped, clenching and unclenching his fingers while he got his thoughts straight. 'It's protecting something,' he finally said. 'Eun-Kyung told me. The folklore about bears around here. They're seen as guardians. Guardian spirits. Protecting the Burren and keeping it safe.'

'Wait – Eomma talked about guardian *spirits*?' Ji-Ah said. 'So, is the bear we saw an actual bear, or not?'

'I don't know,' said Ben.

Fin snorted derisively. 'Will you pair listen to yourselves? Talking about spirit bears and weather goddesses and swords. It's all rubbish.'

Ben whirled to face him. 'Says the guy who wandered out here in the middle of the night because a *dream* told him to,' he retorted.

Fin opened his mouth, but found his words vanished as he tried to say them. 'I – that's not – what

I *meant* was,' he began. 'Shut up, Ben,' he finally finished.

'Look, you can both go home,' Ben said, feeling himself quiver as he spoke. 'But I'm not giving up. We need to find out what's inside that cave. There might be clues about why our family's caught up in all this weirdness. I mean, there's a reason Grandad kept it closed off –'

'Yeah, because there's a *bear* in it,' Fin interrupted.

'No! The bear's there for a reason too. It must be guarding something.' Ben swallowed hard. 'Something Grandad fought hard to keep safe. And whatever it is, we've got to keep it out of the Morrígan's hands.'

'The what?' said Ji-Ah, at the same time as Fin said 'Who?'

'The Battle Crow,' Ben said, the words settling around him like a cold mist.

18

'Ben, this is not happening,' Fin said, standing in front of his brother. He placed one hand flat on Ben's chest and pressed against him, gently, but enough to stop him from walking any further.

'What happened to "we're a fellowship"?' Ben said. '*Bro?*'

'We're a fellowship, yeah!' Fin spluttered. 'When it comes to stuff like sticking up for each other, or lobbying Mam and Dad for more time playing Roblox. Not when it comes to doing *stupid* things like deliberately walking into a cave with a giant *bear* in it!'

'But that's just it!' Why wouldn't Fin just *listen* to him? 'The bear won't hurt me. It won't, Fin! I fell on top of it, before you guys pulled me out, and all it did was take a good long sniff of me. No slashy-slashy, bitey-bitey – none of that. Because it's there for a reason.' He stared up at his brother. 'There are no *actual* bears here. Not any more. They've been extinct for years. Eun-Kyung told me, and she *knows* what she's talking about.'

Fin blinked. Ben could tell he was really trying to understand. 'So, what you're saying is, that's not a real bear?'

'Bingo,' Ben snapped. 'Now, will you get out of the way?' He tried to step around, but Fin grabbed him by the arms.

'Mam will literally feed me my own intestines if I let anything happen to you,' he said.

'Oh my God, that's disgusting,' Ji-Ah muttered.

'*Nothing* is going to happen to me. I absolutely guarantee it.' Ben shook his brother's hands free, irritated at being held.

Fin snorted. 'Just like you *absolutely guaranteed* that ball wasn't hard enough to smash the back window of the shed, that time?'

Ben felt blood rush to his cheeks. 'That was a *mistake*, all right?'

'Yeah, well. Fixing a window is a lot easier than trying to patch a kid back together.'

Ben sighed. 'Look. Just admit it. You've been having dreams, right?'

Fin's bravado fizzled out as he met his brother's eye. 'Yeah,' he mumbled.

'And you've been dreaming about a woman. With, like, black hair and those weird pointy eyebrows and eyes like glacier ice and these lips that look like she's just been eating a rare steak, extra-bloody?'

Fin coughed. 'That's – about it,' he said.

'Yeah. Well, she's the Morrígan. Also known as the Battle Crow. Or the Shadesinger. Or She-Who-Is-Three.' Ben shuddered as he spoke.

Fin looked worried. 'And who is she?'

'Another goddess. Or a witch, maybe? Bit of both, probably. Except she's in charge of stuff like war. And who wins battles, and calling armies together.' He cleared his throat. 'And death. Destruction. That sort of stuff.'

'No way,' Fin breathed. 'That is *so* metal.'

'But – what does she have to do with any of this?' Ji-Ah said, coming to stand beside Fin. She gave him a weird look, and then stared up at Fin with the same strange expression on her face. 'And why are *you* pair dreaming about her?'

Ben took a deep breath, pressing his lips together as he exhaled. 'Look. I have to tell you guys something else too. I – looked in Grandad's office.'

'You literally *what*?' said Ji-Ah. 'Because I told you where the key was? Do you have any clue how deeply Mam is going to ground me?'

Ben looked at her. 'I won't say anything about how I got in.'

'Oh, don't worry,' Ji-Ah said. 'She'll figure it out.'

Fin stared at his brother, ignoring Ji-Ah. 'So, what's it like in there?'

'A mess,' Ben shrugged. 'But I found some stuff. Like, mostly books. But also pictures that Niamh drew, as a kid, which Grandad had treasured, and a photo of Mam and Niamh as babies. He loved them. Don't you see? He loved his family. He wasn't some monster. And there's a connection between the Morrígan, and this area. Something in the landscape around here is important to all this.' He looked at Fin. 'And the Cailleach, from your dream? Well, she's connected to the Burren. And Mullaghmore.'

'This is the smith person, who – makes swords,' Ji-Ah said, raising her eyebrows.

Ben nodded. 'There's one sword in particular, and

I haven't figured out all the details yet, or why it's *us* that are mixed up in it. But – this sword, right? It belonged to a king, a long time ago. He was Nuada. And he fought in a battle where he lost his arm – and also, the use of his sword.'

'Oh my God, I am actually going to throw up right now,' Ji-Ah said, covering her mouth.

'*But,*' Ben continued, quickly, 'the Cailleach made him a new arm, a silver one. And it was given magical powers by some guy called Dian Cecht, so that Nuada could use it just like a real arm. And then, he could use his sword again, he could be king again, and everything was cool for a while. Until he got his head chopped off in another battle.'

'Seriously?' Ji-Ah cried.

'Yeah, okay. And then what?' Fin prompted.

'So that was the end of Nuada, right,' Ben continued, warming to his theme. He found his fingers had started to flick, but he didn't care. 'But the *sword*. The sword was still around. It's missing, nobody knows where it ended up. And it's not just a sword. It's *the* Sword. The Sword of Light. The Sword of the Sun. A treasure of the Tuatha Dé Danann.'

'The actual who?' Ji-Ah said, her eyebrows raised.

Ben waved a hand impatiently. 'They were mythical gods, like thousands of years ago, and they had four really incredible treasures. This Sword is one of them.'

'And what's so special about it?' Fin prompted.

'It's an unbeatable weapon,' Ben said. 'Super-powerful. Like, potentially, the most powerful weapon ever made.'

Fin raised an eyebrow. 'So, you said this crow lady is a war goddess, right? And this Sword is a super-weapon?'

Ben nodded. 'Exactly.'

Fin looked impressed, nodding slowly. 'Yeah, I can see how this would work.' Then, his eyebrows fell and his mouth hardened and he stared down at his little brother with a scathing expression. 'If it wasn't all *completely* ripped off of some kids' comic, or something. I mean, honestly? Is this the plot of some *game* you and your buddies were halfway through when we left Dublin? You seriously thought we'd fall for this?' Fin shook his head and grabbed Ben's arm again, harder this time, so Ben couldn't shake him off so easily. 'Come on, Captain Daydream. We have to get home before we're missed – and I'll try to come up with some excuse as to why the gate over the cave is broken.'

'Fin, come on!' Ben said, digging in his heels. 'You've got to believe me. Grandad *knew* about this stuff too! He wasn't making it up, and he *wasn't* a crackpot.' He looked at Fin full in the face as he continued. 'And – I think, he might have died because the Morrígan killed him.'

'Oh my God, give me a break,' Fin said, trying to drag his brother. 'This is getting worse by the minute.'

'No – wait!' Ben's chest flooded with desperation. He was *right*, he knew it, and he couldn't let Fin take him away before he figured out what to do next. The secret was in the cave. He *knew* it.

'Hold on,' Ji-Ah said. 'You're talking about the feathers, aren't you? In Grandad's study, the night he died.'

Ben turned to her in surprise. 'How do you know about them?'

'Last Christmas, Mam got a bit – well, a bit drunk,' Ji-Ah said, her voice quiet. 'A couple of glasses of wine more than she usually has, I guess. And she started talking about her dad, and about Granny, and about . . .' She looked at the boys in turn. 'About the night Grandad died. And she told us all about the feathers, and how Granny couldn't understand how so *many* got into the room. It was like a whole flock of crows had burst in through the window, except the window wasn't open. And she hadn't heard a thing. No cawing, so scratching, no fluttering – you know how loud crows are, right?'

'The Morrígan is connected with crows,' Ben said, looking up at Fin. 'She *is* a crow, sometimes – she can change her shape. And I think – no, I *know* – that the night Grandad died, she was there. She and her crow army. And she killed him. I don't know why.'

'Maybe he was figuring things out that she didn't want anyone to know about,' Ji-Ah offered.

Ben nodded. 'Yeah. Maybe.'

'Or,' Fin said, 'he already *did* know something, and she wanted to make sure he didn't tell anyone else about it. Maybe Grandad knew something, and the crow lady wanted to make sure it died with him. He never told his wife – our granny – or his kids. And because they never knew what it was, it never got passed down to us either. His grandkids.'

'Well, doesn't that just prove what I'm saying is right?' Ben said. 'If there's stuff in that cave we need to know about, then we've *got* to go and find it.' He looked at his brother pleadingly. 'And I know one thing for sure: the Cailleach and the Morrígan are *not* pals. So, if you were having a dream, and the Cailleach was in it, maybe it wasn't a dream. Maybe you were being brought here. Maybe the Cailleach needs us to do something. Something Grandad would do, if he was here instead of us.'

Fin straightened his shoulders. 'Well – I'm not *sure* the Cailleach was actually *in* the dream,' he said. 'I remember mostly crows.'

Ben quietly made fists, then released his fingers slowly. 'Look. We've got to go into that cave, okay? We've come this far.'

Fin tucked his hair behind his ears. 'Yeah,' he said, putting on his bass face as though he were about to launch into a shredder of a solo. 'No point chickening out now.'

19

Ji-Ah rolled her eyes. 'I'll stay up here. No chance you're getting me underground again.'

Ben nodded, and Fin stepped towards the cave mouth, his phone torch lighting the way. Keeping his arms stretched wide for balance, Ben followed, hoping he wouldn't go careering into his brother's back.

'Hurry!' Ji-Ah whispered, as the boys disappeared. 'I don't really want to be out here if crow-lady shows up.'

'Just shout if there's trouble, or come and get us,' Ben whispered back. Already he could feel the chill of the cave, and hear the steady *plink-plink-plink*. So far, there was no sign of the bear. His foot slipped, but straight away he felt Fin's hand, steadying him.

'Whoa there,' Fin said. 'Take it easy.'

'Sorry,' Ben whispered. He tried to ignore Fin's exasperated sigh.

They made good progress once the floor levelled off, Fin keeping Ben behind him with one long arm stretched out. His phone light shone on the cave's interior, gleaming against the thick, candle-like stalactites and throwing strange shadows.

'We're almost at the spot where we found you last time,' Ben whispered.

'So where's our pal?' Fin muttered. Ben could feel his brother's trembling as they stood, pressed against one another, too scared to continue but not wanting to turn back.

'Ji-Ah said there was a cavern, just past here,' he said. 'It must be in there. Whatever we're looking for, whatever the bear's guarding – it's got to be there.'

'Right,' Fin said, squaring out his shoulders. 'Let's move.'

Together, the boys crept forward, their ears wide for any sound of an approaching wild animal. Then, just as Fin placed his foot down on something that crunched like sand, they heard it. The first low, warning growl.

'Okay,' Ben breathed. 'There it is.'

'So do we continue?' Fin whispered.

'I guess,' Ben replied. 'He didn't hurt me, Fin. When I slid down, practically into his mouth. He didn't touch me. He could've killed me, but he didn't.'

'Maybe he just wasn't hungry enough yet,' Fin grouched, taking another step. His phone light bounced on the sparkling grains beneath their feet, and the whole cavern glowed with something that seemed like bioluminescence – the walls and the floor and the ceiling high above were all bright with a soothing silver-blue light. Fin turned off his phone torch and fumbled the device back into his pocket as they looked around, letting their eyes adjust to the conditions.

'Wow,' Ben whispered, turning in a circle, taking in the sight. 'This is incredible.'

'What's the light caused by?' Fin asked, reaching out to touch a nearby wall. 'It looks –'

His words were cut off by a rumbling roar. The boys turned to face the back of the cavern. Ben's breath stopped dead in his throat, quick and sharp as a guillotine. Even though he knew what he was going to see, there was something so primally terrifying about the approaching bear that it seemed to shut down all his systems, except the one inside his head that screamed at him to get away. The bear's fur was still crackling and its eyes shone with the same silver-blue as the cavern, though the light wasn't so comforting when it was being reflected off the bear's teeth – and its massive black claws. It kept its head down, wary, and its steps were slow and steady as it eyeballed the human intruders.

But, as Ben had hoped, the bear's roar had stopped and it didn't seem like it was ready to attack. *Maybe we're not the enemy*, he thought.

'Okay,' Ben said, once he could breathe again. 'Okay.' He took one step, and then another, towards the bear. Fin snatched at his T-shirt but Ben wriggled loose, continuing his slow but steady journey. As he went, he made himself smaller by crouching and holding his head down. 'We're here. We're your friends. We're not going to harm you.'

'Ben!' Fin's whisper was like a dart. 'Get back here!'

Ben ignored his brother. Instead, he reached out towards the bear, his fingers trembling despite his best attempts to hold them still.

For a long moment, the bear did nothing. Then, to Ben's delight, it shuffled forward and dipped its head even lower, stretching out its muzzle towards his hand.

'Good boy!' Ben crooned. 'Yeah, I see you. Good fella. Good job.' His fingers sank into the bear's fur. It was soft and warm, and crackling with some sort of strange energy. It filled Ben up and made him feel hopeful, even *happy*. It felt like old magic, which had been here since before human memory. He smiled, knowing his own eyes were overflowing with tears as he looked into those of the bear. He wasn't able to name, or even sort out, all the emotions that were running through him – there were too many, and they were too strong. The bear's eyes seemed wet too, or maybe it was just a reflection of the intense glow all around them.

'It *is* magic, isn't it?' he whispered, knowing the bear couldn't answer, but also knowing he was right. Everything in here was magic: the light, the crystals underfoot, the bear itself. Everything. An ancient magic, one that had been here for longer than Ben could fathom. Magic that had to be kept safe and protected. Magic that couldn't be turned to evil, not by the Morrígan, or by anyone.

The bear grunted happily as Ben scratched its muzzle, as gently as he could.

'So, are you the Bear Whisperer now, or what?' came Fin's voice from across the cavern. Ben smiled.

'Come and say hello,' he said, turning to his brother.

'I'm all right, thanks,' Fin said, quickly.

The bear lifted its head and growled, quietly but definitively, in Fin's direction. 'I think you'd better show the bear you're not a threat,' Ben said, his voice tight with sudden fear.

Fin muttered something under his breath, pushing himself away from the wall where he'd been standing. He walked towards the bear, which pushed itself backwards as Fin approached, eyeing him warily.

'Slow!' Ben hissed. 'Fin, come on. Go slowly, and stay low.'

Fin grunted with frustration, but he dropped to a crouch, continuing much more slowly than before. 'Hi,' he whispered. 'I can't believe I'm actually doing this.'

The bear seemed unsure, but finally it flopped forward again and allowed Fin to touch it. His fingers looked like they were carved from darkness as they sank into the bear's silver-bright fur, and Ben smiled to see it. *This is what Grandad was protecting,* he thought. *I've got to tell Mam, and Niamh. They've got to know their dad wasn't awful – he was trying his best to do something good. Something great. And we've got to help him now; we've got to finish whatever he started.*

The bear shuffled backwards even further, and lowered its head to the floor. It huffed out one hot breath, and then another, continuing until the sparkling sand on the cave floor began to move. It billowed away, whirling in the bear's breath, until finally a patch of something pale and smooth was revealed, embedded in the ground.

'What on earth –' Fin began, as the bear continued to use its breath to clear away the sand.

The boys watched as more of the creamy-pale object was uncovered. For a moment, Ben thought it might be a grave-marker, as it seemed to have images carved on it – battle scenes, with horses and warriors and, in the centre, a mighty elk with its antlers raised, light shining from them like a beacon – but then he saw its edges, and realised it was smaller than he'd first thought. He was relieved, as the thought of sitting on top of someone's burial place, even by accident, had made him feel ill for a moment. As the bear continued to blow away the sand, Ben could make out more detail. The object was rectangular, about the length of his practice hurl – *or, the hurl I used to have, when I was in Dublin*, he thought, with a pang – and about twice as wide as a shoebox.

'What is it?' Fin said, curious, coming to Ben's shoulder to look at it with him. Ben felt he could have stared at the battle scene carved on the object all day – there seemed no end to the detail. Giants on the horizon, spears being thrown like hail and, right beneath the elk, a sword. Ben trembled as he stared at it.

'I don't know,' Ben replied. He reached out, glancing up at the bear for confirmation that it was all right, and ran his fingers around the edges of this shape set into the cavern floor. His skin tingled at the touch. 'Hey,' he said, looking over his shoulder at Fin. 'It moves. I can pull it up. I mean, out. I mean, whatever! Move back a bit.'

Fin edged backwards, his eyes on the floor. Ben pushed his fingers down into the crystalline sand, finding that they sank so easily it was like pushing through air. They slid down the sides of the strange object until he was able to put his palms flat against either end of it. Then, setting his teeth, he began to lift it out. The object was a box, made from something solid and smooth and cool to the touch, and it was slowly coming up from the cavern floor, like it was responding to his presence. Every side of the box looked to be carved with scenes from some long-ago battle, and Ben found his brain clicking them into place, spotting things that appeared more than once – the elk, the warriors, the sword – and trying to make sense of the story this box was telling. The figures danced in his imagination, like they were on a screen, but he wasn't the one controlling them. This, Ben knew, wasn't a game.

The bear watched him warily, its silver-blue eyes never leaving the box in Ben's hands. Ben glanced at the animal, hoping its misgivings wouldn't overspill into anger. The atmosphere in the cave felt charged, like it could explode at any moment. *It doesn't trust us yet*, Ben realised, cold sweat beginning to trickle down his back.

Slowly, Ben lifted the box onto the floor and let it rest there.

'What is that made of?' Fin said, in a low voice. 'I mean, it looks like *plastic*, but it can't be. Can it?'

Ben looked around at the cavern. It shone with power, with age, with wisdom beyond anything he'd ever felt. His gaze fell back on the box, which had to be one of the most incredible works of art he'd ever seen. He'd been to the museum in Dublin *loads*, and he'd never seen anything there that could compare to this cavern and the things inside it. Then, he looked at the bear. It was regarding him calmly, its silver-blue eyes steady and glowing. Its breaths were slow, the sound of air passing in and out of its body like the creaking of a ship's timbers.

'No,' he finally said. 'It's not plastic. There's no way.'

He ran his fingers carefully over the surface of the box, closing his eyes as he tried to focus, as hard as he could, on what his senses were telling him. Besides the pattern, Ben could feel imperfections – cracks, and bumps, and tiny spots where things weren't as smooth as you'd expect. *It's something natural*, he thought. *It can't be made by humans, or machines*.

He opened his eyes again and stared at the box. 'It's – I think it has to be made out of bone,' he said.

'Oh my God, *what*?' Fin muttered, scooting back a little.

Ben tried to get his sentences in order. 'It's – I mean,

209

it's natural, okay? Not human-made. And it's *white*, or pale at least, and you've seen scrimshaw, right?'

'Scrim-*what*?'

Ben tried to stay calm. Sometimes, it was easy to get lost in words when he was trying to explain things. 'Scrimshaw – art made out of bone, or ivory. Mostly it was made by sailors, or whalers, a long time ago, during long sea voyages when they didn't have –'

'Yeah, okay,' Fin said, cutting across Ben's train of thought. 'So, people carve out of bone. Right. But what's this for?'

Ben's hands quivered as he reached out to touch the box once more. He looked up at the bear, unwilling to move a hair unless he had permission from the box's guardian. The bear made no move, its gaze calm and eternal. Ben nodded, just once.

Then, he curled his fingers around the lid of the box, feeling smoothly carved grooves there – it made him smile, as they were so perfectly placed and so *useful* – and with hardly any effort at all, he lifted the lid.

Inside, lying on a woven cloth, was a mighty silver Arm.

20

Ben felt his grip on the lid wavering. Quickly, before he could drop it, he put it carefully on the ground. Inside the bone box the Arm lay still, its fingers curled, its silver fittings shining like sunlight on the sea. He stared at it, heart thumping hard, barely able to breathe. Whatever he might have thought his Grandad was guarding, he could never have imagined this. He'd expected an explanation – something he could understand. Something that made *sense*. This made no sense.

But he couldn't pull his gaze from it.

'It's so beautiful,' he whispered. Fin, crouched a few feet away, said nothing. 'I mean, look at how it's made! It's *incredible*.'

The Arm had been constructed from a multitude

of tiny pieces of silver, each hammered and forged so they all sat together like scales. Ben didn't dare touch it, but he could imagine how fluidly it would move, and how amazing it would look in battle. His gaze travelled downwards to the Arm's fingers, which looked as though they were powered by minuscule cogs and gears, so tiny that Ben marvelled at how anyone could see them, let alone work with them – and he *definitely* couldn't imagine anyone being deft enough to make them fit together in such a way that the fingers looked like they could twitch into life at any moment. The skill that had gone into making this object made the inside of his chest prickle with some hard-to-name emotion – like a mixture of pride and fear and amazement, all in one overwhelming ball.

'Fin, come on,' he whispered, over his shoulder. 'You *have* to see this. Seriously!'

Ben felt his brother come near. He could hear Fin's slightly ragged breaths and smell his body spray, and the warmth that radiated from him seemed feverishly hot. It was enough to send a ping of worry and confusion through Ben, like hearing a wrong note in a familiar piece of music. He turned towards Fin, but before Ben could ask if everything was all right, his entire world changed.

Fin threw a handful of sparkling sand from the cave floor right into Ben's face, making him choke and screw his eyes tight shut. The sand was rough and sharp and painful, and Ben felt his eyes start to water as he struggled to breathe. At exactly the same moment the bear began to roar, louder than a jet engine, loud enough to rattle the entire cavern and knock Fin off balance. Ben fell too, completely disoriented by the sand and the sound, but he felt the bear close by. *It's trying to guard the Arm*, he realised. *I've got to help!*

The bear roared again and again, barely pausing for breath in between. It slashed at the cavern wall with its claws, gouging huge marks into the rock, and Ben, blinking away the last of the dust and sand, felt his heart race at the sight. The bear might be a guardian spirit, or somehow not really *real*, but its claws certainly looked real – and *dangerous*.

Somewhere beneath the roaring Ben could hear another noise – a tiny one, in comparison to the bear, but one that was familiar. It was Ji-Ah, calling for the boys from the upper part of the cave. Even though she'd said she wouldn't come into the cave again, the noise must have drawn her down to check if they were all right.

'Ji-Ah!' he shouted. 'Are you okay?'

'Are *you* okay?' Ji-Ah called back, her voice shrill with terror.

'We're –' Ben began, before he felt something knock him to the ground. With a jolt of horror and disbelief, he realised what had happened. Fin had tackled him to the floor and was sitting on him, pressing his shoulders into the ground with painful force. Fin's hair hung down from his face and his eyes were completely vacant once more – open and staring and *empty*, like there was nothing behind them. His lips were pulled back from his gritted teeth and his breath rushed between them, so laboured that it sounded like he was growling. Sickeningly, Ben realised: they had been stupid, coming back down here. Whoever had put that dream in Fin's head, it wasn't the Cailleach.

'Fin, stop!' Ben shouted. 'Let me up! What are you doing?'

The bear seemed torn. One moment it was roaring up the passageway towards Ji-Ah, whose repeated calls of his name reassured Ben that she was still alive and okay, and hadn't been cut to ribbons by the bear's claws; the next, it was facing Ben and Fin, its roar so loud that Ben felt like his eardrums were about to pop. *Two threats*, Ben thought, still struggling to free himself from Fin's iron grip. *Two threats, and only one guardian . . .*

Something shifted in Ben's brain. He remembered the first time they'd been in this cave, and how the bear had appeared only after Ji-Ah had gone exploring deeper into the cave by herself. And this time, the bear had been calm until Ji-Ah had appeared once again – which had happened to coincide with Fin going off the rails, at just the same moment. Perhaps it wasn't *intruders* in the cave, necessarily, that made the bear angry and afraid, or which somehow triggered its defensive magic, but *certain* intruders. He tried to tell himself the story of what was happening here, imagining it was a game, trying to reverse-engineer it to figure out how everything had started. *Fin and me – we're family*, he thought, trying to keep a handle on his logic. *We're family, by blood, to Grandad! And it was him who blocked off this cave, because the Arm was down here – and because he knew the bear was here, protecting it.*

He gritted his teeth, pulling as hard as he could on Fin's arms, but they seemed like two pillars of iron clamping down on his shoulders. *But it wasn't dangerous to Fin and me. It didn't attack me, and it didn't attack Fin, until he started threatening the Arm. There must be something that keeps the bear from attacking us, and it has to be to do with Grandad. Ji-Ah . . . She's family too, but she doesn't have Grandad's blood.* He blinked, the unfairness of it stinging him. *The bear sees Ji-Ah as a threat.* There was only one way to test his theory.

'Ji-Ah, can you go back outside?' he shouted, once the bear's roaring had subsided into wary growls.

'What?' Ji-Ah sounded angry and confused.

'The bear! It's here because it's guarding the cave against anyone who isn't part of Grandad's bloodline!' Ben yelled. 'If you leave, it might calm down.'

He looked back at Fin. His brother's face was red with effort, as Ben wriggled and thrashed beneath him. 'Get *off*!' Ben yelled, but Fin wouldn't budge. He seemed to get heavier, somehow, like something was pressing down on him, and Ben was sure he saw a pained expression cross Fin's face. Then, Fin's head snapped around so he was facing the open box –

the bone box, with the silver Arm still lying in it.

Ben realised, just before Fin moved, what his brother planned to do. *He's going to steal the Arm*, Ben thought, knowing he was right. *And if he manages to do it . . .* Ben thought again about the drawings in Fin's book, and the weird spaced-out spell he'd been under earlier, and the spell he was clearly under right now. Something, or someone, was using his brother to get at this Arm – someone who clearly knew that the only people who could come down here, and possibly the only people who could dig up the Arm, were O'Donnells, related by blood to Grandad. *The Morrigan.*

'*No!*' Ben roared, almost as loudly as the bear. Fin, distracted by the sight of the Arm, was taken by surprise as Ben drew up his knee and whacked him in the stomach. With a groan, the winded Fin released his grip on Ben's shoulders and fell to one side, rolling into a ball on the ground. The bear reared, lifting itself onto its back legs, its bulk filling the entire cavern. Its head brushed against the silver-blue ceiling, and once more its roar rattled the very foundations of the earth. It lifted one gigantic paw, ready to slice Fin into pieces – for he might be an

O'Donnell, but the bear could sense the Morrígan in him too.

Ben fell against the box, staring at the bear which was poised to strike. His thoughts were coming faster than he could process, but all that filled his head was: get the Arm, and use it to defend his brother somehow. If he could make the bear think he was going to destroy the Arm unless Fin was set free, then that's what he'd have to do. Without thinking any further about it, Ben reached into the box to grab the Arm. 'Stop!' he shouted, lifting the artefact in the air and waving it in front of the bear's face. 'Stop it! Leave my brother alone!'

The bear's roar died in its throat, and it turned to Ben with its silver-blue eyes wide. Softly, it slipped back onto all fours, landing so lightly on its paws that it barely disturbed the sand. Ben looked down at the Arm, and his heart skipped a few beats.

He was *wearing* the silver Arm, like a long glove which came right up to his shoulder, and then some. It was hollow inside, and somehow it had wrapped itself around his flesh-and-blood arm, his own fingers sliding down into the mechanical ones that had been crafted and brought to life by the skill of the Cailleach and Dian Cecht, centuries before. He hadn't meant to – he hadn't even realised it was happening. It was as though the Arm had *wanted* him to wear it, like it had moulded itself around Ben's body, or like the metal had flowed up and around his arm, encasing it completely. Gently, and then with a little more force, he tried to pull the silver Arm off, but it wouldn't shift. It didn't hurt, but Ben realised as he flexed his fingers – flexed the *silver* fingers – that the Arm of Nuada was clamped over his own arm, and that it wouldn't budge.

'This is not good,' Ben whispered, staring at it.

The bear was now completely quiet. Its eyes were steady and calm, and it gave off an air of readiness, like a soldier preparing to take a command. Ben felt his breaths get shallower and shallower, until he was afraid he would pass out. He sat down heavily on the floor, leaning his non-silver arm against the rim of the bone box, and tried to calm his panicked heart.

'Ben!' Ji-Ah shouted, shattering the stillness. Her voice was sharp with fear, carrying all the way from the cave mouth. 'What's going on?'

'It's okay,' he managed to call back. 'Ji-Ah, you can come back. The bear – the bear's not going to hurt you now.'

There was a pause, and then Ji-Ah's voice came again, echoing around the cavern. 'Are you for *real*?'

'Just trust me, Ji-Ah,' Ben called. 'It's going to be okay.' *No it isn't*, his thoughts screamed, as he stared down at his new silver arm, and then at the slumped form of his brother. *How can any of this be okay?*

Minutes later, a scrambling, scuffling noise at the entrance to the cavern alerted Ben to the fact that Ji-Ah had arrived. The bear whuffed, shuffling back a little to make room for her to enter, and Ben saw the eerie light from the walls, floor and ceiling shine on the lenses of her glasses, and in her wide brown eyes. She stared fearfully at the bear but it remained entirely calm, its eyes downturned, as she crawled past, slowly at first and then quickly gathering speed once she'd passed the bear. She came to a skidding halt in front of Ben.

'What in the actual – I mean, *what* have you guys been doing in here?' She was staring into Ben's face, so intent on searching him for some sort of head injury that she didn't see the silver Arm until Ben lifted it, flopping it into his lap. It landed heavily and stayed there, like a stunned carp.

Ji-Ah's eyes opened even wider. 'Wha – what did you do? Ben! Ben, what did you do? I mean – what *is that*?' She stared at him. 'Put it back! Like, now! If you haven't damaged it then *maybe* we won't all get sued by the government, or whoever.'

Ben tried to start explaining, but found his brain short-circuited every time he tried to put his thoughts into words. 'I – can't,' he finally managed.

'You can't? You can't what?'

'I can't take it off. Or explain,' Ben said, his voice so quiet it was barely there. 'Fin,' he whispered, pointing with his ordinary arm. 'Is he – is he –'

Ji-Ah scrambled over to Fin's slumped form, helping him to sit up. 'Fin?' she said, gently. 'Fin, are you all right? Come on. Let's get out of here, okay?'

Ben watched as his brother's eyes popped open – but they weren't Fin's eyes. They were black from lid to lid, no iris or pupil visible, just the deep darkness of a crow's wing. 'Ji-Ah,' Ben called. 'Ji-Ah! Come back over here, now!'

The bear rumbled as Ji-Ah looked into Fin's face and saw his eyes. She moaned with horror and fear as she pushed herself backwards, skidding across the shining sand to Ben's side. 'What's wrong with his eyes?'

'It's magic,' Ben said, realising it was true as he spoke. 'The Morrígan's magic. We've got to –'

But before Ben could finish speaking, something drowned out his words – a loud noise made up of claws and beaks chittering and scratching and scrambling and scraping as they burst their way down into the cave, and bird voices screeching and squawking and cawing, and what sounded like thousands of wings fluttering and clattering and beating as the birds pushed their way forward. All at once, as if a tap had opened, they began to pour into the cavern like an oil slick, like a storm cloud gathering, like midnight distilled into some sort of viscous liquid.

And then the bear reared once more, roaring for all it was worth as it lumbered around to stand in front of Ben, slashing and tearing at the oncoming murder of crows.

Ji-Ah pulled Ben to his feet. They reached out to drag Fin to his. Then, together they ran towards the back of the bear's cavern, dragging Fin with them, fear guiding their steps.

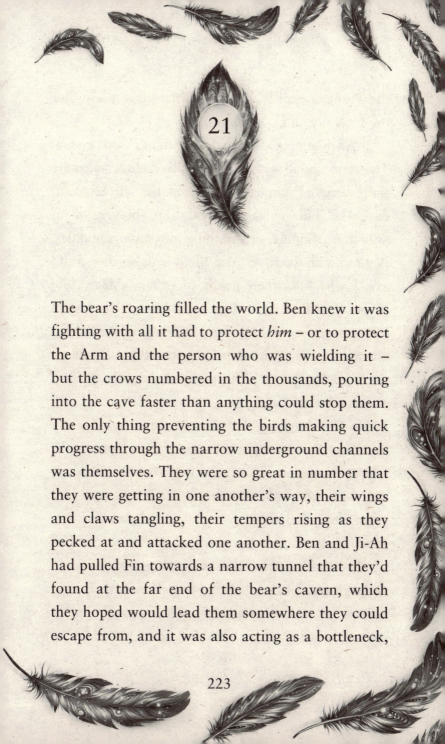

21

The bear's roaring filled the world. Ben knew it was fighting with all it had to protect *him* – or to protect the Arm and the person who was wielding it – but the crows numbered in the thousands, pouring into the cave faster than anything could stop them. The only thing preventing the birds making quick progress through the narrow underground channels was themselves. They were so great in number that they were getting in one another's way, their wings and claws tangling, their tempers rising as they pecked at and attacked one another. Ben and Ji-Ah had pulled Fin towards a narrow tunnel that they'd found at the far end of the bear's cavern, which they hoped would lead them somewhere they could escape from, and it was also acting as a bottleneck, thwarting the birds' progress for a short while. But they were coming, Ben knew.

Ji-Ah whimpered in fear, but didn't miss a step. The Arm shone with a gentle silver glow, meaning they weren't completely alone in the subterranean darkness, but it wasn't enough to prevent them falling, or slipping, or splashing into unseen puddles. Ben ran with the silver Arm lifted high, so they could avoid whacking their heads off any suddenly low parts of the cave roof. They ran desperately, with no idea where they were going, taking turns at random, always on the lookout for a route that seemed to slope upwards or which promised a trickle of fresh air from the surface.

Fin was dragging his feet, mumbling incoherently under his breath. At times he seemed more like himself, and at others less. The closer the terrible crows got, the worse Fin was becoming. 'Come on, come *on*,' Ji-Ah whispered, trying to pull him forward. Ben too, felt his grip on Fin slipping, and he was terrified of what would happen if they were caught in this dark, underground place when the birds found them. *We have to get out of here*, he thought, just as an earth-splitting roar of rage from the bear echoed along the passage. Something about the sound, and about the fact that the bear was still there, still fighting, gave Ben hope.

Then the tunnel rattled with the bear's roar, much louder than before and so suddenly that Ben lost his footing. It sounded so near, like the bear was right behind them, and they realised the bear had to be close on their heels – which meant it had given up the fight in its cavern and was following them instead. *That means there's nothing at all stopping the birds from coming*, Ben thought.

Just as this thought crossed Ben's mind, the air around them filled with crows. He and Ji-Ah threw their hands over their heads instinctively, trying to protect their faces from the beaks and claws of the pursuing birds. Panic and fear pushed them forward, running recklessly fast down the rocky tunnel. The crows were so big, so *impossibly* big, that Ben didn't understand how they could all fit down here. Feathers choked him, and he felt his skin being scratched and torn wherever it was exposed. The crows drove them on and on, until eventually Ben and Ji-Ah realised at the same moment that, in the chaos, they'd lost hold of Fin. They'd probably run twenty paces without him, and to Ben it was like a punch in the stomach. How could he have left his brother behind?

'We've got to go back for him!' Ben shouted. Ji-Ah's face was pinched with fear, but she nodded, right away.

They turned, facing the wave of feathers and rage that was the pursuing crows. Ben held up his silver Arm to try to light the way, palm flat with fingers spread, and felt a pulse of power through his whole body as the light that shone from it suddenly increased. To his amazement, it began to push the crows back. It cost him huge effort, and very soon his muscles began to tremble with exertion, but Ji-Ah held him up and helped him to walk, one step at a time. The Arm's power forced the birds to work ten times as hard to reach them, as it seemed difficult for them to pass through the barrier of light. Some did manage it, and Ben and Ji-Ah used their free hands to punch and push them away.

'It was here,' Ji-Ah gasped, her arm tight around Ben's shoulders. 'We lost Fin here.'

Ben looked around. There was no sign of his brother. Outside the glowing wall that was the power of the Arm, all he could see was a mass of writhing black.

'Where is he? Fin!' Ben shouted. '*Fin!*'

There was no sign. The light showed every crevice, every nook and cranny and hollow of the cave, but Fin was nowhere to be seen. Ben felt a gush of cold anxiety grip him like a clamp. His free hand started to spasm, his fingers twitching, and he clenched his fist over and over, trying to stay calm.

The crows battered the light-barrier, throwing themselves against it in waves and, in the midst of their darkness, Ben saw the silver-blue eyes of the bear, their brightness like twin lighthouses in a thunderstorm. In the next moment the bear itself became visible, its roar deafening, crows scattering as it came – but as fast as the bear could disperse them, they re-formed and came pile-driving at the magic of the Arm. Ben's own arm quivered with the effort of keeping the magical barrier in place, and he knew it was all that was sparing himself and Ji-Ah from the full power of their fury.

'Ben, come on!' Ji-Ah shouted, ducking aside as a crow careered right towards her head. 'Our only chance – and Fin's – is to get out of here through another cave entrance in the karst, get back home and get help. We can't stay here!'

Ben's heart thudded painfully. He knew she was right.

With a sickening, painful feeling, he turned and ran, knowing the crows would follow – and with them, the Morrígan, she who was the power that was driving the birds on. The bear's roar shattered the air once more and he knew it was fighting, trying to give him and Ji-Ah a chance to get out of here, to find another path to the surface. Ben's mind reeled as he raced down the tunnel, his non-silver hand in Ji-Ah's. How much trouble they'd be in when they got home, how worried his parents were going to be, how sick Fin might be and how they were going to try to make him better . . . Ben's vision blurred as he thought about his brother's crow-black eyes, and the fury with which Fin had attacked him back in the bear's cave.

And with a lurch of absolute despair, he realised: *I might never get him back. The Morrígan has him now.* He felt he should have seen it coming – first Fin's dreams, then his strange, hypnotic drawings and finally here, deep underground, when the Morrígan was so tantalisingly close to her goal, her magic had reared up like a grasping fist, finally claiming Fin as her own. The thought made Ben feel like vomiting. *It was like she'd chosen him to steal the Arm for her*, Ben thought. *She sort of forgot about me, until I got myself stuck right into the middle of things . . .*

'This way!' gasped Ji-Ah, pulling Ben to the left. A narrow, steep chimney of rock seemed to lead straight up – and, hopefully, out. Ji-Ah didn't wait to check. She threw herself into it and began to climb, dislodging smaller pieces of stone as she went. Ben put the silver Arm up to shield his face before following her, crying out as crows began to spill into the narrow passage behind him.

'Ji-Ah!' he shouted. She reached down to help pull him up, groaning with effort, her feet braced against the rocky walls. Eventually, Ben found a crevice he could grip with his silver fingers and he managed to haul himself up far enough to grab hold of Ji-Ah.

'We're almost there,' she said, her voice weak with exertion. 'I see it – this leads to the surface, Ben. I know it does.'

All Ben could do was nod. They kept climbing, the passage narrowing as they went and changing direction, almost like the turn of a screw, as it reached upwards. Ben felt his panic shrieking in his ears, but he had to muffle it – the terror of staying here was greater than the terror of continuing. Slowly, Ji-Ah pushed herself up and through the narrow part of the passage, calling for Ben to follow. Her voice echoed weirdly, and Ben struggled to breathe as he pushed himself up, further and further. The roof and the ceiling were too close together, the walls were too narrow, and it was almost too much to take, but Ben followed Ji-Ah's voice, using the fingers of the silver Arm to drag himself on. The bear was still roaring, its voice more distant and muffled than before, and the passage behind them was filled with fluttering and creaking, cawing and scratching, but the crows seemed unable to make it up past the twist in the rock. As terrible as it was to feel pressed on every side, and fearful of running out of air, Ben was glad to be free of the crows at least.

And then he felt Ji-Ah's warm fingers on his palm as she pulled him up, and up, and *up*, out into fresh air and freedom. He flopped, gasping, his head spinning and his stomach sick, onto the ground. After a few minutes he realised: he was out. *He was out*. There was nothing above him but the emptiness of the night sky and the quiet stars.

Ji-Ah grabbed his arm and pulled him into a sitting position. 'Ben!' she called, shaking him gently. 'Are you all right?'

He stared up at her, frowning, not sure if she was joking. 'No?' he answered, in disbelief.

Ji-Ah crumpled to the ground, and it took Ben a minute to realise she was laughing. 'You're *you*, and not some – weird *god*, or something,' she finally said.

'What are you talking about?' Ben asked.

'I mean – have you seen your arm?' Ji-Ah said, prodding it. 'I'm glad it hasn't, like, taken over your brain. Maybe there's so little of it that the Arm's not bothered.'

'I'm fine,' Ben grouched, getting to his feet. 'But Fin's in trouble.'

Ji-Ah stood too, looking around. They had no idea where they were. The moon illuminated a landscape that was flat and rocky all around, and there was no sign of the house. A few hundred metres away there was a low mound, on top of which stood a strangely shaped pile of rocks, looking almost like a garden shed. It had gappy walls and a sloping stone roof, and Ben found he could hardly look away from it. Somehow, in the strange light, its walls and roof gleamed as though veins of shining metal ran through the rock. 'That's Poulnabrone dolmen,' Ji-Ah said, staring at it. 'We must've run for miles.' Her voice was barely more than a whisper.

'What is it?' Ben asked.

'A tomb, I think,' Ji-Ah said. 'Like, thousands of years old? Eomma would know the details.'

Ben glanced at her. Ji-Ah's eyes were tight shut. 'I wish she was here, too,' he said, but Ji-Ah could only nod in reply.

A roar sounded from deep underground, and then another. 'The bear,' Ben gasped.

Ji-Ah's eyes popped open and she wiped her cheeks. 'It's still fighting?'

'Maybe it's looking for a way out,' Ben said, meeting her eyes. For the first time he realised how battered they both were. Ji-Ah had a gash on her cheek and her hair was full of feathers. She was filthy, covered in slime and dirt. Ben doubted he was much better.

'So do we try to find our way back home, or –' Ji-Ah began, before her sentence ended in a shriek of fear and surprise. A flood of crows suddenly burst out of the ground, from every crevice in the rock, like endless dark water being forced out under high pressure. Ji-Ah and Ben staggered, holding one another up, their heads swivelling as they tried to see. The birds blocked the moonlight, shattered the silence, filled up every corner of their senses. All the world was crows.

And then, just as suddenly, they were gone. Ben shuddered with horror as he watched the birds speed into the distance – and he realised, like a dousing of cold snow down his back, where they were heading.

A silver-blue glow hung over the summit of a hill that lay on the horizon. It was a lot further away now than it had been back at the house, and he understood just how far he and Ji-Ah had travelled – and how far they were from home. The crows floated towards it like a malignant, shrieking cloud, their noise gradually fading into the distance.

'Mullaghmore,' he said, staring up at it. 'That's where the crows are going.'

22

'Mullaghmore? It can't be,' Ji-Ah said, as though trying to convince herself of what she was saying. 'There's no way we've managed to come so far – it's just not possible.'

'It *is* Mullaghmore,' Ben insisted, knowing he was right. 'Can't you see the light?'

Ji-Ah looked faintly appalled. 'Did you whack your head when we were underground, or . . .'

'You can't see it?' Ben stared at the mountain. There was a glow there – he was sure. It looked like the glow given off by the silver Arm; a comforting sort of glow, one that didn't hurt Ben's eyes or make him scared. A soft silver-blue, something that made him feel like he could trust it, like it meant him no harm. *But if the crows are going there . . .*

His thoughts were flipping quickly through his head as he tried to work things out. *If the crows are going there, surely the light belongs to the Morrígan?*

And then he remembered: *the Cailleach.* Her forge was up there, wasn't it? On top of Mullaghmore, somewhere, was the place where the Sword of the Sun had been made, where the Cailleach had used her magical hammers to create the greatest weapon of all time – the one thing that the Battle Crow was looking for. So, the light could mean the Cailleach was in trouble, maybe?

Or that the Sword was in danger.

The thought pulsed through Ben's head. 'That's where it is,' he said, the realisation landing in his chest as he spoke. 'That's where it's been, all this time – right back with the person who made it in the first place.'

'What are you talking about?' Ji-Ah wrapped her arms around herself, looking like she was on the verge of tears.

'The Sword of the Sun,' Ben said. 'It's on Mullaghmore. And it knows the Morrígan is coming for it.'

Ji-Ah closed her eyes tight and threw her head

back. '*Why* couldn't I have gone to LA this summer, oh my *God*,' she moaned.

'We have to get to Mullaghmore,' Ben said. 'I think the crows are going there, and I think – I'm pretty sure they have Fin.' He paused, trying to think. 'I mean, you saw his eyes, didn't you? How they'd turned completely black? He's been taken over by her power. I know he has. She wants him for something, and I bet wherever her crows are, the Morrígan is – and wherever she is, we'll find Fin.'

'This is ridiculous, *Brendan*,' Ji-Ah snapped. 'We need to get home, get our parents and get help. Fin's down in those caves! He's not being flown by Corvid Airlines to the top of a *mountain* in the middle of *nowhere*!' Her voice rang out over the karst, echoing strangely in the night air.

For a moment Ben just stared at her, at a loss to understand why she couldn't see things the way he did. 'She's taken over his body,' Ben began. 'The Morrígan's wriggled her way inside his head, inside *him*, and she used him to try to take the Arm – and to try to hurt me. She made him do that! That wasn't Fin. He'd *never* hurt me. Not like that.' He blinked hard. 'She used him to try to get what she wanted, and that's this Arm. And the other thing that she wants? The Sword, which is somewhere on that mountain. She can't wield one without the other. So I know she has my brother, and I know she's got him because *she* knows that, wherever he is, I'll come for him. She needs the Arm, she wants the Sword and I'm the key. And Fin's the only thing that will bring me to her. So that's how I know she's got him. And she'll keep hurting him unless I stop her. So I don't have a choice. I know I'm doing exactly what she wants me to do, and I know that's dangerous, but I'm going to the mountain.'

Ji-Ah didn't say anything, and after a minute Ben realised he hadn't spoken out loud – he'd made his argument inside his mind, which was why it had sounded so logical and reasonable and *right*. He shook his head, unwilling to say it all again – and knowing that, no matter what he said, Ji-Ah probably wouldn't believe him, or understand. He wished they were in a game, where he could just push a button to reset things – but he knew that was impossible.

'I think he is,' he said, eventually. 'If you want to go home, then go home. But I'm going to get my brother back.'

He strode around her, making his way towards

the distant shape of Mullaghmore. He didn't turn around, even when he heard her shout of frustration a few moments later. 'Wait for me!' she called, and Ben paused. Her muttering grew louder the closer she got. 'I cannot *believe* this is happening, what on earth am I doing, I'm going to have to listen to a lecture from *all* my aunties as *well* as Oehalmeoni . . .' She continued muttering as she passed him, eventually turning to glare back in his direction. 'Well? Come on.'

Ben jogged to catch up, just as Ji-Ah fished her phone out of her pocket. She unlocked the screen and frowned at it, as though the device had done something deliberately rude. 'Literally zero service,' she whispered, before switching on the torch. 'We've got to be careful,' she said. 'It can get tricky underfoot, in the dark.'

They picked their way forward, slowly and carefully, and every few minutes Ben looked up to check – but the light around the summit of the mountain was still there. Once or twice he saw it dim, as though blocked out by the flock of crows that passed in front of it and their raucous cawing could be heard in the distance. He swallowed his fear of what they might be doing and focused on *getting* there – on getting to where he was sure his brother was, where he was being held captive, for reasons he couldn't yet fathom. The memory of the empty tunnel filled his mind. No matter what Ji-Ah might think, Ben knew: Fin wasn't in that tunnel any longer. He was *gone*, taken by the Morrígan. Ben had made the mistake of letting his brother go, and it had cost him dearly – it had given the Morrígan her chance, and her birds had claimed Fin. Then, Ben remembered the way Fin's eyes had changed, how they'd turned completely black, like two voids in his skull, and he made his brother a promise – one he couldn't hear, but which Ben meant every word of, just the same. *I promise to get her magic out of you, Fin*, Ben said, inside his head. *It's my fault any of this is happening – if I hadn't been so stubborn about the cave, you'd be okay. I'm going to make you okay again. I promise.*

As he walked, Ben's ears registered a strange sound, one that he'd been hearing for the past few moments without really paying attention. It was low and distant, like the rumbling of a faraway engine. Something about it made his hackles rise suddenly – perhaps it was a change in volume, or the sense that it was drawing nearer to them. He looked at Ji-Ah at the same moment she looked at him, and they both drew to a halt.

'Do you hear –' Ji-Ah began, right as the sound burst the air all around them.

Ben shouted in fright even as his brain registered what the sound was. 'The bear!' he gasped, spinning on the spot. Beside him, Ji-Ah did the same.

'There!' she cried. 'Ben, *look*!'

He turned to see her pointing – and under Poulnabrone, the ancient dolmen, they saw a silvery glow burst out of the earth. It lit the portal tomb from the inside, shining between the stone slabs that made up its walls and shimmering on the underside of its capstone roof. As they watched, the light started to move, gradually solidifying into the shape of the bear, which came lolloping out of the stone structure and down the slope. As it ran, it raised its head to the starry sky and roared again, a sound of freedom so overwhelming that Ben found his hands and fingers flexing, over and over, as the emotion passed through him. He didn't even try to stop himself.

Ji-Ah's breaths were fast and panicky, her grip on Ben's arm tight. 'It's all right,' Ben said. 'It's not going to hurt us.'

'It's a *bear*!' Ji-Ah squeaked. 'Of course it's going to hurt us! Do we run? I can't remember if you're supposed to run or pretend to be dead! We're going to *be* dead in a minute, so we won't need to pretend!'

Ben held up the silver Arm. It shone, as though all the light from the moon overhead was being reflected from it. The bear corrected its course, roaring again as it spotted the glow from the Arm, and began to lope towards them.

'Ben, please!' Ji-Ah cried. 'I'm scared!'

Ben looked at her. In the glow from the Arm, she looked like she was made of pearl. 'I'm scared too,' he said.

They kept their eyes on one another as the bear drew closer. Ji-Ah's eyes finally closed, scrunched tight in fear, as the bear – its fur still crackling with light – reached them, and drew itself to a snuffling, scrambling, breathless, stinking halt. It was bleeding from a thousand different injuries, the darkness of the wounds like holes in the light from its fur. Ben gasped to see them, realising how much of the crows' fury the bear had truly saved them from.

'I'm sorry,' he whispered to it, reaching out to touch its leg with the fingers of the silver Arm.

Ji-Ah put her own trembling hand out a few seconds later. 'Thank you,' she said.

The bear licked its muzzle and gazed towards Mullaghmore. Then it met Ben's eye, its gaze steady, a quiet and insistent rumble rolling in its chest. The glow from the summit was reflected in the bear's dark eyes, and Ben was glad to see it. *I'm not dreaming*, he told himself. *Not this time.*

'I know,' Ben said. 'We've got to go there, right? That's where they've taken Fin.'

The bear nudged Ben with its head, pushing him closer to itself. Before Ben could react, the bear repeated the action, butting at Ben. Its actions were gentle, but definite. Then, to his amazement, the bear flopped down onto the karst, grunting as the air left its lungs, settling itself comfortably on the ground. Its head was about level with Ben's face, and the bear regarded him with infinite patience, blinking slowly as it waited. Ben's thoughts whirred as he tried to make sense of them.

'It – this cannot be right. It wants you to get on its back,' Ji-Ah said. 'Don't you think? That's got to be why it's doing that.'

'I think so too,' Ben said.

'Well, then – do it!' Ji-Ah urged. 'You go. I'll try to get home, wake Mam and Eomma and your parents, and we'll come after you as soon as we can.'

'I'm not leaving you here, Ji-Ah,' Ben said, aghast. 'Anything could happen to you out here, in the dark, by yourself.'

Ji-Ah raised her eyebrows. 'You're going to climb a mountain on the back of a mystery bear in order to find a magical sword before some crow-features battle goddess does,' she said. 'I think all the anythings that could have happened to us have *already* happened.'

Ben choked out a laugh. 'Well. When you put it like that.'

Ji-Ah pushed Ben towards the bear's back, helping him to climb up and get a grip on the animal's shimmering fur. 'Right. Okay. Well, I'll see you later?' she said, her voice brittle. 'I'll get home! Don't you worry. And Eomma will give that stupid witch a kick when she finds her. She'd *better* run, when my mams are on the warpath.' She tried to smile, but Ben was too full of thoughts to put anything into words. The bear didn't move a muscle, not even as Ben wriggled on its back, yanking handfuls of its fur in his attempts to make himself safe. Ji-Ah stared into the bear's face.

'Go,' she whispered to it. 'You can go now, okay? Hurry up!'

The bear licked its muzzle again, its eyes on Ji-Ah, still waiting in that quiet, patient way. She looked up at Ben. 'I don't – I don't get it,' she whispered. 'It's like you said, right? Back in the cave? I'm the problem! I'm the *intruder*, aren't I? The outsider, the one who's not part of Grandad's *blood* or whatever.' Her chin wobbled, and she fought to control it as she continued. 'I'm the one who woke the bear up in the first place, who set off the magic. So why is it still here? It's like . . .' She paused. 'It's like the bear's waiting for me.'

'Well, would you quit feeling sorry for yourself and just get *on*, then?' Ben said, shuffling himself forward a little. 'The magic bear express is leaving, right now!'

23

Ji-Ah clamped her arms around Ben's waist as the bear lumbered to its feet. He could hear her fast, anxious breaths in his ear as they were rocked from side to side, the animal's muscles rolling beneath them as it readied itself for the journey ahead.

'It's okay,' he whispered to her. 'We're going to be okay.'

Ji-Ah's only answer was to tighten her grip.

Then, the bear was off, moving slowly at first but quickly working its way up to a canter, its paws batting the earth and its shoulders and hips rising and falling with every step. It leaped from one flat limestone rock to another, avoiding the shallow channels that lay between them, its pace never flagging, with Mullaghmore always in their sights – and then, the bear unexpectedly changed direction, darting to the right, though it didn't slow down.

'Hey,' Ben called, craning his head to watch the mountain as they left it behind. 'Hey! We're going the wrong way! Bear!'

'What's wrong?' Ji-Ah shouted. Her eyes were clamped shut.

'He's leading us away from Mullaghmore!' Ben felt his panic rising. *Why are we leaving Fin behind?* 'Bear, please! Come on! We've got to –'

Unexpectedly, Ben heard the sound of splashing. He looked down to see the bear was making its way through shallow-looking water, and he held up the Arm to watch its glow light up the face of a turlough at the mountain's foot – and he finally understood. The bear wasn't leaving Mullaghmore behind – it was just bringing them to it by another, safer, route. As they skirted the edges of the lake, Ben wondered whether he and Ji-Ah might have stumbled right into it, if they'd been left to their own devices – and he wondered how deep it might be, the further in you went. A sudden wave of gratitude for the bear, still doing its best to fulfil its duty and guard the Arm, washed over him.

'Sorry, buddy,' Ben whispered, stroking the bear's fur. 'I shouldn't have doubted you.'

The bear's only reply was a soft grunt.

Very quickly they left the lake behind and turned again for Mullaghmore, and the bear's breath began to sound like it was tearing through its lungs, gasping and rasping as it ran. The mountain wasn't steep, but the shale underfoot meant that the bear struggled to keep its grip, and Ben hoped his tight hold on the bear's fur wasn't adding to its pain.

The bear skidded a little as it leaped from one rock formation to the next, making its way up the gently sloping hill much more quickly than Ben and Ji-Ah would have managed alone – especially in the dark. Ben held his breath as the bear made one particularly risky jump, its back paws scrambling as it struggled to keep purchase on the tricky ground, and struggled not to cry out in fear – but in the next moment that fear was forgotten as he felt a sharp, scratching, tearing pain on his scalp and the back of his neck. Behind him, Ji-Ah shrieked. The air all around filled with the ripping, raucous cries of the Morrígan's crows. The bear roared in rage, its pace quickening.

Ben put the Arm over his head to try to ward off

their attack, and immediately the crows descended on it, using their claws and beaks to try to prise away its silver scales and get at the mechanism inside. Ben wondered in horror if they were trying to loosen his grip, to pull the Arm off him and carry it away, right into their mistress's hands. It certainly felt that way. His flesh recoiled at the touch of the beaks, wriggling their way in beneath the Arm and his own skin, pushing and tugging as they did their best to separate him from it. In a rush of overwhelming emotion, Ben realised he couldn't bear it. Somehow, the birds seemed to be pulling at his insides, at his heart and lungs and liver, rooting around with their questing, cruel beaks, not caring what they pulled apart in their efforts to get what they wanted. The Arm was stuck to him, but in some other, deeper way, it was *part* of him now. He was its bearer, and the only way to separate him from it was to wait until he was ready to give it up – or to destroy him.

'Get off me!' he shouted, swinging the Arm as much as he could, trying to dislodge the birds. Ji-Ah freed one hand from its death-grip on his waist and started batting away as many as she could reach too, crying out whenever their claws drew blood.

All the while, the crows wheeled around behind them, pushing the bear on and up, faster and faster, until with one last scrambling leap it reached the summit. Its breath came in huge gasping gusts, and Ben could feel every injury, every strained muscle, every sharp stone pressing painfully into the pads of its paws. Its shining fur was dimmed, but hadn't completely gone out. Ben clung to its back, his brain spinning as he tried to think. How was any of this even happening? And *why*? His chest ached as he thought about home – Dublin, and Clare, and his parents, and most of all Fin, his brother who was smelly and annoying and loud and full of insults and prone to causing him injury, but who meant 'home' most of all. Without Fin, there would be no more home. Without Fin, none of this would matter. Without Fin, it would all be over.

He had to find his brother.

The bear ran towards a dark opening in the mountainside, a gaping cave mouth that stretched high over their heads. It was narrow as they hurried through it but quickly widened, opening into a large space which seemed to swallow the scrambling, breathless noises they were making. Ben felt, strangely, like his ears were stuffed with cloth – as soon as he entered the cavern, his hearing stopped working the way it should. He didn't have time to think about that, so he pushed the idea away, shaking it loose from his head.

The bear padded to a stop, then with a lumbering groan it sank to the rocky floor, allowing Ben and Ji-Ah to slide off its back. Ben stood, his knees wobbling, still convinced he could feel the crows all around him – but they were gone.

'Where'd they go?' Ji-Ah whispered, her voice bouncing lightly around the cavernous space. 'The birds. Where are they?'

'I don't know,' Ben answered. His stomach hurt and his fingers were clenching and relaxing, over and over.

'It's like – it's like they *herded* us,' Ji-Ah said. 'Like we were sheep and they were dogs, and they got us where they wanted us to go.'

The bear whuffed out a heavy breath. The glow from the Arm was dim, but bright enough for them to see the expanse of the cavern they'd ended up in. The ceiling arched far above them, with a bunch of long stalactites hanging down like chandeliers from the highest point, right at the centre. They seemed to glow, faintly, with a muted light, and the longest and thickest of them looked like it was tipped with some dark metal – *iron*, Ben thought, his brain ticking over into all the things he knew about it. *Fairies can't touch iron.* He remembered how that fact had helped him once in *Fae Wars: Attack on Titania*, a game he'd loved a couple of summers back. *It can stop magic. Can't it?* He looked away from the stalactites and around at the rest of the cavern. The walls seemed smoother than those in the bear's cave beneath the karst, almost like they'd been shaped that way on purpose. Near the back of the space was a raised platform, but the light wasn't strong enough for them to see it clearly. It looked like there were steps up to it, and something like a table, or an altar, on top.

'What is this place?' Ben asked, huddling close to the exhausted bear. Ji-Ah stayed close too, unwilling to stray far from their only real source of light. She pulled her phone out of her pocket and pressed the power button. The screen glowed. Ben watched her frowning.

'Wherever it is, there's still no phone signal,' she said. 'Not even to send a text.' She put the device away, staring around at the cavern walls. Then, her face scrunched up as she rubbed hard at her earlobes with the heels of her hands. 'What's going on with my *ears*?' she muttered.

'So it's not just me,' Ben said. 'There's something off about the sound in here, right?'

Ji-Ah nodded. 'It sort of feels like being underwater, or something.'

'And where's Fin?' Ben's teeth began to chatter, with cold and exertion and shock. 'I thought he'd be up here. I was *sure* this was where she was bringing him. But he's not here. There's nothing here.'

'You don't know that,' Ji-Ah said, coming to stand beside him. She kept her arms wrapped tight around her body, but Ben was glad of her warmth and her company. 'We haven't looked around properly. Come on. Let's see what's here.'

A sudden, overly loud scrabbling, followed by a crow's caw, made them both look back towards the cavern entrance. It was hard to see, but they were both certain that the crows were just outside, waiting like sentries, guarding the opening to the cave. Ben shuddered at the thought of what might happen if they ventured outside – they'd be divebombed in a frenzied attack, shredded completely by the beaks and claws of the Morrígan's corvid army. More flutterings and angry calls, ricocheting weirdly around the walls of the cavern, confirmed his fears. It felt as though the cave had been built to amplify sounds at the entrance, while muffling noise from inside, and Ben knew that wasn't helping his anxiety. It sounded like there were thousands of crows out there, which he knew probably wasn't true but he also knew the damage that one or two could do, if they had a mind to. 'Well, we can't go out there, I guess,' Ben whispered. 'Doesn't really give us much choice.'

Using the light of the Arm, and with the bear padding slowly behind them, they made their way around the room. There was nothing of note to be seen anywhere, besides the strangely smooth walls, which were – Ben discovered – slightly warm to the touch. Silvery threads ran through the stone, like rivulets left behind from some ancient rainfall. The room was almost perfectly circular, with an odd-looking rock formation around the back half of the space. About as high as Ben was tall, it shimmered a little like the walls of the bear's cavern, with strange patterns in its whorls which *almost* seemed to make sense to Ben, but just as he thought he'd figured it out, the meaning would slip from his mind again. There were leaves and sticks and smaller stones somehow embedded in its folds, like they'd grown there – or been placed with deliberate care. As Ben moved the Arm, the rock formation seemed somehow to move with it, the light flowing over its pitted surface and making it seem alive.

'Urgh, come on,' Ji-Ah said, pulling at Ben's arm. 'That thing's giving me the creeps.'

They approached the raised dais they'd seen from the doorway and, as soon as they drew near, they could see something like a giant bowl was set into it, definitely carved by someone – or something – with deliberate precision and skill.

'There's no way erosion did that,' Ji-Ah said, gazing down into the depression in the rock.

Ben nodded, angling the Arm to illuminate the entire platform. The 'bowl' was almost as large as a bathtub, though not as deep. The sides and base looked darker than the surrounding rock, and Ben used his free hand to reach in and touch the inner surface, very gently. His fingers came back covered in something soft, and shiny, and black.

'Soot?' he whispered.

Ji-Ah shrugged, her eyes on Ben's hand. 'Something like that, I guess,' she said.

'A fire burned here,' Ben said, his brain turning over. 'And you need fire for a forge to work.'

Ji-Ah looked at him, her eyes wide. 'The sword thing,' she began. 'You were trying to tell me and Fin about it, back –' She paused, swallowing nervously. 'Back when we'd managed to get out of Grandad's cave.' *Back when we were close enough to home that we could have hopped over the fence and made our way upstairs to bed, and none of this would've happened*, hung in the air between them, unsaid.

'We're in the Forge of the Cailleach,' Ben said, wiping the soot from his hand on his jeans as he looked around. He felt lightheaded for a moment at the thought of this place, straight out of a book of legends, which was all around him, as real as the clothes on his back. 'But – if that's true, then where is she? Why did the bear bring us here?' He fought to keep his fear under control. 'And why does the Morrígan want us here?'

'It looks like nobody's been here for, like, a million years,' Ji-Ah said. 'Everything's cold and dirty, and there's no sign of anything you might need to make a forge work.'

'None of this makes any sense,' Ben said, despair clawing at his guts. He felt Ji-Ah's hand on his shoulder, warm and comforting, and behind them the bear stalked back and forth, the clicking of its claws on the stone floor swallowed by the Forge's strange acoustics and its hot breath coming in agitated puffs. It seemed as confused as they were, which didn't help to settle Ben's worried mind.

'I think you'll find that depends,' came a voice, seeming to speak directly into their ears, 'on who you ask.'

24

Ben and Ji-Ah whirled on the spot. In the cavern entrance, silhouetted in moonlight, a dark figure hovered in mid-air. From behind the children, the bear's chesty rumble began, building up momentum until it seemed to roll endlessly around the stone chamber, the sound overlapping as it went. The bear padded past them until it was standing, its fur sparking and fizzing, between them and the newcomer.

Ben couldn't find his voice to speak. It was like his breath refused to stay inside his lungs long enough to push any words out.

'Who – who's that?' Ji-Ah said, her words sounding muffled and soft as a whisper. Ben felt her fingers grab his unsilvered arm, her hands wrapping tightly around his. Even if he hadn't already been sure who the speaker outside the door was, the tingling pain on his feather-mark would have given it away.

'It's her,' he finally managed, swallowing hard into his suddenly dry throat. 'It's the Morrígan.'

'Oh, well done!' the figure laughed, the sound strangely amplified, landing right in his skull. Her words were tinged with a sneer. 'And they say that humans are too *dull* to have any fun with. How wrong they are.'

'Where's my brother?' Ben shouted. His voice sounded muffled to his own ears, but the sound evidently carried to the cavern entrance.

'All in good time,' the Morrígan replied, her words crisp and clear. 'He's remarkably resistant to my magic, but I'll break him. He'll make a good crow, one of these eons.' Ben couldn't properly see her face, but he knew she was smiling a cruel and bitter smile, and it filled him with cold, queasy horror.

'I want to see him, right now,' Ben said, forcing the wobble out of his voice.

'And I *said*,' the Morrígan's voice was sirocco-hot, an angry storm, as it blew into the cave, 'that it will happen all in good time. Don't you understand what that means, puny child?'

258

'Our parents are on their way, you know!' Ji-Ah's voice was so sharpened by fear that Ben could hear it, even through the strange sound-fog. 'They're coming, right now, and when they get here –'

'When they get here, I'll enjoy showing them the same care and attention I showed their father,' the Morrígan purred.

Ben's jaw dropped. He felt his head swim as his imagination filled with the image of a desk, covered in papers and books, a man slumped across it, the room filled with swirling black feathers . . . 'You killed our grandad,' he said, barely loud enough to be heard.

'A good artist always takes credit for their work,' came the reply, wrapped in a throaty laugh.

'But *why*?' Ji-Ah shouted. 'You've hurt my Mam, and you destroyed Granny's life – and my Aunty Aisling's!'

The floating figure seemed to grow larger, filling the doorway, her cloak billowing around her and shedding feathers with every flicker. The bear's growl grew deeper and more threatening, and Ben had the sudden urge to duck behind the dais he was standing on, to try to get out of the Morrígan's eyeline, to hide away in the shadows of the cave and never come out – but he pushed against that urge with everything he had. Together, he and Ji-Ah stood tall, their vantage point on the dais giving them a clear view of the doorway.

'Quiet, beast,' the Morrígan snapped at the bear. 'You cannot touch me unless I set foot into the Forge of the Cailleach, as you rightly know. So quell your ridiculous noise.'

'Tell us why you killed our grandfather,' Ben said. 'Please.'

'Such good manners,' crooned the Morrígan.

'He knew something, right?' Ben persisted. 'He knew something you didn't want him to pass on. You wanted Granny to put his work away – you *wanted* his work to be forgotten. So you took him before he could explain, and before he could tell his family what he was doing.'

'He was frighteningly easy to kill,' the Morrígan mused. 'I feel nature would have dispatched him sooner rather than later, even if he hadn't been mixed up in my affairs. I know humans are *fragile*,' she sneered, 'and their hearts all too easy to stop, but in your grandfather's case? It practically happened all by itself.'

'You wrecked my mam's life,' Ben said. 'Don't you care?'

The shadowy figure seemed to pause, very briefly, as though considering the question. 'Not in the least,' she finally answered. 'It may be difficult for you to understand, but human lives are already so brief, so meaningless, that ending one a little early cost me no more than a fleeting thought.' She chuckled. 'As for causing pain? Causing pain is what I live for, little mayfly.'

'I've read his book, you know,' Ben said, flexing the fingers of the silver Arm as he spoke. 'Or bits of it, at least. I know what he was doing. I *know* what he knew about you.'

'You think so?' The Morrígan's voice was eerie – and somehow close. She seemed to speak directly into Ben's ear.

'I know about the Sword,' Ben said, failing to stop his teeth from chattering in terror. 'I know what you were trying to do to it, trying to make it turn evil, like you. I know why you want it, and I can guess what you want to do with it.'

'You can *guess*?' The Morrígan laughed, and it sounded like the teeth of a saw biting into bone.

'Your imagination is not *capable* of guessing what I will achieve, once the Sword of the Sun is mine. Once the blade answers to me, I will free my sister-selves from their prisons, and my three Aspects will once more be as one.' Her voice remained low, controlled and calm, and Ben's nerves jangled with the strain of listening, and watching, afraid to drop his focus for even a split second in case that was the moment the Morrígan chose to pounce. 'But don't let yourself fret about what will happen once my sisters are free. It won't concern you.' She gave a cold, tight smile. 'Nor will it concern anyone you care for. Very soon, you'll all have nothing to worry about, ever again.' Ben swallowed shakily, realising what the Morrígan meant.

'No,' Ben said, his words thready and barely there. 'I'm not going to let you do that.'

The Morrígan said nothing for a few moments. Finally, she began to laugh, a low gurgling noise bubbling up from the pit of her throat. 'It seems my work was ill-done, and my efforts in vain,' she began, mockingly. 'Despite everything, I have not succeeded in breaking your family's notions of guardianship, your ideas far above your station. It seems destroying your grandfather and his scribblings – stopping him in his misguided tracks before he could hand down his *sacred* task to his descendants – was not enough to separate you from the nobility of your cause. You still truly believe you can stop me, don't you? You still honestly think that *you*, because of some long-ago promise made by an ancestor whose name you can no longer even recall, and because of the ties that bind you to your home and the land it sits on and the Seandraíocht –' she spat the word – 'the *Old Magic* that has kept me from my destiny for all these years, that you are capable of standing between me and my plans?'

Ben focused on pulling his breaths in and out, and on the feeling of the silver Arm encasing his own flesh-and-blood version. *Grandad's sacred task*, he thought, the words settling into his mind. Thoughts and ideas flashed through his imagination faster than he could keep track of, leaving him with little more than an overall sense of the truths the Morrígan was unfolding before him, the realities of what his grandfather had done, and what he'd given his life for. He knew he didn't understand everything yet – and that maybe he never would – but one thing was clear. *Our family made a promise to keep this Arm safe. Grandad did his best to keep that promise. I'm not going to let him down – not now.*

'I believe in whatever it'll take to stop you,' Ben said, quietly.

'Me too,' Ji-Ah added, squeezing Ben's hand as she spoke.

'You,' the Morrígan jeered. 'You're not even of the blood, girl.'

'No,' Ji-Ah said, her voice strong. 'But I'm of the family.'

'*Enough!*' the Morrígan roared. The scorching wind that gushed into and around the cavern was enough to knock Ben and Ji-Ah off their feet. They clung to each other as they landed, hard, on the stone floor of the cavern. 'Enough with this nonsensical babbling, this *pointless* discussion of inanities long past! What matters now is *you,* boy, and that Arm you wear, and how quickly you can use it to find me the Sword.' Ben was sure he saw the Morrígan's eyes gleam. 'And how quickly I can relieve you of both of them.'

She flung her hands towards the cave entrance, and from all around her came a seemingly never-ending flow of crows, each bird like a sharp-edged fragment of darkness come to life, a sentient shadow-blade. The bear, finally permitted to defend the cavern and all inside it against the Morrígan's intrusion, rose onto its back legs, raising its front legs high and baring its fearsome claws as a roar exploded from it, so loud that it rang around the entire chamber, swirling and whirling and growing in volume as it went. Ben clamped his hands over his ears, forgetting, momentarily, that one of those hands was encased in silver and jumping in shock at its touch on his skin. In the next moment the bear's fur was alive with light, crackling and leaping and arcing over its body as it gathered power to itself, growing so bright and silver-blue that it lit up the whole cavern.

But it didn't run towards the entrance, as Ben expected – it didn't seem to want to face the Morrígan at all. Instead, the bear lifted its head and focused the power of its roar into the roof of the cavern, where it rattled the massive stalactites at their root, making them buzz. Through his muffled ears, Ben realised that while the *sound* the bear was making was somehow directed to different parts of the cavern, including out through the doorway where it pushed back at the Morrígan with the strength of a tidal wave, the power and vibration remained, shaking dust from the ceiling. Ben curled up, feeling Ji-Ah wrap herself around him, and together they waited for the walls to fall, for the ceiling to crumble, for the floor to crack beneath them and send them tumbling down into the depths of Mullaghmore, where they'd never be seen again.

Ben had almost given up hope when he noticed something unexpected. One of the strange patterns in the rock formation suddenly seemed to make sense, to seem familiar and recognisable somehow, though even as he watched, the swirls in the rock were changing faster than his brain could process. Ben stared, barely breathing, at the back wall of the cavern, brightly lit by the power of the bear, and saw a whorl in the cave wall become an eyelid, which wrinkled in a frown, the eyeball behind it rolling, bigger than a basketball.

And then, sudden as a lightning flash, the eyelid opened.

25

The massive eye looked around the cavern, rolling weirdly in its socket, and Ben could see the pupil contracting in the unexpected light. The eyelid closed over once more, the 'skin' – somehow stone, and yet alive, becoming less like stone with every moment – wrinkling as the eye's owner struggled to focus. Then the eyelid opened again, and the whole wall began to move.

Ji-Ah and Ben scrambled across the cavern floor, desperate to get away – but there was nowhere to run to. The air was alive with feathers and beaks and claws, the buzzing of the bear's roar reverberated around the inside of the cavern like a swarm of hornets inside a jar, and outside the entrance was the Battle Crow, blocking their only means of escape.

The 'rock formation' continued coming away from the wall, unfolding like inexplicable origami, stretching and rumbling and clicking itself into a shape that somehow began to look familiar. It was a human shape – albeit on a huge scale – and as it stood, rolling out its massive shoulders and stretching its aching neck, its thundercloud hair like wire on top of its head, the leaves and stones and hibernating animals that had gathered in its folds began to rain down out of the figure, skittering all over the smoothly polished floor. As the giant took in a huge breath, Ben saw that in each of her hands, she held a hammer as big as a car.

'The Cailleach,' Ben breathed, staring up at her. She'd been here the whole time – they just hadn't realised.

'I hear you, guardian of the Arm, and I am awake,' came the Cailleach's voice, seeming to rumble through the earth itself. She gave the bear a respectful nod before glancing around her Forge. Then, she filled her lungs with another breath before blowing the air back out again, aiming it at the crows. They smashed against the walls and one another, and many were blown entirely out through the cavern opening, making the Morrígan raise her arms to protect herself against them. She shrieked with rage.

'You,' the Cailleach said, staring at the hovering battle goddess in front of her. 'You may not set foot in my Forge, Anand, She-Who-Is-*One*.'

'I have not set foot in it, Hag,' the Morrígan spat back, gesturing at the air all around her body. 'I am keeping to the letter of our agreement.'

'I will not have your trickery, Battle Crow. You are not welcome here,' the Cailleach roared, her voice shaking the mountain. She swung her hammers, clashing them together, and Ben and Ji-Ah's cries of terror were lost in the noise of their collision. It was like being inside a thunderstorm, Ben thought, right at the heart of a thick black cloud as it tore itself to pieces. The gush of wind created by the clashing hammers flung Ben and Ji-Ah across the floor, making them slide on their backs until they hit the wall.

The pulse of sound pushed at the Morrígan, shoving her backwards out of the cavern despite her best efforts to cling on. She dug her talons into the rock as she was washed back through the door on a wave of noise, leaving wide gouges in the stone walls, and her face was twisted with fury as she vanished into the night.

The Cailleach turned back to the bear. It rose once more onto its back legs and met the Cailleach's gaze. 'I see why you have disturbed my slumber, old friend,' the Cailleach said. 'We do not have long until the Crow returns, and her bloodthirst will be all the greater for having been shamed.' The bear grunted, looking exhausted, before flopping back down onto all fours. It padded quietly towards Ben and Ji-Ah, drawing the Cailleach's attention to them.

Her eyes widened in surprise as she saw the huddled children, and they widened further when she noticed the silver Arm, which reflected the sheen of the bear's glowing energy as Ben held it up. He waved at the Cailleach. 'Hi,' he said, weakly.

The Cailleach was speechless. She began to walk towards them, shrinking as she came, until she'd dwindled to the size of an extremely tall human woman – and she carried a sledgehammer in each hand. Around her waist she wore a thick leather belt with tools of all descriptions hanging from it – hammers, pliers, tongs and more. She looked immensely strong, the muscles of her arms as solid as rock. Her reddish hair was braided around her head like a crown, and her eyes sparked silver like metal being shaped. 'By the Dagda's beard,' she breathed, getting down on one knee to examine Ben and Ji-Ah more closely. 'Mortals.'

'We need your help,' Ben began. 'The Morrígan – she's got my brother and –'

'You bear the Arm of Nuada,' the Cailleach said, staring at it. Her gaze lifted to take in Ben's face. 'How is this possible?'

Ben licked his lips, trying to think. How on earth could he put it all into words? 'My – I mean, *our* grandfather,' he began, glancing at Ji-Ah. 'He tried to protect it by locking it in a cave and telling everyone to stay away from it. But I found it, by accident, I swear, and – it sort of found me too.'

'Accident?' The Cailleach looked thoughtful. 'If the Battle Crow is involved, I fear nothing that has transpired has been an accident.'

'What do you mean?' Ji-Ah asked, her voice barely more than a rasp.

'We are barely past midsummer, and my strength is low,' the Cailleach said. 'You saw how your defender, the guardian bear, was forced to wake me from my sleep. I am at my strongest over winter, in the days of cold and dark, when the storm winds blow – during those months, my power is indeed formidable and more than a match for the Morrígan. So, she has acted now, with planning and forethought, to strike at a time when I am weak.' She looked at Ben again, meeting his eyes with an intense, almost painful, stare. 'And it is no accident that she has targeted you, mortal boy, for your blood sings with the Seandraíocht, the Old Magic, that has tried to protect this land since the Tuatha Dé Danann walked here, and cast their net of protection over the whole of this island. You are an O'Donnell?'

Ben gulped and nodded. 'Yes,' he whispered.

'So the bear could not deny you the Arm.' The Cailleach looked sad as she continued. 'The Arm of Nuada cannot be taken by force – it must be given, voluntarily, by the guardian. That was a magical protection put in place centuries ago, to try to guard against the Morrígan's attempts to take it through violence. We did not consider, alas, that she might worm her way into the family who swore to protect the Arm and override that protection. We were foolish.'

'My family swore to protect it?' Ben said, barely able to believe the words.

The Cailleach nodded. 'Your ancestor and I came

to an agreement, many years ago. In exchange for my protection against storms, floods and winter damage, your family agreed to act as custodians of the Arm, permitting it to lie in a cave beneath your land. They undertook to ensure there would always be an O'Donnell on that land, an O'Donnell who knew the significance of what they guarded, and that the responsibility would be handed down from parent to child, in an unbroken chain.'

'But it did get broken,' Ben said, his voice wavering. 'My grandad – he died. I mean, he was killed by the Morrígan. And nobody knew about . . . about the magic. He didn't get to tell anyone. And my granny wouldn't allow anything about him, or his work, to ever be talked about.' He blinked hard. 'His daughters – our mams – they hate him, and his memory.'

The Cailleach's face fell. 'And so the Morrígan has created her opportunity.'

'We have to stop her,' Ji-Ah said. 'We have to *beat* her. Right?'

The Cailleach turned her gaze towards her. 'The Morrígan cannot be beaten,' she said. 'She can only be bested, for a time. For she, like many of us who have lived since the days of the gods, is as eternal as the turning of the seasons.'

Ji-Ah's breath hitched as she stared at the Cailleach. 'So – what do you mean? She's going to *win*?'

The Cailleach smiled, but it was as sad as it was kind. 'She and I have fought many battles. In some, I have prevailed. In others, she has held the upper hand. So the cycle has always been.'

'But – no,' Ben said, urgency taking him over. 'Not this time. She wants the Sword of the Sun. She wants to change it – to break it and make it dark. She told me! She wants to use it as a weapon, to destroy the world. She wants her sisters back, and she thinks once she has the Sword, that she'll rescue them – and then, together, they'll make the world pay.'

The Cailleach's eyes darkened. 'Then she wants to break the cycle and claim an eternal victory,' she said. 'She would befoul the Old Magic, as she tried to do before, in order to make it bend to her terrible will.'

'She tried before?' Ji-Ah asked, her voice shaky.

The Cailleach looked at her. 'Once we fought, and the damage we wrought in that battle is remembered still. Manannán Mac Lir aided me in reclaiming

274

the Sword before she could make it her own, and I returned it to my Forge, where I beat the darkness out of it with the strength of my hammer.' Ben listened, thinking of the story of the lightning on the mountain on the Night of the Big Wind, and imagined the sparks leaping from the metal with every blow the Cailleach struck. 'It was after that the O'Donnell clan and I came to our agreement.'

'We can stop her, can't we?' Ben said, desperate hope flaring in his heart.

The Cailleach sagged as she turned to him. 'I cannot deny the Sword to anyone who bears the Arm,' she said, sadly. 'If she succeeds in taking the Arm from you, then I will be compelled to surrender the Sword and all will be lost.'

'But – that must mean, Ben can take the Sword right now. Can't he?' Ji-Ah spoke quickly.

'What?' Ben said, staring at her. 'Take the *Sword*? I don't want it. What on earth would I do with it?' He gestured with his silver Arm. 'I didn't want *this* either, and look what's happened!'

'I know it's not going to turn you into a superhero, or whatever,' Ji-Ah snapped. 'And it's not like I want you to fight the Morrígan with it or anything – you'd probably take your own eye out. I just meant, we could take it and hide it somewhere.'

'There is nowhere on or in or underneath this earth where she will not find it,' the Cailleach said, her voice hollow.

Ji-Ah shook her head, staring incredulously at the Cailleach. 'But – this is stupid! We've *got* to stop her. We can't just give up! You said it yourself. Our family guard the Arm, and *you* protect us. So, protect us!'

The Cailleach opened her mouth to respond, but her words were drowned out by a howling gale that began to whip around the Forge, carrying leaves and stones and grit and debris with it like tiny, cruel weapons. The entrance darkened as crows in their hundreds began to pour through it – but this time, they weren't alone. In their midst, carried by a never-ending whirl of claws and beaks, was a slumped human shape.

'*Fin!*' Ben shouted, and the desperation in his voice was louder than the wailing wind. 'It's my brother!' he called to the Cailleach, begging her to understand. 'She's got my brother, and she's hurting him!'

Ben looked back at the swirling crows. Fin hadn't responded to his cry – he looked unconscious, or deeply asleep. His head lolled to one side, his hair flopping over his face, and Ben thought there was a smear of blood across the front of his shirt.

In a blink, the crows vanished, becoming a twist of darkness in the air. Fin fell to the floor, crumpling like a pile of dirty laundry. He lay there, still and quiet, while the darkness solidified into the form of the Morrígan. She drifted slowly to the ground, landing lightly beside Fin and taking two or three insolent steps towards the Cailleach, the bear and the children.

'Well, then,' the Morrígan said, with a triumphant sneer. 'Are we ready to put this nonsense to rest, once and for all?'

26

Ben felt like his head was bursting. He was frozen to the cavern floor, indecision and fear making him feel like something was sitting on him, pressing him down, down, down, into the rock. He couldn't stop staring at the slumped, motionless shape on the ground that was his brother, and the taunting figure of the Morrígan, standing between him and Fin. Sounds began to fade, as though they were happening a hundred miles away, and he was vaguely aware of Ji-Ah's hand slipping out of his.

'Fin,' he whispered.

The Cailleach suddenly reared into action, stepping around in front of Ben. The muscles in her powerful arm tensed and worked as she raised one of her hammers, before flinging it end-over-end at the

Morrígan, who looked momentarily surprised before waving one hand in the air. A swirl of dark magic solidified between her fingers like a whip, wrapping itself around the handle of the hammer and diverting its force towards the bear instead. Ben watched as the bear took the hammer's full impact, sending it sprawling towards the cavern wall. Stunned, it slid to the floor, its glow fading.

'How careless of me,' the Morrígan said, one eyebrow quirked. 'I'll be sure to destroy it, next time.'

The Cailleach met Ben's eye, and he could see the desperation in her gaze. She was out of breath, barely able to lift her own hammer from the floor. The effort of making a stand against the Battle Crow seemed to have exhausted her, and she was beginning to turn grey around the edges, like she was returning to stone. He glanced around but couldn't see Ji-Ah anywhere – he pushed his worry down beneath his hope that she'd made it to the doorway and out, somehow dodging not only the Morrígan but also her murderous crows. His fear was doubled without her, but Ben gritted his teeth and forced himself to will her onwards, to send her far away with the power of his thoughts. *Go, Ji-Ah!* His voice was loud inside his head. *Go and get help!*

'Give me back my brother,' Ben said, hardly sure he was even speaking. The sounds weren't reaching him properly, and they didn't seem to make sense anyway. Fin still hadn't moved. His hair was flung over his face, as usual, and Ben couldn't see whether his brother was wounded, or bleeding – or alive at all.

'How lucky, to have two sons of O'Donnell to choose from,' the Morrígan laughed. 'After so many years without a true, blood member of the family in the house, now you've all descended on it once again. All that opportunity for me. Little did I guess, however, that the *younger* brother would be the stronger – but it hardly matters, now.'

Ben pulled his gaze from Fin and stared at her, trying to understand. 'What are you talking about?'

'Your family, Ben,' she began. 'If one has the power to manipulate Clan O'Donnell, then one has the power to manipulate everything under their protection. And with every passing generation, your family has weakened, slowly but surely. I had only to bide my time, and now my time has come.'

'But – my granny,' Ben said. 'She always lived here. There was always an O'Donnell here.'

'Your grandmother might have *married* an

O'Donnell, but her own blood came from far afield. So she was no use to me.' The Morrígan paused to laugh, lightly. 'And in any case, after your grandfather's . . . *passing*, her mind was like a fortress – quite impressive, for a human. I couldn't find the slightest crack in her defences, nothing to exploit, no way to get in and wriggle myself around, enticing her to fetch me what I needed.' She waved her fingers in the air, her claw-like talons extending as she spoke. 'And her daughters? They learned well from their mother. Their hatred and pain were most nourishing to my soul, feeding me up and making me strong for as long as they lived here – but I hadn't considered that the very same hatred and pain which gave me such delight would also keep me out, as effectively as their mother's anger had locked me out of *her* mind.' She folded her arms, her face settling into a pout of impatience.

'Your grandfather was a scholar, not a warrior; he wasted his efforts on trying to *understand* me, on reading about ways to imprison or defeat me, and so I did not owe him the honour of facing me in battle. But I admit, destroying him as I did was a mistake. Not only did I lose my chance with him, but I also destroyed my advantage over the other members of his family. So, I realised my miscalculation would mean waiting for a new generation to be born – a weaker generation, one not so fuelled by grief and loss and rage.' She gave Ben a tight smile. 'And finally, with your arrival, my patience was rewarded.'

'But – what?' Ben felt like the floor was falling away beneath him. 'You've been *here* this whole time? Like, watching my family?' A strange crackling sound made him look towards the Cailleach. Stone was still growing over her skin, like rock forming on cooling lava, and he saw the light start to fade from her eyes. Swallowing his panic, he turned away.

The Morrígan shrugged, unconcerned. 'I did not linger, like an unwanted guest, on your family's threshold, but I kept my eyes on the comings and goings, the meaningless flutters of what passed for life, on the land that housed the Arm. For years, I drew on and encouraged the darkness that settled over your home, but not even at the end, when your grandmother's mind began to crumble and wear away, did I have a chance to make her one of my own.' The Morrígan gave Ben a cold stare. 'She began to forget, you see. She forgot your grandfather, forgot her pain, forgot her children, forgot it all. In the end, all that was left of her was a gentle ball of light – pure *love*,' she spat, looking revolted, 'for something, or someone, she couldn't recall. I can't work with that.' Her gaze hardened. 'But you, and your brother. Now, those are things I can fashion after my own heart.'

'You'll *never* make me yours,' Ben said, drawing on every last scrap of courage he had left. 'My grandad knew what you were doing, and he would have stood against you, no matter what. He would have found the courage. I know he would've!'

'I'm sure you're right,' the Morrígan replied, falsely bright. 'But I killed him before he could.'

Ben pushed himself off the ground, running with a roar towards the Morrígan. Her face twisted with delight – but before Ben could get near her the bear reared into life, leaping into the space between the boy and the Battle Crow, its fur shining brighter than the sun.

'Argh!' Ben yelled, throwing his hands over his face to shield his eyes, as his ears filled with a scream – but not a scream of fear, or pain. A scream of delight, a warrior's battlefield cry, a roar of conquest. As he hit the floor once again, Ben saw the Morrígan's magic rip the bear to pieces, the long sharp strands of her dark power acting like blades, dissecting the bear-spirit and reducing it to a fading spark of silver-blue and a pile of ancient-looking bones, which the Morrígan kicked roughly to one side. They clattered against the cave wall, their sound dulled by the strange acoustics and by Ben's despair.

He turned to the Cailleach, who was mostly stone once more – only her shoulders and part of her face remained, and she rolled her one working eye towards Ben. 'Take my hammer!' she gasped, her rocky fingers cracking and snapping as she forced them open. The hammer fell to the floor with a bang, and Ben – using both hands – began to drag it across the flagstones, as somewhere in the cavern the Morrígan laughed.

'I can't abide these easy victories,' she said. 'I truly *have* grown powerful on your family's pain, young O'Donnell. You stand alone, with a weapon you cannot wield, another you do not know *how* to wield and no concept of the enemy you face.'

Ben didn't answer. It was taking all his strength to drag the hammer. He wasn't even sure why he was bothering – the Morrígan was right. It was too huge and too heavy for him to lift, let alone swing. He had nothing, and nobody, to fight with. His brother was beyond help, his protectors had been destroyed and the cavern was thick with magic and death. It was over. His body knew it and he slumped to the ground near the dais, his grip still tight on the handle of the hammer as his eyes slid shut.

Vaguely, he thought about Ji-Ah, wondering whether she'd made it down the mountain. A wave of sorrow rose inside Ben as he realised no matter what she managed to do, help wouldn't arrive in time to save him. Mullaghmore was so far from home and Ji-Ah was on foot, stumbling across the vastness of the karst in the dark, alone . . . And he could imagine her trying to get his parents to understand, trying to tell them what had happened and make them believe it. By the time they got here, the Morrígan would have won. So what was the point in fighting any longer? Strength began to leave him as he sank further and deeper into thick, oppressive darkness, suffocating and inescapable. His mind felt as though he were being lowered into a bog, soft and peaty and cold, where he would lie for ten thousand years, completely undisturbed. His limbs felt as if they were floating and his thoughts drew to a halt, almost completely . . .

But she doesn't have the Sword yet, came a tiny

voice inside his head, like a pinprick of light shining through a heavy curtain, needling him right in the centre of his brain. *The Sword of the Sun is still safe.* Ben felt his body react, and his muscles start to fight against the sucking downward pull. His brain sparked awake again, suddenly aware of how close he'd been to surrendering to the darkness – to allowing the Morrígan's magic to claim him and quench his flame. *She doesn't have the weapon yet*, the voice continued. *She hasn't won yet, Ben!*

He opened his eyes, turning to look at the Morrígan. Her face was a picture of horrified surprise, as though he'd done something completely unexpected. The tiny voice inside his head grew stronger, the light growing from a pinprick into a wider beam. *Come on*, it urged, in a voice that was somehow familiar. Ben couldn't place where he'd heard it before, though he felt sure it was there to help. *Don't let her magic smother you. Fight back!*

'*Danu*,' the Morrígan hissed. Her face twisted further, her rage growing. 'Get out of him, you Old Magic witch!' Ben had no idea who, or what, she was talking to. 'The Seandraíocht has no place here. I swear, as I did before, that none who bear it in their veins will ever wield the Sword of Darkness.'

It is still the Sword of Light, said the gentle voice in Ben's mind, and the beam of sunshine in his imagination grew wide, as though someone had pulled open a dark curtain that had been blocking a window filled with bright daylight. The Morrígan shrieked with anger, and Ben pushed away the last strands of her magic, the spell she'd been using to try to trap and extinguish him, to break her way inside his head and take him over.

'I'm not going to let you take it,' Ben said, hauling himself to his feet. He glanced at the handle of the hammer. For all his effort, he'd barely managed to drag it more than a metre from the Cailleach's stone fingers. He looked back at the Morrígan, undaunted. 'I'm *not* handing over the Sword to you. Not today. Not ever.'

The Morrígan's eyebrows raised and she took a deep, pained sigh. 'Well. In that case, I'll simply do what I did to poor old Nimhfola, and take the Arm and all,' she said, raising her hands to strike.

And then, out of nowhere, came a loud noise, so sudden and startling it felt like an explosion – a crashing, squealing, pained mess of roaring guitars, and a voice shouting out, '*One, two, three, four!*'

27

Music – overwhelmingly loud and disconcertingly close, just like the Morrígan's voice had sounded when she'd been standing in the cavern's doorway – filled the air. Ben spun on the spot, looking for the source, and finally his eyes fell on a familiar figure near the cavern entrance. They were huddled carefully, hidden from view by a groove in the stone, a brightly lit mobile phone in their hand. The person looked at Ben, the light from the phone screen reflected in the lenses of their glasses, with their other hand raised in the rock salute.

'Ji-Ah!' he shouted, a confused smile lighting up his face.

The Morrígan was completely wrong-footed by the noise. The magic she was about to use against

Ben sputtered and sank back into her skin as she pressed her hands to her ears. She dropped to one knee as the music continued, smashing and crashing around the cavern, amplified and distorted by the cavern's acoustics. Ji-Ah must have worked out that a sudden loud noise, in just the right part of the cave where its strange construction would carry the sound and weaponise it, would be an excellent way to use the element of surprise and gain an advantage – but Ben knew he had to *use* that advantage, fast. He also had to fight back against his own senses, as the music was making his brain feel like a ball of tangled yarn – and that was *before* the wailing vocals began. They sounded like cutlery scraping across an endless plate and put his teeth, and his whole body, painfully on edge.

Sudden movement to his left made Ben turn. He was amazed to see the Cailleach pulling herself free of her stone prison as the Morrígan's power started to weaken. Flakes of rock cascaded off her, revealing soft flesh underneath, and Ben saw her draw in a huge breath just as a cloud of crows started attacking on the cavern entrance. She blew hard against them, making Ji-Ah duck for cover, and the birds were pushed back and away, wheeling off into the darkness. As Ben looked, he saw dawn beginning to soak into the horizon, the faintest line of pink and gold announcing the start of a new day.

The Cailleach sprang to grab her remaining hammer, lifting it with a roar of effort. She balanced it in her hand as she pulled its weight back, aiming for a point high in the ceiling, and then she threw it.

She, Ben and the Morrígan watched the hammer fly, hearing its heavy *swush-swush-swush* as it spun through the air. It smashed into the stalactites that hung from the cavern's highest point, causing a noise like an explosion in a crystal factory, before the largest stalactite – its iron-tipped point sharp as a sword – dropped straight down from the ceiling. The Morrígan tried to dodge it, but she wasn't fast enough.

The stalactite passed right through her, pinning her to the floor.

Her screams of rage were loud enough to be heard over the crashing, tinkling noise of the still-falling stalactites, as well as the music. For a moment, it seemed like the entire ceiling was about to collapse, and Ben raced, skidding across the floor to pull Fin to safety, dragging him by an arm and a leg away from the cascading rock. He saw his brother trying to open his eyes behind his curtain of hair, not yet fully clear of whatever magic the Morrígan had used to overpower him. He frowned, his face contorting as he tried to fight it off. Ben could have whooped for joy at the sight.

'Fin!' he shouted. 'Fin, come on!'

'Tell Ji-Ah to turn that muck *off*!' Fin mumbled, his eyes opening properly – and they were *his* eyes, no longer darkened by the Morrígan's spell. Ben laughed, holding his brother tight.

Suddenly, the silver Arm began to shine, and Ben's breath stopped as he stared at it. He glanced towards the Morrígan, who was flailing and kicking, trying to use magic to escape the stalactite which was still holding her down, but her power appeared to stutter and short out every time she tried to call on it. As Ben watched, he saw her try to turn herself into a swirl of darkness, only for her body to re-form, over and over again, but her shriek was one of fury, not distress. He remembered the iron on the stalactite's tip, realising that it must be having a dampening effect on the Morrígan's magic, but he knew she would free herself before too long. *I've got to find the Sword before then*, he thought, staring down at his Arm. *And either use it to destroy her* – he gulped at the thought – *or do something to keep it out of her grip.*

'Look!' shouted the Cailleach. She pointed towards the ceiling, to the spot where the stalactites had once been. Their shattered remains were still there, sharp and angled and broken off, but hanging among them – and entirely hidden, until the point when the Cailleach had brought the stalactites down – was something that gleamed with the sheen of metal. It pulsed with the power of a deadly predator. Ben saw its cross-shape, the breadth of its blade, the sharpness of its point, and almost forgot how to breathe. It was made of polished sunlight, powerful and terrible as the heart of a star.

'The Sword of the Sun,' he whispered.

From the floor, where she was still pinioned, the Morrígan shrieked even louder, pouring all the magic she had into the stalactite that was keeping her prisoner. It began to shake, as though it were in imminent danger of loosening.

'Ben, you have to call it!' the Cailleach shouted. 'Call the Sword!'

'What?' Ben's heart quailed. 'I don't know how!'

'You bear the Arm of Nuada,' the Cailleach said, her eyes urgent. 'It has to be you. The Sword won't respond to anyone else!'

Ben laid Fin's head gently down on the floor, trying not to be worried by the fact that his brother hadn't fully woken up yet. 'I'll be right back,' he whispered, hoping Fin could hear him over the still-wailing music that was shredding the air. Vaguely, he was aware that Ji-Ah had changed the track, from one of Atomic Eyeroll's hits to a song by Fin's own band, the sound so familiar that it gave him strength. Then, he stood, his silver Arm outstretched as he walked to the centre of the Forge. Right beside the raised dais, Ben looked up into the ceiling. The Sword was hanging over his head, a teardrop from the centre of the universe.

'*Eddie Ate Dynamite!*' screamed the music. '*Good Bye Eddie!*'

Ben raised the Arm.

A blue-white beam burst from the palm of his silver hand, shining straight up at the Sword. It loosened from the ceiling, spinning gently as it came, falling slowly through the air and catching the light with every turn. It was a magnificent weapon, the blade wide and true and so bright it was painful to look at. The grip was wrapped in fine-grained leather, gleaming and well-oiled, and the pommel was a heavy piece of polished steel, shining like precious metal. Embossed into it were four symbols, one on each of its four faces – a cauldron, a spear, a sword and an upright stone.

The Sword came to a stop with its point touching the floor at Ben's feet and the pommel level with his heart. He closed his fingers around the grip, watching his silver Arm finally take possession of the weapon it was made to wield.

Ben felt relief, and giddy joy, well up through him as he settled his hold on the Sword. It was almost as long as he was tall, so he knew it wasn't a weapon he could yet use in a real battle, but he felt complete – holding it made him feel like he had finally achieved the one thing he was made to do. *Nothing* would ever come close to this. He blinked away tears as he thought about his grandad, about all his ancestors going right back to the first O'Donnell, the one who had sworn to guard this Sword. He wished they could all see him now – and his mam and dad too. How proud they'd be! How *amazed* –

A gush of something dark and stinking suddenly engulfed the Sword and Ben gasped, horror-stricken. He stumbled backwards, losing his grip on the weapon, trying to understand what had just happened – and then he heard the Morrígan's foul laughter, just as Ji-Ah's phone battery went flat and her music finally fell silent. In the sudden stillness, Ben's head rang, his ears buzzing and his heart pounding hard. He stared at the Sword, still balancing on its point, and then he looked towards the Morrígan. In her hand she held the shattered remains of a small vial, the shards of which were still coated with the same dark liquid that now sullied the blade of the Sword. Ben saw she had sliced open her own skin with the broken glass, mixing her blood with whatever had been inside the vial.

He looked back at the blade as its light began to fade, horrified to see tendrils of darkness snaking their way through the metal like ink creeping through water.

'What have you done?' he shouted.

'I have done,' the Morrígan said, straining against the stalactite which she'd almost freed herself from, 'exactly what I needed to do.'

'The blood of Nuada's line,' the Cailleach gasped, staring at the Sword.

'But of course,' the Morrígan replied, her voice a taunt. 'Nimhfola spilled so much of his blood the day my sister-selves cut him down. It seemed a shame to waste all of it on the snow of Mweelrea.' She laughed, thickly. 'Long have I kept that vial, waiting for this day.'

The Cailleach turned to Ben. 'She is using blood magic to adulterate the blade, mixing her own blood with that of the heir of Nuada. While the Sword still answers to the Arm, we must unmake it!' Her voice was urgent. 'Quickly – or all is lost.'

Ben turned to see the Cailleach pour a reddish liquid into the hearth of her Forge, muttering a spell over it to make it light. As it grew white-hot, she began to pump something with her foot, pushing air through into the fire.

'What do I do?' Ben shouted.

'Grasp the Sword and place it in the flame!' the Cailleach called, her face almost hidden behind the licking, fiery tongues rising from the hearth. 'And hurry!'

The Morrígan roared, pushing at the stalactite.

She extended her limbs, her bones and muscles cracking terribly, using every inch of herself to lever her body out of the floor and toss the stalactite aside. Ben felt sick as he watched her, knowing they only had moments before the Battle Crow was free – and, judging by the blade of the Sword, her weapon would be ready before she was.

'*Now!*' cried the Cailleach. 'You must do it now!'

Ben wrapped the fingers of the Arm around the grip of the Sword of the Sun. It was only inches away from being transformed into the Sword of Darkness, and Ben felt the weight of it like a heavy stone in the centre of his chest. This was what his grandfather had feared. This was what he knew the Morrígan was planning. *This is what I want to stop from happening*, Ben told himself. He saw the darkness dripping down the blade, almost completely engulfing its light, and already he felt the weapon's desire to answer the Morrígan's call instead of his own – he felt his muscles quake and struggle as he tried to control it, a struggle that hadn't been there before.

He placed his feet steady on the ground, glancing over his shoulder to see Ji-Ah and Fin, pale-faced and exhausted but *Fin* once more, with his eyes clear and his expression one of pride and concern and worry, as they huddled together against the cavern wall. *If I don't do this, they'll die*, he thought, the words ringing bleakly through his head. The Morrígan, her body grotesquely deformed, elongated and multijointed, insectile and creeping and wrong, was almost free.

Ben gritted his teeth, focused his attention, steadied the fingers of his silver Arm – and lifted the Sword of the Sun.

28

Ben cried out, feeling like his muscles were tearing and straining, his joints dislocating, as he tried to heft the Sword. He saw the Cailleach's face moving as she shouted, but the words didn't reach his ears. Ji-Ah was weeping and Fin was pale as bone, reaching out for Ben as though in slow motion. All he could hear was the beating of his heart, fast and feverish, and a strange scream that seemed to come from somewhere very far away – and yet close, at the same time.

After a moment he realised: it was the voice of the Sword.

The Sword was singing, a song of past glory and battle prowess, a song of times long gone, before any living mortal had ever set foot upon the earth. It sang of fighting alongside Lugh, a god made of light and courage; it sang of blood and loss and terror and destruction. And then the tone of the song changed, twisting and ripping and becoming a growl, and Ben knew: this was the song of the darkness, the terrible magic that sought to engulf the Sword of the Sun and snuff out everything that made it noble and courageous and true. *The darkness will swallow it, its brightness will die* . . . The words floated into Ben's memory. He both remembered them and knew them, the words of the poem his grandfather had translated – the warning he had tried to give, in his own way.

He braced his legs, using everything he had to lift the Sword high enough to reach the Cailleach's fire. The song rang louder in his ears, the power of the light pushing aside the darkness again, and his heart broke with the anguish of it, for the sorrow and the farewell. The Sword knew its days were done. It would never be wielded in battle again. It was going to its unmaking, willingly, somehow knowing that there was no other way.

Then the darkness reared in the blade once more, and the sticky, tar-like substance the Morrígan had used to work her magic on it began to reach out tendrils, rolling and glooping down the blade and sucking its way down over Ben's silver Arm, sending out tacky fingers to try to stop itself from falling into the fire. Ben knew the last remnants of the light inside the blade were working with him – the Sword itself was trying to help – but the dark magic had almost completely engulfed it.

But he was nearly there. Without stopping to think, Ben plunged his silver Arm into the flames of the Cailleach's Forge, slamming the Sword down into the fire. He tried to release his fingers but found the black tarry tendrils had fused the metal of the Arm to the grip of the Sword. He yelled in pain and fear, the blistering heat feeling as though it were raising welts on his face.

'Ben!' Fin's voice was ragged with terror. 'Let it go!'

Ben didn't have breath to answer. He tried once more to release his fingers, but when he attempted to pull himself out of the flames, the Sword came too. It shifted, the blade lifting free of the fire, and instinctively Ben reached out with his other hand to push it back. His palm touched the tip of the Sword, which still shone silver-blue, the last remnants of the Old Magic not yet overwhelmed by the Morrígan's terrible spell. Instantly he felt a sharp burning pain, and he knew the Sword had drawn his blood – hopefully, the last blood it would ever draw.

But he didn't lose his grip.

Using all the strength he had, he pushed the Sword back into the fire. Fin and Ji-Ah scrambled up from the floor, coming to stand on either side of him, and Ben felt their hands sliding around him. Fin held him round the waist, pulling him backwards, and Ji-Ah pushed herself between him and the fire, wrapping him in a desperate hug as she tried to push him clear.

Ben caught sight of the Cailleach on the far side of the hearth. In her hands she held a sharp-edged tool, like an axe. She raised it above her head, ready to bring it down hard, her eyes focused on the spot where Ben's arm – inside the silver Arm of Nuada – was stuck to the handle of the Sword.

'Wait!' Ben yelled, feeling sure she was going to drive the point of the axe right through him – but instead, he heard a metallic *clang* and saw a shower of sparks explode from the point where he was hit. She raised the axe again and with the second blow, the Arm separated, opening up like an egg being cracked. Instantly, it released its hold on Ben and he fell backwards, away from the fire, on top of Fin and dragging a fumbling Ji-Ah down with him. They hit the floor in a painful jumble, falling right down the steps of the Forge.

Breathlessly, Ben watched as the Cailleach swapped her axe for a hammer – not the sledgehammer she'd used to free the Sword and trap the Morrígan, but a smaller tool, one with a head that looked like it had been cast from a lump of solid iron. It glowed bright, like a comet, as she smacked the blade of the Sword once, twice, three times, her muscles shifting and shuddering with the power of each blow. Finally, she used both hands on the hammer's oak handle, raising it high above her head and bringing it down on the Sword's blade with a roar of pure sorrow and effort and love – and with that, the Sword of the Sun shattered into a million shards, shedding the dark magic that had sought to transmute it as they flew up and out, peppering the walls and ceiling of the Forge. The shards drove themselves deep into the rock, so deep that they would never be found again – so deep that they would never again be whole, nor remade into the Sword, or anything else. The holes each shard made in the rock glowed for a moment –

303

red at first, then cooling to blue like a profusion of stars, before finally winking out – and then, like footsteps being washed away by an incoming tide, they vanished, disappearing forever into the fabric of the Cailleach's cavern.

Ben blinked hard as he stared up at the ceiling and tried to come to terms with what had just happened. He knew they had done the only thing they could – the only thing that would stop the Morrígan from trying, again, to steal the Sword of the Sun or change it utterly. Nowhere was safe to hide it. The Morrígan would always come looking, destroying whatever she wanted in her attempts to find the thing she sought. Her efforts to bend the weapon to her will would never stop. And the only way to ensure it could never happen was to destroy it outright – to break the magic of the most powerful weapon the gods had ever wielded, and to sever forever one of the last links to the Old Magic, to the Tuatha Dé Danann and to the Seandraíocht that they set in place to protect Ireland, longer ago than anyone could remember.

Ben and the Cailleach looked at one another. Her face was lit by the flames of her Forge, and her eyes shone with tears. Ben knew he was crying too, his heart aching with the sadness of the Sword's last moments, and his whole body heavy with despair and what felt like defeat.

'You're bleeding, Ben,' Ji-Ah said, holding up his hand – the hand he'd used to touch the Sword's blade. He looked down. The wound was long and straight and deep, and it bled freely, but he couldn't bring himself to care.

Then, an unearthly screech tore through the air, quickly followed by a roar that sounded like someone making a monumental effort, and a loud, tinkling crash. Ben, Ji-Ah and Fin turned to see the Morrígan, finally freed from her stalactite prison. She pushed the stalactite aside, letting it shatter to pieces on the floor. Its iron tip burned bright red, as though being inside her body had heated it, and Ben realised he'd been right, and that the metal was somehow implanted with a spell to dull and delay the Morrígan's magic. Certainly, it seemed to have had some terrible effect on her power. As he stared, Ben thought she resembled the strings of dark magic that had sprouted from the Sword in its last moments; her limbs were horrifyingly long, bending and twisting on too many joints, and her torso had a gigantic hole in the centre, her flesh stretching and oozing as it tried to repair itself. Her face was unrecognisable. Where before she'd had a terrible, cruel beauty, her red lips and ice-violet eyes enough to strike fear into anyone who saw her, now she had a mask of bitter anger and loss, her features distorted, and her hair thin and straggling over her weirdly pale skull.

She stared at them all, breath heaving in and out through spittle-flecked lips. Her eyes were wild with rage and despair, and Ben realised: *she didn't get her sisters back*. That was what the Morrígan had wanted, more than anything. More than war, more than death, more than destruction, she had wanted her other selves, had desperately tried to reunite the separated Aspects of herself that she'd been without for so long – and it had been denied to her. Her gaze fell on him, and for a moment that seemed to go on forever, they stared at one another.

'I'm – I'm sorry,' Ben finally whispered. 'I'm sorry about your sisters.'

The Morrígan's lips pulled back from her teeth and she shrieked again, this time with disgust and a blood-chilling hatred, before bursting into a cloud of ragged-looking crows, which wheeled drunkenly about inside the cavern before finding their way to the door. In the next moment, they were gone. Ben sagged with relief, feeling Fin's arms wrap around him.

'It's over,' Fin whispered, stroking his brother's hair, and Ben did his best to believe it. 'Everything's over, little dude. Now, we get to go home.'

The Cailleach doused her fire and settled her tools. Then, she turned to Ben.

'I thought you might like this,' she said, pressing something cold and hard into his hand. Ben looked down. He was holding a piece of polished steel, which fit neatly into his palm, with an image pressed into each of its four faces. He recognised it straight away.

'It's the top part of the Sword,' he said, staring up at the Cailleach.

'The pommel,' she smiled. 'Yes. I was proud of that piece, when I made it. And I thought it might be best going home with you now.'

Ben rolled the metal around in his hand, looking at each image in turn. 'What are they?' he asked, though somewhere deep inside himself, he felt sure he already knew.

'The Cauldron. The Spear. The Sword. The Stone.'

The Cailleach looked sad, and fond, as she gazed down at the pommel in Ben's hand. 'Each of them a treasure beyond measure. There were four. And now there are only three.'

'This is all that's left of the Sword of the Sun,' Ben said, sadness pressing his heart once more.

'And it belongs with the last person who wielded it against a foe,' the Cailleach said, placing one large hand on Ben's shoulder.

He looked up into her ancient eyes, half-wild and full of fearsome, unknowable power. 'Thank you,' he said.

She gave a brisk nod. 'Now, let's get you three home, before you do any more damage to my forge.'

Ben slid the pommel into his pocket as he, Ji-Ah and Fin took one another's hands and stood in the doorway of the Cailleach's cavern. The karst landscape stretched out before them like a gigantic jigsaw puzzle, fitting together in its own unknowable pattern. The risen sun glinted off the surface of the lake at the foot of Mullaghmore. The morning air was cool and new, suffused with fresh hope, like heavy rain had washed all the darkness away. Ben wondered, vaguely, whether his parents had noticed they were missing yet, and how much trouble they'd be in once they got back.

The Cailleach filled her lungs once more and blew, carrying the children on the wind, until they landed – Ji-Ah fairly gracefully, the boys in a tangled heap – right outside the cavern their grandfather had tried to make safe. The gate was still open, the lock still in pieces on the ground.

Ben stood outside the cave, thinking about the bear that had done so much to keep them safe and tried to do its duty in guarding the Arm, right to the very end. He felt the sorrow of its loss fill his chest and make his eyes prickle around the edges. 'Thanks, bear,' he whispered. 'And thanks, Grandad.'

'Spud-brain!' Fin shouted, shattering the moment. 'Are you coming?'

Ben turned. The others were waiting for him at the garden fence. 'How did you know?' he asked Ji-Ah, as he walked towards them.

'Know what?' she frowned.

'When you played the music,' Ben said. 'How did you know it would do – *that*?'

Her face brightened. 'I figured the Cailleach had built her place to muffle the sound of her hammers and stuff, so that she didn't drive herself crazy with all the bang, clang, wallop. You know?' She shoved her glasses up on her nose. 'So all the noise from *inside* got pushed out, to sound like thunder. But just at the entrance, there was a place in the rock that made all the sounds from *outside* sound louder. Right? That was why the Morrígan's voice sounded like she was speaking right into my ear –' Ji-Ah shuddered at the memory – 'but you, standing right next to me, sounded like you were a million miles away. It was really clever, on the Cailleach's part. Like an alarm system, or security, or whatever. So, she'd always be able to hear if someone was attacking, or trying to come in, no matter how much noise she was making at her Forge.'

'Genius,' Fin breathed.

'Thanks!' Ji-Ah chirped.

Fin rolled his eyes. '*Her*, not you.'

Ji-Ah shrugged happily. 'Whatever.' She turned and made a leap for the fence, and was over it before Ben managed to close his mouth.

'All right,' Fin said, indicating the house with a jerk of his head. 'You ready to face the music?'

Ben grinned at his big brother before darting

towards the fence. 'Last one there has to listen to Atomic Eyeroll non-stop. For a week!' he shouted, laughing at Fin's shout of disgust as he swung himself over the top.

Epilogue

Three weeks later

Ben rested his spoon in his half-finished bowl of Chocko Pops and flexed his hand. It still stung, but it wasn't so bad. He sat on the same kitchen stool by the sliding doors that he'd been sitting on three weeks before, as his mam had done her best to clean and disinfect and bandage up his wound. It had turned out to need stitches, but right then and there his mam hadn't cared about that. All she'd cared about was the fact that her boys were home.

Ben glanced at the kitchen table, remembering how two of their four parents had been sitting there that morning, mobile phones in hand, cold cups of tea left forgotten, exhaustion on their faces, and how they'd looked up as Ben, Fin and Ji-Ah stepped into the room, their mouths falling open in shock and disbelief.

'Oh my *God*!' Aisling's voice had been stricken as she'd rushed to embrace her sons. Niamh had wrapped Ji-Ah in a similar hug, and for several minutes all that could be heard were the sounds of a family reunited. Niamh had phoned John, who'd been out on the karst, and Eun-Kyung, who'd taken to the roads in her massive car, searching for any trace of them. Ben had heard his father crying down the phone when he heard the kids were safe, and that they were home.

Ben blinked out of the memory. None of the grown-ups had even been that angry; all they'd been worried about was that the children would get lost underground. And as far as the adults knew, Ben had gone wandering over the limestone, Ji-Ah and Fin had gone to find him, they'd had some minor bumps and scrapes, but thanks to Fin's superior orienteering skills (Ben tried not to roll his eyes), they'd all come home safe. The kids hadn't even been aware of the massive rainstorm that had suddenly come down, or the thunder and lightning around Mullaghmore – they'd somehow missed all of it.

That was the story they were sticking with, and so far, it had worked.

The past three weeks had been a blur. Ben had

started sleeping better, the silver pommel nestled in his dice-jar on a shelf beside his bed where he could see it every morning, first thing. So far, none of the grown-ups had even noticed it. He and Fin and Ji-Ah had a sort of private language now, something only the three of them understood – though Ben occasionally wondered whether Fin and Ji-Ah were trying to convince themselves that none of it had really happened. He shrugged, taking another mouthful of cereal as he stared out into the garden. It *had* happened. He knew it had. And, like that feeling you get when you know you've forgotten something but you can't remember what, exactly, he was aware of a nagging, pulling sensation in his mind – a sense that, despite everything they'd been through and all that they'd done, it wasn't really over.

He tried to push his thoughts away and focus on the view outside the window. It looked like it was going to be a nice day. They'd decided the evening before that a trip into Ennis was in order, to get some school supplies, a new pair of shoes for Fin and to visit the library. He winced a bit, realising that the books he'd borrowed last time were a little late in being returned. He hoped the nice librarian would be

314

on duty again. Hopefully, she wouldn't mind.

After breakfast, they piled into Aisling's car. It was a tight squeeze in the back seat, and Ji-Ah and Fin spent the first ten minutes of the journey squabbling over seatbelts, but Ben let his gaze and his attention drift, focusing on the summit of Mullaghmore for as long as he could. He smiled, unseen by anyone, as he finally lost sight of the mountain, hoping that the Cailleach was peacefully asleep once more, and that there'd be no more light around the summit for a while.

The library was as peaceful and welcoming as he'd remembered. Ben hefted the stack of books awkwardly as he approached the scanning machine. He'd forgotten to get his library card ready and it was hard to keep hold of them while he fished around in his pocket for it.

'Hey! Whoa there – you look like you could use some help,' came an amused voice. Ben turned to see a familiar face, one with kind eyes and a knowing expression. She had a T-shirt with pink, white and blue stripes on it, and her hair was now dyed a light purple, but he was fairly sure he recognised her. He glanced at her name on her lanyard, just to be sure –

and there it was, its final letter still smudged halfway between 'u' and 'i'.

'Hi, Dani,' he said, smiling. He paused for a moment, frowning at a half-formed memory. *Or Danu*, he thought. *Where have I heard that name before?*

'Give me those before you hurt yourself,' she laughed, reaching out for the books.

He handed them over, gratefully, while he pulled his library card free. Dani made a show of inspecting it, as though she were a police officer checking a driver's licence. 'You don't even need your card to return books,' she whispered, winking as she handed it back. 'Proceed!'

She handed him the books one by one as he placed them on the scanner, where they were removed from his library account. He paused for a while over *Old Irish Myths and Legends*, stroking the cover gently.

'You can renew it, if you like,' Dani said, in a quiet voice. 'No questions asked.'

Ben grinned up at her. 'Nah, it's okay. I've read all of it. I just – enjoyed it a lot. You know?'

Dani nodded sagely. 'I get it. I loved it too, when I was your age.'

Ben looked down at the book once more. 'Do you

ever think –' he began, before stopping himself. 'No, never mind.'

'Do I ever think what?' Dani prompted. 'Go on. We're in a library, don't forget – no such thing as a silly question in here.'

Ben looked up at the librarian's face. He blinked, frowning a little as he looked into her eyes. Was he imagining it, or was there a tiny flash of silver-blue in her irises? The same silver-blue that had animated the guardian bear; the same silver-blue he'd seen around the top of Mullaghmore; the same silver-blue he sometimes noticed shining on his pommel, back at home. He stared, but Dani blinked and her eyes returned to normal. Ben shook his head. *Get a grip*, he told himself. *You're seeing that silver-blue glow everywhere! And now, in someone's eyes? Don't be so stupid!*

'Do you ever think that the stories are real?' Ben finally managed to say, looking back into Dani's face. 'I mean, that the people were real people and that the stuff they did – actually happened?'

She smiled at him, so warmly that it felt like he'd settled down in front of a roaring fire. 'What do you think?' she replied.

Ben swallowed. 'I – think I'm not sure,' he said. Sometimes, looking back over the memories of the past few weeks gave him something like vertigo – it made him dizzy and disoriented and confused. It *had* happened – he knew that. But had it happened exactly as he recalled? 'I mean, I think so. I really *hope* so. But I don't know.'

'I think,' Dani began, 'that there's a truth, and a level of wisdom, in these old stories that we'd do well not to ignore. Things might not be *exactly* as the tales have them, but – yes.' She leaned down a little, focusing completely on Ben. 'I do believe they're real. I *know* they are. There's no doubt in my mind.'

Ben glanced back down at the book. 'It talks about something called the Seandraíocht in here,' he said. 'Is that, like, Old Magic? I know that's what it literally means, but what is it, exactly?'

Dani's eyes gleamed again, and Ben held his breath as he looked at her. 'It's an Old Magic that protects Ireland, put there a long time ago by the Tuatha Dé Danann,' she said. 'We all carry it inside us, though some more than others, I think.'

'Do I have it in me?' Ben asked.

'More than anyone I've ever met,' Dani replied.

Ben finally recognised the voice he'd heard in his head as he'd fought the Morrígan's dark magic, up in the Cailleach's Forge – the voice that the Morrígan had recognised and tried to silence, the voice that had encouraged him, that had helped him, that had come to his aid when he desperately needed it, reminding him to fight and filling him with the courage to carry on. *Just like a librarian helped me out when I was really scared, that time.*

'Thank you,' Ben said, hoping Dani understood everything he was thanking her for. 'I think, probably, the Old Magic is in you too.'

Dani smiled. 'Go on with you! I've got work to do.' She held out her hand for *Old Irish Myths and Legends*, and Ben carefully gave it back to her. 'But if you ever need help, you just ask. All right? That's what I'm here for.'

Ben nodded, feeling like a weight had been lifted off his shoulders. Dani winked and walked away, and he wandered over to the children's section. Flopping down on a beanbag as he looked out of the window, he felt himself sinking into it, like his body was finally able to relax. He realised his fingers were flexing and flickering, making patterns in the air, but he grinned at them, realising he didn't mind who saw. If people thought he was weird, so what? Ben knew his 'weirdness' had helped him save his brother, and he was never going to hide it again. With one last flex, his hands fell still and Ben sighed with satisfaction. There were books within reach and he stretched to pick one off the shelf, wriggling himself deeper into the beanbag as he got settled.

Then, something outside the window caught the corner of his vision, reminding him of all the times he'd walked past a door and felt his arm yanked back as his sleeve got stuck around the handle. He looked out, his chest clenching in surprise to see a familiar sight.

On the fence that ran around the small sensory garden outside the library window, a large black-and-grey crow was perched, staring in at him, its eye shining with darkness and its beak cruel as grief. Ben felt his breathing quicken, and his grip on the book grow loose.

Then, Dani appeared, her arms filled with books for reshelving. She stopped a few feet away, staring out at the crow, and Ben was reminded of the woman in the friary, the woman who'd faced the Morrígan without fear. And as he looked at Dani, he knew: it had been her he'd seen that day, already helping and protecting him, before he'd even realised he needed it. The crow let out one raucous caw, before fluttering away until it was nothing more than a dot in the distance.

And this time, when Dani turned to meet Ben's eyes, he was sure her irises glowed a beautiful silver-blue.

Characters

I've made use of the rich and wonderful mythology of Ireland for this story, and some of the characters had a long (and sometimes complicated) history before they ever landed in my imagination. Read on for some more information about how I shaped and reshaped mythology to help create this book.

The Cailleach (pronounced a little like *kye-loch*) is a figure found in Irish, Scottish and Manx folklore. She is the bringer of winter, and she's often associated with horned animals. Her name, in modern Irish, means 'hag', 'old woman', or 'witch', and she is connected to an area of County Cork called Beara. In Scottish folklore, she uses her hammers to shape the mountains and the landscape. She doesn't have a particular connection to the Burren – that's something I borrowed her for! – but the most southerly tip of the Cliffs of Moher (spectacular cliffs found at the edge of the Burren in County Clare) is called *Ceann na Cailli*, or the Hag's Head. In *Sword of the Sun* she is a skilled smith, using her hammers not only to shape mountains but also to create magical silver arms – but this is something I invented for her and it isn't part of her existing folklore.

Cú Chulainn The greatest Irish hero, a demi-god. Cú Chulainn literally means 'the hound of Cullen'. He was known as Setanta until he accidentally killed a hound which belonged to a man called Culainn while playing hurling one day, and to atone for his mistake he swore he would live the rest of his life as 'the hound of Cullen', and so became known as Cú Chulainn. (The Irish word for 'hound' is cú, and his name is pronounced Coo Cullen.)

Dagda The king of the **Tuatha Dé Danann**; the god of plenty, agriculture, hospitality and wisdom. His name is pronounced *Dog-da*.

Danu is thought to be a mother goddess in Irish folklore, but there are no actual references to her in the written sources. Her name is taken from the Tuatha Dé Danann – the People of the Goddess Danu – and it may be connected to the word *dán*, which means 'skill'. She is also sometimes connected with the goddess Anu, who is named in an Irish text as the mother of the gods. Her name sounds like *Dah-noo*.

Manannán Mac Lir is often understood as a sea god, but he's more strictly a ruler of the Otherworld in Irish mythology. His surname, Mac Lir, means 'son of the sea' ('Mac' meaning 'son of', which appears in many Irish surnames), and he is often connected with the sea. When the Tuatha Dé Danann were overthrown by the Milesians (the final 'tribe' to conquer Ireland, usually seen as humans) Manannán became the king of those Tuatha Dé Danann who remained. He is the owner of a fantastic sword, Fragarach (pronounced *frag-arr-ach*), the Answerer, which is also connected with Nuada Silverarm; nobody could tell a lie when Fragarach was pointed at them, and any wound it gave proved fatal. As well as this, Manannán had a self-navigating boat named Wave-sweeper, and a horse that could travel over water, named Aonbharr (pronounced *Ayn-var*). His name is pronounced *Man-an-awn Mack Lirr*.

The Morrígan is one of my favourite characters from Irish mythology. She is a member of the Tuatha Dé Danann, the group of ancient gods and goddesses of Ireland who were eventually defeated and driven underground, where they became the fairies of later folklore. As Danu in *Sword of the Sun* explains to Ben, she's not wholly 'good' or 'bad'; she's simply extraordinarily powerful, and sometimes unpredictable! She is connected with war and fate; she's a shape-shifter; she's a triple-aspect goddess, and one of her aspects, Badhbh (pronounced *Bowv*) is called 'the battle crow', which is why crows and ravens are often seen as being connected to this formidable warrior goddess. Her name is pronounced *Moor-ree-gan* or *Mor-ree-gan*.

Nimhfola I made this character up for this story. His name literally means 'poison blood', which hints at his role. In *Sword of the Sun*, Nimhfola is a descendant of Nuada Silverarm, and therefore he can wield the Sword – which leads the Morrígan to take an interest in him! I imagined him tall and long-limbed, blue-skinned, with long silvery hair. His name is pronounced *Niv-full-ah*.

Nuada Silverarm (Nuada Airgeadlám) is a member of the Tuatha Dé Danann. He was their first king and led them into war at the First Battle of Moytura, where they faced the Fir Bolg. In this battle, Nuada lost his arm when it was severed by a warrior named Sreng. The Tuatha Dé Danann required their kings to be physically perfect, so losing an arm meant that Nuada had to relinquish his kingship and he was replaced by a half-Fomorian warrior named Bres, who was not kind. The healer Dian Cecht and the silversmith Creidhne forged Nuada a new arm to replace his own (and it was eventually replaced again, with a flesh-and-blood arm, by Miach, the son of Dian Cecht) which meant Nuada could reclaim his throne and get rid of the nasty Bres. Nuada is pronounced *Noo-ah-da*; Airgeadlám as *Arr-ghet-lawv*.

Tuatha Dé Danann A legendary race of deities who once ruled Ireland. The **Fir Bolg** and the **Fomorians** were their enemies. Legends say they eventually dispersed, becoming the Aes Sídhe (*Ace Shee*), or the fairies of folklore. Pronounce their name like *Too-ah Day Dan-unn*.

The Four Treasures of the
Tuatha Dé Danann

At least three texts written in an old form of Irish known as Middle Irish talk about the legends of the Tuatha Dé Danann and the treasures connected to them. It's generally taken that the treasures are:

The Lia Fáil (*Lee-ah Foil*), or the Stone of Destiny, which was brought by the Tuatha Dé Danann from the island city of Falias. The Lia Fáil was said to cry out whenever the true king of Ireland was crowned, and its cry could be heard all across the land. A stone still stands at the Hill of Tara, which some believe to be the real Lia Fáil.

The Spear of Lugh, which was brought by the Tuatha Dé Danann from the island city of Gorias. The spear of Lugh was said to always hit its mark.

Claíomh Solais (*Cly-iv Sull-ish*) or the Sword of Light, (called in this book *the Sword of the Sun*, a name it doesn't bear in mythology) which belonged to Nuada Silverarm, and which was brought from the island city of Findias. Like the spear, the Claíomh Solais could withstand any attack.

The Cauldron of the Dagda, also called the Coire Ainsic (*currah an-sich*) in Middle Irish, which came from the island city of Murias, was always my favourite of the treasures. It was said to fulfil the needs of anyone who came upon it. (You can read more about the Cauldron and the Lia Fáil in my book *The Silver Road*.)

Irish Culture

Guardians of the Peace/Guards

Early in the book, Anand mentions the Guards, or 'Guardians of the Peace'. This refers to the Irish police force, which is known as the Gardaí Síochána (pronounced *Gor-thee Shee-uch-awna*). It's usually shortened to 'Gardaí', or just Guards. Their full title in Irish literally means 'Guardians of the Peace'.

Objects

Sword of the Sun mentions an object called a **hurl**, which might not be familiar if you've never heard of the brilliant sport of **hurling**. Hurling is an ancient game, and it's been played for so many centuries that there's no record of when or how it first came to Ireland! It's played outdoors, using a **hurl** (or **hurley**), which is a stick made from the wood of the ash tree, curved at the end. This rounded head is known as a **bas** (pronounced like 'boss'), and the goalkeeper's bas is larger than the other players'. The hurl has a band of metal around the bas, to prevent it from cracking or splitting during play. The ball used in hurling is called a **sliotar** (pronounced more or less like 'slitter'). Points are scored by hurling the sliotar over the 'bar' (the top of the goal), and goals, which are worth three points, are self-explanatory. It's an extremely fast game and very exciting to watch. Every county in Ireland has a county hurling team, as well as many smaller local teams, and every year there's an All-Ireland final in hurling and in other Gaelic games. Hurling is technically only played by men and boys; the women's version of the sport is known as **camogie** and is played in much the same way.

Historical Events

Oíche na Gaoithe Móire, the Night of the Big Wind, was a real historical event that took place on 6 January 1839. It began with a sudden heavy snowfall on 5 January, which was followed by a sudden thaw on the sixth. During 6 January, an Atlantic depression moved across Ireland and collided with the warmer air over the country, resulting in a massive storm. By nightfall, winds were hurricane force. Massive damage was done countrywide, including flooding from a storm surge along the west coast. In the east, up to a quarter of the houses in Dublin were damaged or destroyed by the high wind, and many boats were submerged or destroyed as they tried to shelter in harbours. It's estimated that about three hundred people were killed. Crop and grain stores were destroyed, which led to shortages and hunger in the months after the storm. The wind eventually passed across the Irish Sea, striking Britain and causing damage in Liverpool, before eventually blowing out as it made its way towards continental Europe. It was the worst storm to hit Ireland in over three hundred years. It's still remembered today in folk memory, historical record, songs and stories.

Places

The Burren

The Burren is a real place – as is the Burren National Park – though I have taken huge liberties with its geography in this book! The Burren is found on Ireland's west coast, in County Clare and parts of County Galway, and covers an area of over 500 km^2; however, its exact size is debated. It is a karst landscape, which means it is formed from a type of rock that is soluble (this means it can 'dissolve' when slightly acidic rainfall wears it away over time). The Burren is formed mostly of limestone rock, and – like all karst landscapes – it's filled with caves, openings, underground passageways, springs and sinkholes. Karst landscapes are found all over the world, but the Burren is internationally famed for its unique features, including the fact that it's also a glacio-karst landscape. This means the top layers of rock and mud that developed over the limestone in the Burren were worn away by the actions of glaciers many millions of years ago.

As well as the large, flat, cracked and weathered

limestone pavements that characterise the landscape, the Burren features glacial deposits like boulders and drumlins. It's also dotted with bodies of water that are not there all the time, like turloughs (lakes which can come and go, depending on water levels and weather conditions) and is home to hundreds of species of flower, some of which are extremely rare. Several animals, including bats, goats, pine martens, stoats, badgers, foxes and many species of moth and butterfly are at home in the Burren – though, sadly, it is true that the bears which once roamed the landscape are now extinct. However, the earliest evidence of human activity in Ireland comes from a cave in the Burren known as the Alice and Gwendoline Cave (named for two little girls who lived on the land under which the cave is found, many years ago). Bear bones with marks of butchery – marks made by human tools, showing the bear had been hunted and eaten – found in this cave were dated to around ten thousand years ago.

There are many caves in the Burren region with some you can explore, such as the marvellous Ailwee Cave network. If you visit it's important that you don't go anywhere you're not supposed to. Not all the cave networks beneath the Burren have even been mapped yet! You must care for the landscape, leave the flowers and wildlife untouched and undamaged and never explore anywhere by yourself.

You can learn more about the Burren National Park on its website: nationalparks.ie/burren/

You can learn more about the Ailwee Cave on its website: aillweeburrenexperience.ie/

Mullaghmore

As Eun-Kyung explains to Ben in *Sword of the Sun*, Mullaghmore is a high point on the largely flat landscape of the Burren – but it's not the highest point. That honour belongs to Slieve Elva, which is 345 m above sea level. Mullaghmore, which is only 180 m above sea level, is a mountain with a very unusual 'folded' shape, almost like the swirl of an ice-cream cone! This happened because, many millions of years ago, the mountain was subject to the huge pressure of a continental collision (when two continental masses bumped into one another), which meant all the rocks of the Burren tilted and the mountains started to look folded. At the foot of Mullaghmore, there is a turlough named Lough Gealáin – a turlough is a seasonal lake, which means its size and depth varies depending on time of year, conditions and rainfall. In real life, it's nowhere near as deep as it seems in *Sword of the Sun*, but you should never wade through a body of water if you don't have to (and if you're taking a shortcut on the back of a bear, all the more reason for caution!) Also, there is no Cailleach's Forge at the summit, in reality, but instead you might find a prehistoric 'cairn', or burial chamber, on top of Mullaghmore. It can be climbed, but only if you're a sturdy hillwalker or mountaineer – and never by yourself!

Mweelrea

Mweelrea (pronounced *mweel-ray*) is a mountain in County Mayo. It's the highest point in the province of Connacht. There are four provinces in Ireland: Ulster (in the North), Leinster (in the east), Munster (in the south) and Connacht (in the west). Mweelrea overlooks Ireland's only fjord, Killary Harbour, and it is 814 m above sea level. Its name translates from Irish as 'the smooth bald top'!

Poulnabrone Dolmen

The Poulnabrone Dolmen is Ireland's oldest megalithic tomb. Megalithic means 'constructed with huge stones', and the majority of these structures are dated to between 5000 and 1500 BCE. Megalithic tombs and sites are found in many coastal areas in Europe and in parts of the UK. The Poulnabrone Dolmen is a portal tomb, which means it has two large standing stones (forming the sides of a portal, like a doorway) topped with a huge slab of stone to form a roof. This roof is known as a capstone. At Poulnabrone, there is also a second capstone which now lies on the ground; it may once have covered the back of the dolmen, like a wall. Archaeologists have discovered at least thirty-three people buried beneath the Poulnabrone Dolmen, and their remains date to between 5,200 and 5,800 years ago. The name 'Poulnabrone' can be translated as 'Hole of the Quernstone', a quernstone being the large stone which is used to grind grain into flour, but sometimes it is more poetically rendered as 'Poll na mBrón', which is Irish for 'Hole of the Sorrows'.

A note on Korean words

Ji-Ah uses a few Korean words in this book, and I'm very grateful for the help of Sojung Kim-McCarthy for her help with this. For clarification, here they are, with some explanations and a pronunciation guide.

Bulgogi Meat, usually beef, which is marinaded (soaked in a flavoured sauce) before being cooked in thin strips over a griddle or barbecue. It can also be stir-fried in a pan. In Korea it is a commonly eaten food, and a favourite on pizza! It's pronounced *bul-goh-ghee*.

Eomma This means 'mum' or 'mam', in Korean. Pronounced *Oh-ma*.

Oehalmeoni This word means 'grandma', specifically the grandmother on your mother's side. Korean has two words for 'grandma', depending on whether it's your mother's mother or your father's mother you're talking about! If it's your dad's mother, you use the word **Chinhalmeoni**. Oehalmeoni is pronounced *weh-hal-moh-nee*.

Acknowledgements

I wrote this story for my younger self – for the kid who, like Ben, had flickering fingers, a lot of anxiety and a universe-sized imagination. The kid who loved mythology and folklore, playing guitar, listening to loud music, spending endless hours drawing and taking quiet time just for thinking. And, of course, *reading*, which brought me more joy than anything else. It's a story for the kid with a head full of wonder, and the kid who hoped for enough courage to say 'yes' if adventure came calling.

I hope it's for a reader just like you too.

This year marks my tenth as a working author, and I'm overjoyed that I still get to talk to the people inside my head for a living. But, as with all dreams, this one couldn't have been achieved without a lot of help.

So many folks need thanking, as ever: my agent, Polly Nolan of PaperCuts Literary Agency and Consultancy, whose quiet nod of affirmation is all I'm looking for when I pitch her an idea; my publisher, Piccadilly Press, and my editors Ruth Bennett and Aimee White, whose guidance was (as always) invaluable; my marketing and PR gurus Pippa Poole, Samara Iqbal and Isobel Taylor for being *extremely* patient and supportive; Dominica Clements my cover designer, and my cover artist, Manuel Šumberac, whose work never fails to leave me overwhelmed; Anna Bowles, my copy-editor, for killing all my commas (joke, mostly) and for ensuring things are as smooth and neat as possible on the prose front, Margaret Milton my proofreader, and Sojung Kim-McCarthy, my absolutely brilliant Korean sensitivity reader, who saved me from making some extremely silly mistakes in my depiction of Ji-Ah and Eun-Kyung. Any errors that do remain are, of course, entirely my own fault. I'm so grateful to everyone on this dream team for bringing this book together so superbly.

My family, as always, deserves so much gratitude. My husband Fergal, our daughter Clodagh, my beloved parents Doreen and Tom, my legend of a brother Graham, and his wonderful wife Lisa, my parents-in-law Gretta and Michael, my brother- and sister-in-law and all my extended family – aunts, uncles, cousins, the lot. Rock and roll will never die!

My partners in crime, the writing community, also

deserve thanks. I've been lucky enough to make some stalwart friends over the years, and I'd like to thank in particular the team behind Discover Irish Kids' Books, who have done so much to promote and support the work of Irish-based and/or Irish-born creatives. I'm proud to be part of this group and to shout about how we celebrate the diversity, beauty and uniqueness of Irish writing in everything we do. I urge you to check out the website discoveririshkidsbooks.ie and find your next favourite Irish-created story.

My heartfelt thanks to my friends and fellow authors, Susan Cahill and Rachel Delahaye, who were early readers of a draft of this book, and who gave me not only the benefit of their knowledge but also the sort of cheerleading support that we all need from time to time. Thank you both.

To the teachers, bloggers, librarians, TAs and booksellers who give their time and expertise to bring children to books and books to children: thank you. You're always there to help, just like Dani (or Danu?) and it's deeply appreciated.

I thanked Pat O'Shea in my previous book, *The Silver Road*, and I'd like to thank her again here. Without Pat's work, I don't think I'd be a writer – and I certainly wouldn't have written the book you're holding. I'm grateful to her, and to my dad for buying me my copy of *The Hounds of the Morrígan* one hot August, long ago. The Seandraíocht must have been looking after us that day.

And – as always – my best thanks go to you, the reader. To make a story in my head and then give it to you is the greatest, deepest, wildest magic there is. *Go raibh maith agat.*

About the Author

Sinéad O'Hart is a children's author, a children's literature podcaster (she co-hosts *Storyshaped*, available on all podcasting platforms) and a parent, all of which keeps her busy (but not too busy to read). She's the author of *The Eye of the North*, *The Star-Spun Web*, *Skyborn*, *The Time Tider*, *The Silver Road* and *Sword of the Sun*, and sometimes she can't quite believe she's lucky enough to do what she loves most (putting fictional people into frankly dangerous situations) as a job!

Discover a world of magic hiding
beneath your feet in . . .

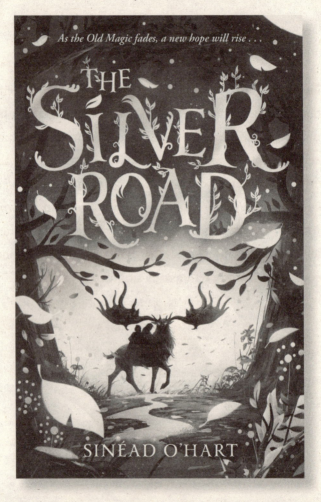

As the Old Magic fades, a new hope will rise . . .

THE
SILVER
ROAD

SINÉAD O'HART

'Charming and action-packed, *The Silver Road*
is a reminder that we can change the world with
just a little bit of *cróigíní* – courage.'
Children's Books Ireland